ROGUE DEFENDER

By John R. Monteith

Stealth Books

D1430760

Table of Contents

CHAPTER 1	CHAPTER 14	CHAPTER 26
CHAPTER 2	CHAPTER 15	CHAPTER 27
CHAPTER 3	CHAPTER 16	CHAPTER 28
CHAPTER 4	CHAPTER 17	CHAPTER 29
CHAPTER 5	CHAPTER 18	CHAPTER 30
CHAPTER 6	CHAPTER 19	CHAPTER 31
CHAPTER 7	CHAPTER 20	CHAPTER 32
CHAPTER 8	CHAPTER 21	CHAPTER 33
CHAPTER 9	CHAPTER 22	CHAPTER 34
CHAPTER 10	CHAPTER 23	CHAPTER 35
CHAPTER 11	CHAPTER 24	CHAPTER 36
CHAPTER 12	CHAPTER 25	About the Author
CHAPTER 13		

CHAPTER 1

East Asia burned, and Admiral John Brody felt the world crushing him.

"I can save Taiwan," he said.

A dark pinstripe suit rose and extended thick ebony fingers onto the table. Secretary of Defense Gerald Rickets responded with authority.

"You need your resources elsewhere," Rickets said. "Taiwan stands alone."

"The president agrees?" Brody asked.

"Yes."

"China launches electromagnetic pulse attacks, North Korea crosses the DMZ, and God knows who has sunk five warships on both sides, but you're restricting my response."

"Taiwan doesn't count," Rickets said.

"American submarine sailors died defending them five years ago, and now they don't count?"

Brody sighed as Rickets straightened his jacket.

"I'm taking fifteen minutes," Rickets said. "When I get back, I want to review sorties over Seoul and Patriot missile positioning."

The other Joint Chiefs turned to aides for updates, but Brody followed Rickets into the hallway, the soles of his mirror-polished shoes clapping tiles like hooves digging dirt. He tugged stuffy navy blue wool from his neck, his starched uniform serving as the flank strap Rickets had cinched around his chest. Bracing to buck his rider, Brody flared his nostrils and lowered his horns.

"What the hell was that?" he asked.

"Doing my job," Rickets said.

"You know I can knock China back ten years and keep our naval supremacy," Brody said, "But you're doing what? Playing politics?"

"Why would the Chief of Naval Operations mention politics during a military crisis? Did you hear a certain powerful senator mention that the next Republican presidential candidate would be a black leader with a background in national defense?”

“Yeah,” Brody said. “The whole nation did. So what?”

“Flexing the Navy’s muscle by hitting China hard would put you in the lead for the position.”

“Keeping the Joint Chiefs in check behind a delicate diplomatic response would favor you,” Brody said.

Rickets’ tone became soft.

“I don’t want to yield to China any more than you do, but it would cost too many American lives to undo what’s been done, just to protect an island.”

“Taiwan is a vital cog in world commerce and a de facto ally. For the sake of the free world, I’ve got to do something.”

“Follow me to my office.”

“Why?”

“I’m introducing you to someone.”

“Who?” Brody asked.

“The guy who’s doing something for the free world.”

*

Brody sank into a leather armchair and watched a face appear on a screen. A silver-haired man in a gray blazer looked back with eyes of blue steel framed by crow’s feet. A gold-plated lighter sparked flint into flame under a cigarette.

Rickets spoke from a chair beside Brody.

“I thought you quit,” Rickets said.

“I did,” the man said.

Brody found the man’s French accent misplaced before a Taiwanese flag in the Keelung naval command center.

“Is that a Marlboro?”

“I am permitting myself the luxury during the stress of the campaign.”

“How is the stress level?” Rickets asked.

“Thick when I arrived, but optimism is taking root. The Taiwanese are my best clients for a good reason.”

“Who is this guy?” Brody asked.

"Allow me to introduce myself," the man said. "My name is Pierre Renard. You almost killed me a decade ago when you sank the USS *Colorado*. I commend your successful career and rise in rank to the Chief of Naval Operations."

"You know about the Colorado Incident?" Brody asked.

"I am the Colorado Incident."

Curiosity melted Brody's agitation.

"You stole nuclear warheads for Taiwan, but failed," Brody said. "And now they and Secretary Rickets trust you?"

"Since the Colorado Incident, I've proven myself quite reliable. I helped Secretary Rickets defeat the renegade Pakistani *Agosta* submarine off Hawaii and reacquire the hijacked Israeli *Dolphin* submarine."

Brody glanced at Rickets, who nodded.

"And I rid the Taiwanese of Chinese *Kilo* submarines during the blockade five years ago," Renard said. "I'm sure you remember the outcome."

"I do," Brody said. "So, what makes you think you'll keep up your track record? China has boots on the ground this time."

"The Taiwanese are prepared," Renard said. "I foresaw this distasteful scenario you see unfolding across East Asia and advised them appropriately."

"I don't care who you are or what you planned," Brody said. "They're outgunned."

Renard exhaled smoke.

"I fought beside Admiral Ye five years ago, and he accepts my advice. For this he will be rewarded. He has prepared his arsenal, and I will consult him to victory through restricted tactical nuclear warfare."

Brody glared at Rickets.

"You're allowing this?"

"Hear him out, admiral."

"The subject is broached, admiral," Renard said. "The terrorist electromagnetic pulse attack over the United States three years ago employed a nuclear weapon. Restricted nuclear hostility is in play on the world stage."

"And China all but pulled the trigger for the North Koreans to copy the pulse attack maneuver over Seoul," Brody said. "I get it. That doesn't allow escalation to tactical nukes."

"Restricted to naval warfare, the smallest of warhead yields, miles from the shoreline. It will be permissible."

Brody wanted to doubt Renard but couldn't convince himself the Frenchman was wrong.

"Let's say Admiral Ye uses restricted nukes at sea. How long will his arsenal last?"

"I'm not at liberty to speculate," Renard said.

"Not to me as your audience," Brody said. "But you'll at least tell me where you plan to use the nukes."

"Of course. I've already sent Secretary Rickets an advanced copy of the international announcement that the Taiwanese Minister of Foreign Affairs will soon release."

Brody turned to Rickets.

"This is wrong," he said. "If you let me handle this now, we won't need nukes."

"The decision is made," Rickets said.

"I'll risk the Seventh Fleet on Taiwan now, but not if you let it escalate. Anything Taiwan dishes out, tactical nukes or not, China can and will hit back harder."

"The decision is made, admiral."

"Are we done here?" Brody asked.

He pulled himself forward on his chair but froze with the Frenchman's voice.

"Have you made contact with Jake yet?" Renard asked.

"Who?" Brody asked.

"Jake Slate is alive," Rickets said.

The periscope-framed image of Jake Slate escaping the *Colorado* on a life raft flashed in Brody's mind, but he had been unsure if his friend had survived.

"Bullshit."

"I wouldn't lie about this," Rickets said.

"You've known since the Colorado Incident?"

"I've kept his existence a secret to protect him."

"You couldn't trust me with that knowledge?"

"You had no need to know."

"Damn you."

"You need to know that Jake is involved now," Rickets said, "so you know that you can trust Renard."

Brody looked to the monitor.

"I've selected him to command an important submarine," Renard said. "The first of the indigenous *Hai Ming* class, based upon the French *Scorpène* design."

"That ship's a year away from being commissioned," Brody said.

"Disinformation," Renard said. "Even Secretary Rickets didn't know, but it's ready and it's needed. It will support stealth patrol vessels in countering China's submarine fleet."

"Those are tiny stealth patrol craft," Brody said. "They won't beat the Chinese submarine fleet."

"Agreed, admiral," Renard said. "But they will fend off Chinese submarines with tactical nukes and targeting assistance. I just need a submarine commanded by an ace to break them free of the minefield surrounding Taiwan."

"You've given Jake back to me in this conversation just to send him on a suicide mission?" Brody asked.

"I would never send him to his grave," Renard said. "In fact, I am convinced he is charmed. He will surprise you, if you can get him here in time."

"I'll stash him on a diplomatic flight," Rickets said.

"Smuggling him here is not my concern. His commitment is. He's been reluctant to join me in the past."

"Have you contacted him since the fighting broke out?"

"He won't answer my calls," Renard said. "His zeal for valor may be waning, and we've both run out of carrots to tempt him."

"He needs the threat of something taken away," Rickets said.

"I would never," Renard said. "I would command the ship myself before I would violate his trust."

Rickets stood and straightened his Jacket.

"You don't have to," he said. "I know where he's weak, and I have eyes on him. My men know what to do. I'll have him there in twenty hours."

CHAPTER 2

East Asian hostilities beckoned Jake Slate, and he summoned his oracle to confirm it.

"Welcome to Michigan," he said. "You look tired."

"You just flew me in on a private jet in the middle of the night," his elder brother, Nick Slate, said.

"You stink. Do you ever wash those things?"

He glanced at a rainbow tie-dye imprint on a hemp shirt that draped over Nick's lithe frame and then returned his gaze to the highway.

"I was sleeping in these when you called."

"Right," Jake said. "Maybe this was stupid. Maybe I'm just being paranoid."

"No," Nick said. "You're not."

Jake pressed on the accelerator of his Ford Fusion and passed a truck.

"How do you know? You haven't read me yet."

"I don't have to. If you believe you're in danger, then you are."

"That's paranoia," Jake said.

"No, that's the gift."

"I'm not even sure I believe in your powers or abilities or whatever you call them."

"You flew me here for a reason."

Jake swore under his breath as truck headlights blinded him in his rear view mirror.

"Paranoia," he said.

"Actually, I believe that if a child has the gift, then it's likely that the siblings do too. And it gets stronger with the younger siblings. I might be the least gifted of all of us."

"Then why is Joe an imbecile?"

"Mom's passing hurt him the worst because he was too young to cope."

Jake snorted.

"You give him too many excuses."

"You give him too little understanding," Nick said.

"Forget him. Can you read me while I'm driving?"

"It's best to be still."

"I don't want to wait," Jake said.

"You sense the danger," Nick said. "I already sense it, too. You don't need a reading."

"I want to know if I should run."

"Yes," Nick said.

"Yes, what?"

"Yes, you should run."

Jake craned his neck and cut across two lanes of traffic on I-275. Gravel crunched under the Fusion's tires, and a sign indicating the I-96 interchange appeared in his windshield. He kept the motor humming and trotted in front of the hood.

"Get out," he said.

He whipped the door open and yanked his brother up.

"Careful," Nick said. "Not so rough."

"Sorry," Jake said and extended his hand. "Read me."

"Fine."

Jake watched Nick bow his head and felt him clasp his palms over his hand.

"Relax and free your mind," Nick said.

Nick squeezed with alarming strength and collapsed to a knee.

"What the hell?" Jake asked. "Are you okay? You're freaking me out."

Nick staggered, and Jake reached with his free hand to help him stand. His brother looked ghastly in the moonlight.

"You're in danger," he said.

"No shit," Jake said. "We've established that. How bad?"

"You know how I've said these feelings are never one hundred percent."

"Yeah?"

"I lied."

*

Jake drove in silence. Nick appeared nauseous and his voice

strained.

"I collapsed worse than that after a really bad reading once," he said.

"Is that supposed to cheer me up?"

"I knew someone was going to die. All I could do was tell him to prepare for his passing. He died of leukemia seven months later."

"What does this mean for me?" Jake asked.

The phone rang on the Fusion's infotainment system. Jake glanced at the console and noticed a restricted number.

"Damn it," he said. "Probably Renard. I'm not answering."

"No," Nick said. "It's someone else."

"You've said I'm in danger, and there's naval warfare in a part of the world where he always sticks his nose. I know when he wants me. Who else could it be?"

"He wants you, but that's not him."

The phone rang again but a name accompanied the chime. It was Gerald Rickets.

"Holy shit," he said.

"Who is it?"

"The Secretary of Defense. Apparently on his personal line."

"A friend?" Nick asked.

"Not exactly."

He answered the phone and heard an authoritative voice fill the Fusion's cabin.

"Slate?"

"Rickets," Jake said.

"Thank you for answering," Rickets said.

"Since when do you thank me for anything?"

"I've learned a few pleasantries in my new job."

"And I hear you're a frontrunner for president."

"This is my personal, unsecure line," Rickets said. "Careful what you say."

"What do you want?" Jake asked.

"I need you."

"Obviously."

"I'll get more specific if you'll call me back on my secure line. Someone is texting you the number now."

"When I get home in ten minutes."

"You don't have much time," Rickets said. "You're traveling tonight."

Jake saw the exit sign for Farmington Hills.

"Three years of nothing, just letting me have a normal life, and now you need me," he said.

"It's not just me who needs you."

"Is it my country? One of its allies? Perhaps an old friend with a French accent?"

"It's a worthy cause."

"My dues are paid, Rickets."

"Nobody's chasing you."

"Because you know I can't run. Doesn't your CIA intern pay attention during my monthly interviews?"

"The latest intern is FBI, actually," Rickets said. "You were reclassified as a domestic case for good behavior."

"Whatever. I'm tied down."

"This is the life you chose."

"I didn't choose you calling me when you had something too dirty to handle yourself. This is bullshit."

"Say goodbye to your wife then call me," Rickets said. "There's transportation waiting in your subdivision with bags packed for everything you'll need."

"I'll call you when I'm home."

Jake hung up, exited the highway, and turned onto Twelve Mile Road in Novi.

"You know I have to go, right?" he asked.

"This is consistent with your danger," Nick said.

"Can you look after Linda?"

"You mean–what? I didn't say you were going to die. I mean I sense certain death, but I don't know that it's you. It could just be somebody you interact with."

"I mean stay with her. She gets lonely easily, even with her kids around. She needs someone to just look after her and let her know she's going to be okay."

"Sure," Nick said. "Wait. How long? I have a pretty busy schedule back home."

"I know. I know I've called it hocus pocus, but I'm proud of you for making a business out of your abilities. I'll cover your loses and whatever you need to throw at your clients to keep them coming back happy."

"Sure," Nick said. "I think that'll work. But how long?"

"As long as it takes."

*

Jake stomped through the doorway into his four-bedroom suburban lie. In the entryway, feminine lines drew voluptuous curves under a pink robe, and dark hair touched the woman's shoulder. She greeted him, but her smile faded.

"Something's wrong," she said.

"Linda, you remember Nick, right?"

"Yeah," Linda said. "Hi. What's going on?"

"I went to pick up Nick."

"No kidding," she said. "I mean you have a look."

"Later," Jake said. "Are your kids home?"

"You know where they are. The boys are upstairs. Christina is sleeping over a friend's house tonight."

"Call her. Make sure she's there."

"Jake?"

"Just do it!"

Linda recoiled, and Jake realized he had yelled. He felt Nick's hand on his arm reassuring him.

"I'm sorry," he said. "But you need to call her."

"She's not answering," Linda said.

"Call the parents where she's staying."

"You're scaring me, Jake."

"I'll kill him if he's bringing your kids into this."

"Who, Jake?"

"Call."

Jake watched Linda put the phone to her ear and heard her

apologizing for calling late as he brushed by her towards his office. He closed a door behind him. Recalling his security code, he sat and accessed an encrypted web site. His fingers danced on the keyboard.

Rickets' voice shot from desktop speakers.

"Are you home?"

"Where's my stepdaughter?"

"You assume I follow you that closely," Rickets said. "That's good."

"Where is she?"

"I know she's not home with you. Beyond that, I don't know. Do you need help finding her?"

Phone to her ear, Linda opened the door and mouthed inaudible words about having found her daughter. Jake nodded and ushered her out the door with a stern finger.

"No," Jake said. "I know where she is. I just wanted to make sure you weren't bringing my step kids into this."

"Your cooperation keeps them off the table."

"Keep it that way."

"Are you ready?"

"How long do I have?"

"Thirty minutes," Rickets said. "I recommend you leave sooner. Dragging it out makes it worse."

Jake ran his hand through his hair and reclined.

"Okay. What's next?"

"A taxi is watching and will meet you at your mailbox when you stand next to it. Bring an empty duffel bag so any watching neighbors are less suspicious. You'll have a situation report and tech manuals in the car."

"So, that's it, then?"

"That's it."

"Is Renard involved?"

"Yes. He'll brief you."

Jake found comfort in his friend's involvement.

"Okay, then," he said. "Where the hell am I going?"

"You're going where I know you've succeeded before," Rickets said. "You're going back to Taiwan."

CHAPTER 3

"Who is the other?"

Jeongkwan Kim cringed when he realized he had spoken the words aloud. His bunk mate on the *Romeo*-class submarine rolled to his side, and the room fell silent except for Kim's heartbeat and the deep breathing of sleep.

He scanned faces of his shipmates in his mind, speculating the identity of the other, his secret accomplice. The question had plagued him since leaving the naval base in Haeju, North Korea days earlier, and it had consumed him in the final hours motionless on his back.

He lowered his sneakers to the deck plates, propped open his bunk, and rummaged for canisters of compressed hydrogen cyanide gas. They weighed heavy against his thighs as he slid them into his overall pockets, but they made no sound as he crept away.

He ducked through a door into the engineering compartment and heard the gentle hum of the propulsion motor. Pushing his hands into his overalls, he turned the corner around an electronic equipment cabinet and spotted a man in a sweaty jumpsuit seated before a control panel.

"What brings you back here, Kim?"

"Looking for Li," Kim said.

"Why?"

"Can't sleep," Kim said. "I'm trying to figure out how to fix that lube oil leak."

He hoped the man wouldn't pry further.

"He's near the shaft bearing looking at it now."

Kim nodded and darted away. He turned and descended a ladder through a machined lip welded between deck plates. A cubby hole by his ear caught his attention.

He unlatched the cubby door and withdrew an air mask. While plugging the mask's feeder hose into an emergency air line, he glanced at his watch. He was early.

Considering that the other agent might act ahead of schedule, he pushed the mask against his face. Synthetic rubber pinched his cheeks as he inhaled stale, metallic air from the emergency header.

He heard footsteps on the plates above and pressed his back against a lube oil tank until the sailors departed.

Minutes passed in solitude, and Kim reflected upon the Chinese agents who had approached him with promises and threats. The money would feed his family for years, and his cooperation assured that they would live to spend it.

Hesitating, he doubted his resolve, but the Chinese said that the other agent would strike from the forward compartment while he struck from the aft. The submarine crew was doomed regardless of his compliance, he knew. He swallowed, blinked, and reached for a door latch.

He pulled and heard the grumbling whir of fans. The canister he lifted from his pocket filled his palm, and as his finger curled, the pin yielded slowly. He heard a hiss and saw billowing compressed gas.

He tossed the canister into the fan room and followed it with its twin. He shut the door, backed up against the lube oil tank, and waited.

Minutes passed as he slowed his breathing. He heard a distant thud that he hoped was a collapsing corpse, and the thought relieved and horrified him.

Time slogged forward as Kim prayed that the gas massacred the crew. He pinched the air hose and snapped it free. Holding his breath, he climbed the ladder and sought a new emergency air connection. He reached and pressed the hose into the header and inhaled.

As he caught his breath, he noticed the unmoving form of the last man he had spoken to. He detached his air hose, stepped over the corpse, and plugged in to fresh air.

The body below him revealed pinkish skin from the acute poisoning. Kim balanced his weight above his former colleague and twisted a control knob. The propulsion motor murmured its baritone eulogy and hummed to a halt.

Kim crept forward to a new feeder. He inhaled several breaths before stooping through the door into the main compartment. His heart raced with the anticipation of meeting the other.

Entering the control room, he glanced at the carnage strewn about the deck plates. He snapped into a fresh air line and breathed.

Motion caught his eye, and he saw a man reaching for an air manifold. The man turned, disengaged, and walked toward Kim. The mask scrunched the face into an unrecognizable form, but Kim knew the uniform.

"Captain?" he asked.

"Whom did you expect, boy?"

The captain's mask muffled his words.

"I had no idea," Kim said. "They didn't tell me."

"They told you all you needed to know. Now we have work to do."

The captain snapped his air hose free and joined Kim at his manifold.

"What sort of work?" Kim asked.

Kim saw the captain's hands in front of his mask and felt his head being wrenched down. He resisted, and the mask slid from his face.

He suppressed his instinct to inhale and swatted away the captain's arms. He turned and kicked the captain's stomach. As the captain staggered, Kim mashed his mask to his face and squeezed his lungs empty. Poisoned air blew by his cheeks, and he inhaled. He felt dizzy.

As the captain lunged for him, Kim reached for his enemy's hose, twisted, and pulled. He seized his adversary's lifeline, held its air-starved nozzle against his chest, and moved in front of the air manifold.

He absorbed punches, and his ribs ached, but his arm stayed true holding his mask to his face. The punching stopped, and then desperate hands probed, groped, and tugged at the tubing. His arm burning, Kim denied the captain his hose, and the pulling stopped.

The captain fell to the deck, convulsed, and died.

Kim steadied his breathing and surveyed the control room. A digital display indicated that the submarine had drifted to a stop and was rising to the surface where it would be exposed.

He reflected that surfacing the *Romeo* was necessary in the Chinese plan to steal it. His instructions were to radio an infiltration force once surfaced.

But he questioned his instructions. Knowing the other agent's identity, Kim wondered why the Chinese had plotted his death at the captain's hands. Confusion quickened his pulse, and growing anger in his betrayal pumped throbbing blood through his neck.

A survival instinct focusing him, he calmed himself and changed his plans. He studied a navigation chart and noticed land eighteen nautical miles away. He memorized its direction.

As the submarine bobbed in surface swells, Kim inhaled, disconnected from the manifold, and walked to the hatch. He plugged in, inhaled several times, and detached.

Not knowing the differential pressure between the submarine and the outside world, he rotated the hatch lock half way, heard hissing wind, and retreated to a manifold to breathe.

Returning to the hatch, he grabbed the ladder with one hand and twisted the locking mechanism with the other. The hatch folded open as the cabin pressure equalized with the outside air. Kim climbed, leaned over the hatch lip onto glistening metal, and tore off his mask.

He breathed moist, warm summer air and pulled himself to his feet. He noted the angle of the moon and his memorized direction to land relative to the bow. He expected the water to be uncomfortable but survivable.

Before jumping, he scanned all horizons. He thought he saw a dark ship approaching with a low, ominous silhouette from behind the submarine, but he didn't linger to find out.

As he dove into the Yellow Sea, the riddle's answer revealed itself to his jaded mind. There was only one, the *Romeo's* captain, but the Chinese needed insurance to verify their agent's compliance. He, Kim, the lowly, vulnerable technician, provided that insurance.

He was the other.

CHAPTER 4

Pierre Renard tugged at his gray blazer and sparked flint into flame under his Marlboro. A breeze carried the scent of asphalt and salt across his face as he watched Jake Slate descend the jet's stairway to the tarmac. His protégé appeared tired and agitated.

"It's been a while, *mon ami*," he said.

"Don't you have a war to run?" Jake asked.

"The campaign will survive during my absence from the command center."

Renard blew smoke.

"I thought you quit," Jake said.

"A temporary indulgence during operations."

Renard felt Jake pulling him into a hug and cringed.

"You know how I loathe this."

"Yes."

"Then why do you insist?" Renard asked.

Jake's arms became vice grips as he squeezed. Renard squirmed until the pressure subsided.

"Because I know how you loathe it."

*

Half the world's second tier nations desired Renard's arms-equipping and military advisory services. The other half sought his pelt for their mantles.

He had chosen and abandoned enough sides to mistrust all but his best clients, Taiwan providing him an ecosystem isolated from vengeful furriers but dense with nourishment. An opportunistic feeder, Renard had tracked his Asian clients to rich sources of imported weapons commissions and brilliant military victories. With vulpine cunning, he had crafted a hunt for his den mates, and he expected Jake Slate to pounce on their most prized prey.

Renard had found Jake distant during the ride from the tarmac and wrestled to squeeze banal information from him about his attempt to live a simple life in Michigan. He abandoned hope of reading Jake's mental state while escorting him through security checkpoints.

Jake beside him, he entered the Keelung command center and felt two dozen eyes rise from an electronic navigation chart. The chief of staff stood straight.

"A hero has returned," Admiral Ye said in English. "Welcome, Mister Slate."

Renard sensed Jake's hesitation and whispered.

"Go on. You remember him. Shake the man's hand."

"I'm not feeling it," Jake said.

"There is nothing to feel. You're just fatigued."

"No," Jake said. "It's more than that. Something's wrong. I don't belong here."

"Few welcome combat," Renard said. "But it's our fate. You are pursuing your destiny, man, I assure you."

Renard felt Jake brush by him to greet the admiral. Gestures followed that repositioned planners around the navigational chart.

"We will speak English while briefing Mister Slate on the operation," Admiral Ye said.

Renard nodded to his translator who moved beside the officers he recognized as having the poorest English skills.

As Renard looked down, a myriad of lights representing shipping dimmed, and baby blue lines rose to connect Taiwan across island chains to Okinawa and to the Philippines.

"The sound surveillance arrays," Admiral Ye said, "are operational. They have tracked seventeen mainland submarines in passing east into the Philippine Sea."

Five red dots framed by inverted semicircles shone east of Okinawa and south of Japan's mainland.

"Japanese assets are tracking these five mainland submarines," Ye said. "The other eleven are at large. Since we control the air and surface to the east of the arrays, these submarines are the primary threat."

"What good are sound arrays that tell you you're being overwhelmed by submarines?" Jake asked.

"An excellent question," Renard said. "I advised the construction of these two arrays for a solitary purpose. They were laid to protect incoming shipping from either direction–from Japanese islands or from the Philippines."

"You brought me here to escort convoys?" Jake asked.

"Nonsense," Renard said. "There will be no escorting per se, as there will be a constant influx of supply shipping. But protection to shipping will be provided by air cover and by stealth vessels patrolling the hydrophone arrays."

"So, why do you need me?"

"Admiral Ye, will you demonstrate?" Renard asked.

As Admiral Ye wiggled his thumb across a touch pad, a dot traced an arc on the chart and stopped eighty miles southeast of Keelung in the Japanese waters surrounding the island of Yonaguni.

"You will lead the *Hai Ming* submarine," Renard said, "in a minefield egress operation. The *Hai Ming* is a licensed indigenous replica of the *Scorpène* class. You are quite familiar with it, as is your crew."

"Minefield egress?" Jake asked. "You summoned me half way across the world for that?"

Renard met Jake's stare and exhaled smoke.

"Will you excuse us, Admiral Ye?" he asked.

The chief of staff moved to Renard and spoke softly.

"I need that submarine on this operation–with or without Slate," Ye said. "I prefer with him."

"I will earn his commitment," Renard said.

"He seems hesitant," Ye said. "This is not how I remembered him."

"I think I know the issue," Renard said. "Can you get a video feed to his wife?"

"I need fifteen minutes."

"Thank you," Renard said.

Ye nodded and snapped a command in Mandarin. A sea of naval uniforms followed him through a door. Watch officers remained seated at consoles around the navigation chart where Renard enjoyed privacy with his protégé.

"I'll get you time to speak to your wife."

"I miss her," Jake said. "How did you know?"

"Because you are still resisting who you are," Renard said. "You pretend that you desire a simple bedroom community life, yet here you are."

"I was forced."

"You were nudged," Renard said. "Rickets hardly applied pressure."

"He didn't have to. My wife and stepchildren are open targets. I can't run anymore."

Renard blew smoke.

"Somehow," he said, "I suspect that you are here by your own volition."

"I may be blindly trusting you," Jake said.

"You've done so before."

"But a mine egress operation? Driving a submarine through a minefield is suicide."

"Of course," Renard said. "But your submarine is already free of the minefield."

"That wasn't in Rickets' briefing."

"Taiwan and the United States don't share all intelligence," Renard said. "I'll show you how you're soon to shape the world."

He turned the corner and grasped a handheld touchscreen. He tapped icons and nodded to the chart.

"After the prior episode of Chinese aggression, I advised Taiwan to establish a secret and submerged submarine pen free of contested waters."

"No shit?"

"Indeed," Renard said. "At the first indication that China was laying mines around Taiwan, a skeletal crew absconded with the *Hai Ming*."

"Where?"

"Here, carved inside the Pengjia Islet."

Renard tapped his controller and maneuvered a blue dot to

the northeast of Keelung.

"There's nothing there," Jake said.

"Precisely. It's so small that it's invisible on this chart scale. It was little more than a lighthouse until, thanks to my foresight, it became a safe supply and repair haven for submarines."

"You still haven't said why you want me to lead a minefield egress operation."

"The greatest threat to the stealth patrol craft will not be the mines themselves but the submarines awaiting them at the edge of the minefield."

"Where's the edge and how do you know?"

"China wisely announced the areas of exclusion to keep international shipping away," Renard said. "They are making sure to limit this campaign to a civil affair."

Jake raised his voice.

"It's practically a world war."

"In appearance only. Look more carefully at events."

"Electromagnetic pulse attack over Seoul. Tanks rolling into Israel. North Koreans burrowing through tunnels across the DMZ. The Chinese Navy playing cat and mouse with Japan like the Cold War."

"It's a surgically crafted mélange of misdirection and puppetry designed for one aim–global acceptance of a Chinese military presence on its once-renegade province of Taiwan."

"You see that as the sole outcome, through all this violence? How?"

"Observation, deduction, interpretation of Chinese language from diplomatic channels. They want a permanent force on the island. The rest is subterfuge."

"What about Korea?"

"It was little political risk for them to instruct the North Koreans how to use a nuclear weapon at the proper yield and altitude over Seoul to cripple its electronic systems."

"To what end?"

"For the Chinese, a distraction that consumes American attention. For the North Koreans, respect. No outsiders will risk boots on the ground for a peninsular affair, and a gesture of respect, be it a seat at a council or a lifting of a trade restriction, will earn a voluntary withdrawal of North Korean forces. Though both America and Japan must turn their attention to the peninsula, the outcome is already predicable."

"And Israel?"

"Money and arms were given to her enemies who hope to take back a slice of Israel, but as history has proven, Israeli resolve will prevail. From the Chinese perspective, an American carrier strike group is consumed monitoring and supporting Israel."

"What about Japan?"

Renard blew smoke.

"You said it yourself," Renard said. "It's a game of cat and mouse like the Cold War. The Chinese are violating no laws and intend no act of hostility, but American forces must watch Chinese assets that are harassing Japan."

"And Taiwan is left alone."

"Indeed," he said. "With the magnitude of global stress, any nation who wishes to ally against China can meet its obligations and rightfully claim victory by returning everything else to the status quo, but Taiwan must remain at arm's length."

"The risk is too great to challenge China for Taiwan," Jake said, "and the reward too small."

"Precisely. Each ally will yield to the temptation to coin Taiwan as an internal affair. But financial markets will remain in turmoil for years, and…"

Renard hesitated and reflected upon his life's greatest effort.

"And what?"

"I've worked too hard to let this happen. We both have."

"Then what's my goal?" Jake asked. "If it's all settled, then what's everyone fighting for here?"

"The permanent Chinese presence on Taiwan will vary between a complete and outright occupation and a symbolic outpost, depending who has the strongest position during the ceasefire negotiations. Your job is to assure it's the latter."

"By springing the stealth patrol craft free to protect incoming shipping from submarines and keeping Taiwan fueled for the fight?"

"Indeed."

"You're asking a lot from small patrol craft."

"They have an advantage."

"The hydrophone arrays. I get that. But that's shitty targeting data at best for those little ships without sonar systems."

"Agreed," Renard said. "Except that I've armed them for limited use of tactical nuclear weapons."

Jake raised an eyebrow.

"Seriously?"

"Picture a tactical barrage of small-yield depth charges launched in a pattern around the target. The crudest hint of a submarine's presence yields its doom."

"And the doom of any other submarine that's nearby."

"The weapons can be selectively armed based upon tighter targeting data and the location of friendly assets."

"Sounds like I'll be a Guinea Pig."

"You'll be safe, provided you follow my plan. It's orchestrated to optimize the tactical assets of your submarine and the skill of your team."

"The whole gang is back?"

"I had to hire new junior operators after making millionaires out of their predecessors, but all the senior ones have returned because they are addicted."

"The Taiwanese team? Same arrangement as last time?"

"Of course. Support of your crew, and an executive officer who reports to you but who is formally in command."

"It's not Sean Wu? He had talent."

Renard felt the melancholy of a lost comrade.

"Sadly, our former colleague perished leading the *Hai Lang* into a noble but fateful one-for-one exchange with a Chinese *Kilo*-class submarine."

"That's not–"

"International news. No, nor will it be until this campaign is decided. Your executive officer will be a youngster who is capable but inexperienced. The remaining experienced men are patrolling aboard the *Sea Tiger* or *Sea Dragon*, but the best are entombed inside the *Hai Lang*."

"I see why you need me," Jake said. "I'm ready. How do I get to Pengjia and my submarine?"

Renard cleared his throat.

"Via aircraft."

"What sort of aircraft? That air space is contested, if I'm reading the colors on that chart right."

"An aircraft from which, with the assistance of a tandem professional, you will jump at high altitude and glide via parachute to reach the islet."

"Shit. Fine. I've jumped before. Then what?"

"And then you will prove to me once again," Renard said, "that you are indeed charmed."

CHAPTER 5

Dao Chan barked in Mandarin at his executive officer, Lieutenant Huang Gao.

"Get below! Get below!"

"What?"

Chan pointed at the horizon where he had seen the gun muzzle flash. He watched in horror as he beheld another brilliant burst. A third flash caught his eye, and he cringed as the ocean erupted over his shoulder.

He slapped the shoulder of his executive officer as he brushed by. Terrified eyes stared at him through a mask.

"You've scuttled the ship?" Chan asked.

He nodded at the fishing vessel that had brought his crew to the abandoned *Romeo*-class submarine.

"Yes, captain. It's flooding."

"Take us to full speed and dive. Warm up a salvo and open the outer doors. I will close the hatch behind me."

Gao disappeared into the *Romeo*, and the sea exploded twice again. Droplets pelted Chan's back.

He pressed binoculars against his eyes and stared in the darkness. A silhouette became recognizable, and its cannon fired again.

As water rushed over the bow of the deck submerging below Chan's feet, a projectile whistled over his head. The sea erupted again.

He squeezed his cheeks into his mask and tasted forced air fed from the canister at his chest. He raced down the manhole and closed its hatch. The ocean popped and rumbled as a round exploded outside the hull.

As he steadied himself on the downward sloping deck, the executive officer met him. The fear in his voice came through the speaker of his forced air ensemble.

"We are accelerating through eight knots, sir."

"The weapons?" Chan asked.

"Three minutes remaining on warm up."

The next three cannon rounds shook the deck plates, but Chan's pulse slowed as the *Romeo* plummeted below danger.

"Level us out at forty meters," he said.

"Done, sir," Gao said.

"Is the ship secure?"

"Say again, sir?"

"Secure?" Chan asked. "I sent armed men into this ship first for a reason."

"Initial sweep is negative, sir. The detailed search is underway."

"Good. Where is the commanding officer?"

Gao pointed at the body of the North Korean vessel's former captain.

"Dead, sir."

"That explains why we have no warmed up weapons," Chan said. "Come here."

Chan stepped over a corpse to the shoulder of a sailor at a sonar console. His executive officer joined him.

"Do you have the hostile vessel on the bow array?"

"Only the transient noise of their cannon fire, sir," Gao said.

"Transmit active to attempt ranging," Chan said. "In ninety seconds, I shoot down their bearing."

"What if it's not an antisubmarine vessel, sir?"

"It is," Chan said. "*Pohang*-class corvette."

"You could tell?"

"My best assessment under the circumstances."

Chan glared at the sonar screen. It became fuzzy with the noise of the *Romeo's* own movement.

"Wait," Chan said. "Cease transmitting and slow to five knots. Pass the word for everyone to remain still."

The sonar screen became muted until a loud trace fell upon it. The young sailor seated before Chan pressed ear muffs into his head, nodded, and pointed at the screen.

"That's all I need," Chan said.

"Active sonar emissions from the corvette?" Gao asked.

"Yes. Get a firing solution to that target's active sonar. Box it in with a salvo, one torpedo lagging, one leading. I want to fire when the weapons are ready."

Seconds passed, and another active emission rose on the sonar screen.

"They may have an active sonar return on us."

"If they are steaming fast enough to matter, they may not," Chan said. "Plus our torpedoes are bigger, faster, and will be closing on them head on while we run from theirs."

"They may have called for help, sir, such as helicopters."

"Fight this battle, Gao. Not the next one."

A masked sailor uttered something at Gao that Chan could not hear, but he gleaned the meaning.

"Weapons ready!" Gao said.

"Shoot both tubes!" Chan said.

Pneumatic pressure screeched through pipes and echoed throughout the submarine. Chan glanced at the sonar screen and saw two lines diverging as his weapons bracketed the encroaching corvette.

"Full speed ahead, right ten-degrees rudder, dive to two hundred meters."

North Korean sailor corpses rolled on the deck as men seated in front of control yokes maneuvered the ship. Two faint lines grew on the sonar display that Chan recognized as the corvette's incoming weapons splashing into the water from deck-mounted tubes.

"They are too far away for a trailing shot. Their weapons will run out of fuel if we can maintain propulsion."

"I pray you're right, sir," Gao said.

Chan watched the splashes on the sonar display disappear and give rise to the sound of torpedo blades.

"The shots appear accurate," he said. "We need speed."

"Passing twelve knots, sir. Twenty minutes of battery remaining."

"This will be close," Chan said.

He hadn't expected mortal combat threatening him before he could assume command of his maverick submarine. He noted tension in his muscles but assured himself that he carried himself with confidence.

"Sir, the first group of men have only five minutes of air remaining."

"If we surface to ventilate, we risk being run down and attacked by cannons."

"If we don't, men will die in five minutes, sir."

"Pass the word to have the men find masks for the ship's emergency air system."

"You would have them switch masks in a cyanide atmosphere, sir?"

"If it comes down to that or suffocating, yes."

Chan probed his mind for a new plan.

"There are atmosphere-sensing kits in the engineering spaces, are there not?"

"If this ship is true to our homemade submarines, as it should be, then yes."

"It is. We sold the North Koreans this vessel, and there is no reason they would store the kits elsewhere. Measure cyanide levels in all compartments. Have the men with limited air gather in the cleanest space."

Chan straddled a corpse and looked over the shoulder of a sailor at a weapon control screen. He saw what he wanted.

"Our salvo is active," he said.

A sailor nodded his confirmation, and Chan returned to the sonar operator's shoulder. One incoming weapon angled away, but the other maintained its course toward his *Romeo*.

"Increase speed to flank," Chan said.

"Battery life is now fifteen minutes," Gao said. "Speed is increased to thirteen knots."

A sailor with a glass tube and rubber suction bulb entered the compartment and announced that the cleanest air in the submarine was in the control room.

"Have the men with limited air gather here," Chan said.

A half dozen men crammed into the crowded room, and Chan recognized risk as the cost of command.

"If I pass out or die," he said. "Surface, ventilate, and take down that corvette."

He knelt and lifted the mask from his deceased predecessor. As he plugged it into the ship's emergency air line, he welcomed the high-pressure hiss. He drew in a breath, removed his mask, and pulled the straps of the new one over his head.

While he cracked the air tight seal with his finger, he coughed his lungs empty and forced air from his mask. He released the rubbery seal to his face and inhaled from the header.

His world turned a dizzy red, and his legs felt wobbly. But he stood and he breathed. After calming himself with multiple breaths, he barked his order.

"Find masks and plug in," he said.

"Our lead weapon is in terminal homing!" Gao said.

"Excellent," Chan said. "Estimated distance to nearest incoming weapon?"

"Seven nautical miles. We will make it, sir, if we retain propulsion."

The ocean grumbled and boomed.

"The corvette is no longer a problem," Chan said.

"Shall we surface, sir?"

"Wait until we've cleared distance from the corvette. In case they have called for assistance, I want to be far away when we broach."

"We no longer hear incoming active seekers," Gao said.

"That's encouraging but not definitive," Chan said. "We will maintain flank speed for three more minutes."

Chan waited with a patience that surprised him as the incoming weapon diminished into a ghost.

"Slow to three knots," he said. "Listen for incoming weapons. Line up to snorkel and ventilate all compartments while charging batteries."

The deck rolled into the balls of his feet.

"What's next after ventilating, sir?" Gao asked. "Time with a mast exposed on the surface is time at risk."

"Agreed," Chan said. "We head toward the nearest friendly

waters until I'm sure no hostile assets are tracking us. Chart a course for Qingdao."

While the *Romeo* bobbed at shallow depth, Chan listened to the grumbling engines. The twin diesels sucked air through the induction mast, dragging it through the compartments en route to their intakes.

Chan squinted through his mask at the periscope optics but could see little. Gao appeared before him, reddened skin and sweat outlining his face where his mask had been.

"The air is clean, sir."

Chan tore off his mask and glued his eye to the periscope. The dark horizon became discernible. He rotated in slow circles, unsure of what he hoped or expected.

His stomach sank and his heart raced. He saw a mast on the horizon, and a sick intuition suggested that it belonged to a South Korean destroyer.

CHAPTER 6

Air whipped Jake's cheeks as the black void swallowed him. His lungs froze as his jumpmaster yanked at his flanks and dislodged him from their tandem connection. He tucked and rolled, finding relief in the softness of the dirt.

He pushed himself prone, steadying his world. His muscles knotted as the billowing parachute cast a translucent veil over the moonlit horizon. As the sprawling canvas jetted toward a cliff, its wires entangled the jumpmaster's leg.

Jake rose and sprinted toward his companion, who dragged his free boot on the ground while slashing a knife at his damning cords.

Diving, Jake grabbed the man's waist, rolled, and felt the thump of his helmet hitting a stone. He fought the anger of the gale to spare the man who had guided him through a high-altitude jump with a twenty-mile glide to a tiny rock in the East China Sea.

Through combat fatigues, dirt abraded his leg. As the landing zone's edge approached, he prepared for a fateful decision to relinquish his partner to his death.

He fell back, and the world became silent. Panting, he rolled forward to see his freed companion reclining before him. Wind whipped the parachute up, fluttering it and pumping it like a jellyfish before driving it below the cliff and into the sea.

Jake helped his partner to his feet and served as a crutch to the limping soldier. After a few steps, separated by a language barrier, he reached an agreement with the man that reaching the lighthouse required a piggyback ride.

Adrenaline coursing through his muscular mass, Jake found his companion an ethereal load while trudging through the earth. He paused, reached under his passenger's thigh, and tugged him higher up his back.

While walking, he mulled over the debate gnawing at him since leaving Michigan. He felt drawn to the allure of leading a frontline warship into combat, but part of him hoped to find a crew on the submarine competent enough to handle affairs without him.

When he reached the lighthouse, a bulb shone on a man in slacks and dress shirt who rendered Jake a smile.

"It has been a while," Henri Lanier said.

"Henri, my friend," Jake said.

Henri reminded him of a reserved version of Pierre Renard with an uptick in dignity and impeccable penchant for dress. The aging submarine mechanic kissed the air by Jake's cheeks.

Repositioning the jumpmaster on his back, Jake lifted the oxygen mask at his chest.

"Where can I dump my gear?"

"In the lighthouse."

"And my new friend?"

"Also in the lighthouse. There is no place else."

Jake followed Henri into the circular structure and left his companion on a chair. A keeper approached, exchanged words in Mandarin and nods with the injured man, and gestured for Henri to join him.

The keeper and Henri slid a desk and kicked back a carpet. The Frenchman knelt and pulled open a trap door. He started down steep stairs cut into stone, and Jake followed his silvery hair into darkness.

Florescent lights revealed crude, jagged cuts into rock. Jake's legs ached as he stooped.

"I imagine this resembles the tunnels the Koreans used under the demilitarized zone."

Jake's words echoed through the tunnel.

"Probably," Henri said.

"Not meant for a man of my height," Jake said.

"Nor mine. Pace yourself. It's a long way to the submarine pen."

Ten minutes later, Jake slouched sore shoulders and saw metal plates blocking the level ground ahead.

"What's that?"

"They force a zigzagging path through the final meters to

reach the pen," Henri said. "To slow infiltrators."

"Clever."

"Thank the South Koreans," Henri said.

"Installed in tunnels under the demilitarized zone?"

"In addition to sealing them with concrete, at least for the ones they know about."

After wiggling through the plates, Jake watched Henri punch a code into a console by a steel door. The Frenchman shouldered the door open to a control room no bigger than Jake's suburban living room.

Jake entered and latched the door behind him. Windows at the far wall revealed a cave hewn by nature, with fingers of stalactites, expanded and shaped by explosives.

Halogen lights bathed a concrete dock beside which rose a black conning tower. Jake recognized the *Hai Ming* as the Taiwanese version of the familiar *Scorpène* class. Nostalgia of past deeds rose within him, yielded to anxiety of uncertain dangers, and evaporated with Henri's voice.

"We have a problem," the Frenchman said.

"What is it?" Jake asked.

"From the looks of it, a drone. There's a satellite photograph from the United States with a note from Pierre."

Jake crouched while Henri pointed at the screen.

"This oblong object in the water," Henri said. "It surfaced for several hours before sinking. It probably was intended to sink more rapidly but suffered a malfunction."

"Looks like a torpedo, but torpedoes don't surface, unless they're exercise weapons. This thing's got to be an acoustic drone."

"Pierre agrees," Henri said. "So do the American analysts."

"It's Chinese, right?" Jake asked.

Henri lifted a sheet with black text toward his nose. Jake watched his eyes scan Renard's note.

"Pierre suspects that a Chinese submarine launched it and then abandoned it to its mission. It likely searched around the island on a repeated route for days, if not weeks."

"They know we're here," Jake said. "Shit."

"Not necessarily, he says. The Chinese at least suspect our presence within the island. However, their drone technology is inferior. The drone would have been challenged to hear one of our submarines."

"I'm not sharing your optimism," Jake said.

"This islet has always had a military presence. It may just be a precaution on the part of the Chinese."

"And there's been no sign of Chinese submarine activity around here?"

"Nothing."

"They could have laid mines around the island, if they figured out we're here."

"There are no mines, Jake. Divers check the shallows frequently."

"But not the steep drop off. You can't check there for mines."

Jake sensed himself panicking worse than he had while facing greater past perils. Henri stood straight.

"We have an acoustic array around the island."

"That's comforting," Jake said. "I'm a little on edge."

"I see. It's unlike you."

Jake thought of his wife.

"I have someone I want to go home to this time."

"I know," Henri said. "Pierre warned me."

"Warned you?"

"Yes. You are trying to convince yourself that you would enjoy a quiet life. We have all tried it. Pierre, Antoine, Claude, myself. But it is folly. Once you taste the adventure, you cannot reject it."

Jake tucked Henri's musings into his memory's recesses and sought a distraction to the Frenchman's sharp philosophical insight.

"Why don't we have a defensive minefield?"

"The Taiwanese could not lay one," Henri said. "The act of laying would have risked suspicion of our presence, and the detonation of a mine would have confirmed it."

"Forgive my pessimism," Jake said. "That's looking like the wrong decision."

*

Jake followed Henri down a staircase to the chiseled ledge of rock serving as a wharf and marveled at the brutal elegance of the waterfront.

The Taiwanese had packed spare weapons, fuel tanks, and electronic cables into carved recesses. Fed by fuel and lubricant lines, a diesel generator whirred with air ducts running into the rock ceiling.

"How'd they get all this down here without the Chinese knowing?"

"The cutting took two years," Henri said. "Once the rocks were carved, the concrete and wood arrived aboard submarines. So did any machinery too large to appear appropriate for the lighthouse and encampment."

Jake looked again at the diesel.

"This is cannibalized."

"Indeed," Henri said. "Lifted from the last of the *Guppy*-class submarines in the Taiwanese order of battle. So are the pipes and tanks."

A tank raised in recessed shadows came into Jake's view. Piping connected its underbelly to a centrifugal pump with a discharge line kinking into the water.

"What's that?" he asked. "It's big enough to be spare diesel fuel, but I question the pump and pipes heading into the water."

"That's the hydrazine," Henri said. "Across the basin is the sodium azide."

"I'm not following."

"I see that Pierre did not explain the hydrazine line," Henri said. "I designed the system for him, and we tested a prototype in the Azores. It's a defense system of pumps, pipes, and chemicals. It shares structural supports with the hydrophone system."

"So, on our egress route, just before the drop off to deep

water," Jake said, "you have an underwater piping system running at the edge of the shallows, carrying something called hydrazine."

"Hydrazine and sodium azide, isolated from each other, of course. Only when activated will the compounds react."

"React and blow up?"

"React and gasify," Henri said. "Like an airbag, only there's no airbag. Just the shallow water above. The piping has release valves and aeration holes running its length. The system creates an instant curtain of bubbles."

Jake frowned.

"Countermeasures on steroids," he said. "Either that or Alka-Seltzer for whales. Why?"

"It's quite useful in many circumstances."

Jake wanted to spin the idea of a bubble curtain throughout his imagination, but he considered it distracting.

"Looks to me like Pierre's letting you play with science experiments," he said. "Let's see the ship."

Jake's boots tapped concrete as he trailed Henri onto the dock. An aluminum gangway echoed with his steps and carried him to the back of the black submarine where his soles gripped rough steel.

Orienting himself on the warship spurred his awareness. He realized that the ship pointed toward the cavern's solitary, submerged exit.

"How'd they turn the ship around?" he asked.

Henri pointed toward the deep, dark end of the cave.

"There are capstans on the far wall," he said. "It takes nearly half an hour of line handling, but it is a rather simple exercise to complete."

"And a smart design to turn the ship around on the way in," Jake said. "Allows for a quick exit."

"Not too quick," Henri said. "Lest you drive the submarine into the island. The exit is completely submerged and gives scant room for error. Fortunately, the ship's formal captain, who will be your executive officer functionally, is an expert at piloting the egress."

"I can't wait to meet him."

"Well then," Henri said. "Turn around."

Jake turned, and a diminutive man in a Taiwanese lieutenant commander's uniform extended a hand. Jake shook it and noted pimples, thick glasses, and a goofy smile. The officer looked too young for his role.

"Jake," Henri said, "allow me to introduce Lieutenant Commander Yangyi Jin, commanding officer of the *Hai Ming*."

"Consider me your executive officer, Mister Slate" Jin said. "I will follow your lead. My command is a formality."

"Sure," Jake said. "That's how it worked last time. If you don't mind me asking, what's your experience in hunting submarines?"

"I'm an expert with drone operations. I handled them in three successful anti-submarine missions."

Jake digested the answer's narrowness.

"Then you're a specialist?"

"Yes."

"Have you led an attack against surface vessels?"

"I have not led in combat. Those who have such experience are deployed on the *Sea Tiger* and *Sea Dragon* or perished on the *Hai Lang*. I am here to support basic submerged operations with the joint French and Taiwanese team and to handle the drones during combat."

"Very well," Jake said. "Let's head below and brief the crew on the mission."

Jin disappeared through the hatch, and Jake called to Henri in French to assure secrecy.

"Is he really the best they have?"

"He proved his competence in sea trials with me," Henri said. "And his reputation precedes him in drone operations."

"But no combat leadership."

"The best perished on the *Hai Lang*. The remaining people with experience were shared on their other two submarines, which are searching for Chinese submarine pens. Jin was the only officer available with combat experience."

"He looks twelve years old."

"He was a lieutenant until promoted into this role," Henri said. "Yes, he is young."

"What about the rest?"

"Pierre recruited half a dozen young men from the French Navy. They are even better than the prior crop."

"That's good, but what about their Taiwanese counterparts?"

"A dozen good men," Henri said. "Pierre and I observed them in training drills and sea trials. They are disciplined and bright, but they are untested in combat. They will need leadership."

Jake stared down the hatch into the vessel and prepared to re-enter the dangerous submerged universe.

Fate decreed that the *Hai Ming* was his to command.

CHAPTER 7

Jake beheld the *Hai Ming's* operations room. Six dual-stacked French-designed Subtics system tactical monitors spanned the compartment's left side. Before one panel sat sonar systems expert, Antoine Remy.

Short with a wide head and thick nose, Remy reminded Jake of a toad. He stood, shook his hand, and kissed the air beside his cheeks.

"I am happy that you decided to join us," Remy said.

Jake considered claiming that Secretary Rickets had forced him, but he banished excuses to the other side of the steel shell encircling him.

"It's good to see you, my old friend," Jake said.

As Remy returned to his sonar system diagnostics, Jake noticed young Taiwanese sailors offering hopeful and uncertain stares. Jin made introductions and assurances of the competence of the ship's native contingent. Jake found their English respectable and saw a healthy mix of bravado and fear in their eyes.

After handshakes, the men returned to their stations.

"They are rehearsing drills," Jin said. "To assure proper response during important events."

"Which one are they rehearsing now?"

"Emergency deep procedure."

"Do you have an abandon ship procedure?"

"No."

"Make one," Jake said. "These are shallow waters, and the surface will always be attainable."

Jin appeared frozen in indecision. Jake realized the young Taiwanese officer was processing his first command.

"Yes, Mister Slate," Jin said.

"Call me 'Jake'. It's quicker communication."

"Yes, Jake."

"I will introduce myself to the rest of the crew while I tour the ship with Henri. Have an abandon ship procedure outlined when I get back. Include life rafts, provisions, communications equipment, and fire arms."

"Yes, Jake."

Jake nodded, turned, and ducked through the compartment's aft door. He heard Henri's rubber soles tap the deck plate behind him.

"It's like déjà vu," Jake said. "This ship feels like it rolled right off DCN's construction dock."

"It may as well have," Henri said, "given the droves of French workers Pierre recruited to Keelung for its construction."

Jake passed through the after battery compartment and after auxiliary machinery room, reaching the hull section that contained the air-independent ethanol and liquid oxygen MESMA plant. He looked upward at a high-pressure tank of compressed explosive gas. His fingers tapped cool, dormant piping as he moved by.

He ducked through another watertight door and underneath the wide air ducts leading to the quad diesels. He saw the main motor further aft, hidden intermittently by a man pointing to gauges on a control panel. Four sailors–two wearing Taiwanese uniforms, two Frenchmen in dungarees–stood behind their teacher, who smiled, embraced Jake, and kissed the air beside his cheeks.

Jake welcomed the presence of Claude LaFontaine, former engineer officer on the French nuclear-powered *Rubis* submarine and proven expert on diesel operations aboard *Agosta* and *Scorpène*-class boats.

"*Bonjour*! Welcome, Jake."

"Claude LaFontaine," Jake said. "You haven't changed a bit. Still wiry and fidgety."

"Can't eat enough to gain weight, even at my age. Let me introduce you to some of the engineering team."

Jake shook hands with Taiwanese mechanics and young electricians pilfered from the French navy. One had a thick accent, but Jake judged the English skills sufficient.

"How is the propulsion system?" Jake asked.

"Just like you would expect from a European shipyard," La-Fontaine said. "Predictable. Reliable. Not a peep or hint of protest at depth, speed, or maneuvers."

"The MESMA system?"

"Fine," LaFontaine said. "I ran it hard during shakedown, but I didn't push its endurance. I wanted to conserve fuel. We can't refuel oxygen here. Only diesel."

"You made a good choice, my old friend," Jake said. "Have you exercised the battery through full cycling?"

"Of course. All within specifications."

Held by Henri's hands, an electronic tablet appeared, showing a summary page of systems tested during sea trials.

Jake waved his hand.

"Okay," he said. "I studied the reports on the flight to Taiwan. If you guys tell me the ship is ready for sea, then it's ready."

"It's ready, Jake," LaFontaine said.

Jake watched Henri nod his agreement as he questioned if a submarine of French comrades in a strange land was supplanting a Michigan suburb as home.

*

Two hours later, French and Taiwanese sailors crammed around the control room's central chart table. Jake slid a stylus across a chart.

"When the last patrol craft evades the minefield to the east, we turn north and clear the area."

The faces surrounding him appeared to understand. Jake took comfort that his team learned fast, but he disliked their lack of experience. Nobody had the knowledge to second guess him. Henri knew nothing of combat tactics, and the art of dueling with another submarine remained unknown to Lieutenant Commander Jin.

"Take a fifteen-minute break," Jake said. "Return here for a review of drills."

"We have only two more hours of darkness," Henri said. "It takes well over an hour to egress from this berthing."

"We're not leaving this morning," Jake said. "We'll wait until tonight. We have plenty of time."

"I was allowing for contingencies."

"Good thinking," Jake said. "But I'm training for contingencies of a different sort."

*

Three hours later, Jake's adrenaline ebbed, and fatigue clouded his thoughts as he stifled a yawn.

"One more time," he said. "Torpedo evasion!"

Jake glanced at the Frenchman at his control panel to the right of the central charting table.

"I ring up a head flank with cavitation to the engine room," Henri said.

Jake angled his nose to the other side of the room.

"I warm up countermeasures to be launched on your mark," Lin said

"I prepare a torpedo for a reactive launch, search depth equal to our own depth, range three thousand nautical yards," a Taiwanese sailor seated beside Jin said.

"And I report the bearing to the incoming torpedo every fifteen seconds, whether you hear me or not," Remy said from his sonar station.

The voices sounded tired and the faces looked worn, but Jake judged the team as ready as an ad hoc crew could be.

"Very well," he said. "Everyone get some sleep. We're getting underway in seven hours."

*

Jake awoke with a coppery taste. The commanding officer's wardroom felt confining as he crept to a steel basin to brush his teeth. He stripped and slipped into a shower, spurting water over himself. As the droplets landed against entombing metal, he felt trapped in an alien world he had forgotten.

After drying himself and donning loose-fitting slacks and a cotton dress shirt, he ducked through the watertight door to the control room. He heard Henri's soles slapping ladder rungs and saw the Frenchman stoop through a door.

"Topside is rigged for submerging," Henri said. "The gangway is on the pier, and four lines remain to be cast off to get underway. Each line is mated to a capstan."

"What's next?"

"Divers swim to the capstans on the far wall," Henri said. "There will also be line handling crews at the pier capstans. The line handling crews will pull us from the pier and orient us in the center of the basin."

"Then how do we get rid of the lines?"

"Divers mount us to cast off the lines, and then they swim for the pier. We'll receive word when they are clear so we may submerge. They await your command."

Jake nodded and reached for a microphone above.

"Prepare to get underway," he said. "Man the egress piloting team."

Sailors filled the tiny room, and Henri moved beside Jake, who handed him a radio handset.

"Tell them to center us in the basin."

Henri exchanged words with the command station.

"Line crews are maneuvering us," Henri said. "It will take a good ten minutes to steady us."

"How's our trim going to be?"

"Very light," Henri said. "We will submerge slowly, and there will be a slight down angle."

"How many times have you done this before?"

"Me? Twice. Jin has been through it three times. It will be tight by design, but it will go smoothly."

Jake stepped forward and placed his eye on the periscope optics. Under florescent illumination, a man in a wetsuit whipped a hand crank and coiled nylon rope around a capstan. He stopped and dropped his head below his shoulders, Jake assumed, as the submarine slid toward him.

The man looked up in response to a distant cue and recommenced his laboring with the crank. He released the handle, stood, and shook his arms.

"We are centered," Henri said.

"Lowering the periscope," Jake said.

He twisted a ring concentric to a glistening shaft and watched the periscope glide into the well at his feet.

"Lines are off," Henri said. "We are underway and ready to conduct the egress."

"Attention in the control room," Jake said. "Henri has the conn. I have the deck."

Taiwanese faces looked at him and frowned.

"That means Henri is driving but still taking orders from me," Jake said.

Heads nodded.

"Submerge the ship and pilot us to open water."

"Submerge the ship and pilot us, aye," Henri said. "Open main ballast tank vents."

Jin flipped switches, and Jake felt nothing while the creeping numbers of a depth gauge hinted at motion.

"Subtle," he said.

"Indeed," Henri said. "Each tank level and storage weight is known, be it fuel, sanitary matter, lubrication oil, food stores, or weapons. Even each person on board is accounted for in the neutral buoyancy equation."

Jake waited and eyed Henri.

"We've steadied," he said. "Looks to me like we've hit the bottom of the basin, huh?"

Henri glanced at the depth gauge and blushed.

"The basin floor is covered with a meter of silt in the event that the buoyancy calculation is... just slightly off," Henri said. "I will get us off the bottom."

Henri slid over the shoulders of a seated sailor and stood behind Jin. He pointed and orchestrated the movement of water through tanks, spurring a trim pump to life that caressed Jake's ear with a distant whir. The ship tilted forward, rolling Jake to the balls of his feet.

Henri returned to his side and shrugged.

"I apologize."

"No need," Jake said. "I once drilled a Trident into the bottom of the Atlantic."

"Nevertheless," Henri said. "I will be more careful."

"Take her to sea," Jake said.

"Make turns for two knots," Henri said.

Jake watched a speed gauge crawl through one knot. Henri returned to Jin's shoulder and helped the Taiwanese officer caress the submarine down an underwater ramp. The speed readout indicated two knots.

"Leveling out," Henri said.

Jake rebalanced his weight between his heels and toes.

"We are passing through the basin door," Henri said. "The egress will be complete momentarily."

Henri turned, hovered over the nautical chart, and lifted his head from between his shoulder blades.

"We are clear, Jake."

"I have the deck and the conn," Jake said. "Make turns for four knots. Maintain course."

He stepped to the chart and stood opposite Henri.

"Expand the scale," he said.

Henri lowered his arm and depressed a button. The islet became smaller, the world expanded, and the fathom curves tightened. The islet's defensive sonar array wiggled into the field of view followed by the dark blue hue of deeper water.

"Give me a deduced reckoning," Jake said.

Henri nodded and slid his finger to a second control. Timestamps glowed on hashes crossing the *Hai Ming's* projected course.

"We can go deeper in twenty minutes at this pace," Henri said. "Do you wish to accelerate?"

Jake shook his head, surprising himself with patience.

"Secure the piloting team and set underway watch team number one. Take over the control station from Jin."

Jake stepped back to the elevated conning platform and sat on a foldout seat as bodies snake-danced before him. Ten minutes elapsed, and a new team settled in the room.

He dismissed Henri to explore the submarine for signs that a valve might have been left open, a duct misdirected, or a spoon misplaced. He trusted the veteran's instincts to assure the ship's readiness.

In a moment of quiet, he let himself think about returning home, another game-changing deed accomplished with inner peace as his reward.

"Jake!"

The interruption was a hoarse whisper. Antoine Remy, his eyes huge between the muffs of his sonar headset, had become a petrified toad.

"Antoine?" he asked.

"I think I heard launch transients."

"You think?"

"I wasn't listening for them. There's something out there, bearing one-six-two."

Jake flew to Remy's shoulder and studied his screen. A discernible blip of noise rolled down the Subtics monitor.

"There," Remy said.

Jake nudged the Taiwanese sailor beside Remy.

"Transmit three secure active bursts on that bearing."

Three lines sought acoustic returns on a Subtics monitor. Three blips glowed three miles away on a bearing of one-six-two.

"Shit," Jake said. "Warm up tube one. Three-mile range, bearing one-six-two. Target speed zero."

"High-speed screws!" Remy said.

"Get a bearing rate."

Remy clasped his muffs and squinted.

"Forward. It's leading us, Jake. It's a good shot!"

"Torpedo evasion!" Jake said. "Countermeasures now!"

The submarine shuddered, and compressed air popped as the hull expelled gaseous canisters. A voice Jake recognized through his adrenaline as that of Lieutenant Commander Jin made ready his retaliatory torpedo.

"Shoot tube one!" Jake said.

The rapid equalizing of pressure through the vented torpedo tube hurt Jake's ears as an ejection pump thrust a slug of water cradling his weapon into the sea.

He remembered that returning fire disoriented an attacker who controlled his weapon via a command wire. Then he realized his attacker didn't need a wire. Someone had surprised him and shot from point blank range.

His pulse racing, Jake accepted that his counter fire shot was spite against an enemy who had already won.

CHAPTER 8

Restraining his coiled power wore out Brody's patience, and he banged his horns against his pen's steel gate. If Defense Secretary Rickets wanted to straddle his broad shoulders and ride him to victory, he'd first have to prove he could hold on.

"Let me invade Taiwan," he said.

"No," Rickets said.

"You're being weak," Admiral John Brody said.

"You're being irrational. America won't tolerate the risk, and neither will I."

Brody suppressed an urge to swear.

"You mean your political career won't tolerate it," he said. "You're positioning yourself as a moderate conservative presidential candidate, the guy who can land a soft jab on China's face but hold back the haymaker."

"This isn't about obliterating an enemy. We're too intertwined with China economically. It's about wielding measured power to strengthen a diplomatic outcome."

"Damn it," Brody said. "I can end this."

"The conclusion is already known. Korea is backpedaling. Israel has taken the hit but will push back. Japan is just being harassed, and China won't attack them. These were only distractions using diversion and puppets. All China cares about is Taiwan."

"Then why are my forces elsewhere?" Brody asked.

"You have to address the other fronts," Rickets said. "You need to keep the pressure on, the air sorties going, the counter-harassment games in the Sea of Japan. You are the demonstration of strength."

Brody wanted his career to culminate in more than a demonstration.

"Then close the diplomatic deals on those fronts so I can redeploy to Taiwan," he said. "I can win there."

"It's not about winning," Rickets said. "It's about American lives."

"American lives are being lost now."

"Not in the numbers they would be if you engage China. Losing pilots or a squad of marines is one thing. Losing hundreds of lives when a naval vessel is attacked is another, and that's what's going to happen if you take China on directly."

"That's what my warriors signed up for," Brody said.

"America isn't on board."

"I've drawn up plans that minimize the risk. The commandant is ready to support with his marines. The time to attack is now, while China thinks they've got us spread thin elsewhere."

"They do have us spread thin elsewhere," Rickets said. "That's why I'm letting the Taiwanese defend themselves."

Brody checked himself. He questioned if he was letting an urge for personal glory cloud his judgment. He wondered if political ambition was driving him too hard to position himself as the Great American Conqueror.

"I might agree," he said, "if you can convince me they can succeed."

"The nukes will enable it."

Brody sensed a new air of smugness. He glared at Rickets in a silent conversation of facial expressions.

"You gave them the nukes, didn't you?" he asked.

Rickets glanced at the floor, smirked, and looked up.

"That's an interesting theory. I admit I had plenty of opportunity to do so, but you probably already knew that."

Brody sensed he had stumbled onto a truth that struck like an ice pick on steel before its shock receded into the acceptance of a warm bath–a truth both obvious and necessary in retrospect of the complexities that led him to the precipice of nuclear hostility.

Rickets had not just spent years moving nuclear fuel to Taiwan, enabling the island to fend for itself, but he had overseen its growth in strength.

Somehow, Brody thought, Rickets also controlled Taiwan through the subtle and murky machinations of a politician–through the fragile economics of favors traded, promises made, and expectations insinuated. And a Frenchman named Pierre Renard served as his governor of such arrangements.

Rickets' wielding of power over a nation with a perfect delicateness intimidated Brody, and he struggled to hide his doubt.

"So, the fact remains that they are armed and ready to strike," Brody said. "There's a conflict brewing that will change the shape of warfare forever."

"That's why I called you here," Rickets said. "We're getting ready for the minefield egress operation, and nukes will be used. I want an update. Renard is standing by."

Rickets raised a remote from the arm of his chair, and the speakers bracketing the monitor chirped. A dark screen yielded to the sagging cheeks of the Frenchman Brody remained uncertain he could trust.

"Good morning, gentlemen," Renard said.

"You look tired," Rickets said.

"I shall rest soon. I have time set aside before the patrol craft make for sea."

"When are they leaving?" Rickets asked.

"The operation is on schedule," Renard said. "The first patrol craft will leave port at dawn."

"Taiwan controls the airspace?" Rickets asked.

"The hold is tenuous but should last," Renard said.

"Good."

"Only eighteen patrol craft are available. One was lost on a reconnaissance mission, and another–the one in the greatest state of disrepair–was cannibalized to make the others seaworthy."

"You estimate needing twelve craft to hold the line at the choke points?"

"Yes," Renard said. "Four to the south to the Philippines and eight to the north along the Ryukyu Island chain. I expect losses in the minefield egress, but I predict fourteen to fifteen survivors."

"That's acceptable," Rickets said.

"There are no further deviations," Renard said. "You have the most updated operations schedule."

"Admiral Brody," Renard said.

Brody wiggled in his seat.

"Yes, I'm listening," he said.

"The official nuclear exclusion zone remains unchanged," Renard said. "But I can share with you the less restrictive zone where the Taiwanese truly intend to operate. You'll want to assure that your assets are clear of the coordinates which I will send you immediately after our discussion is ended."

An international criminal telling him where he could deploy the United States Navy pushed Brody over the edge.

"A maverick doesn't tell the Chief of Naval Operations where he can deploy his forces."

"He's on our side, admiral," Rickets said.

"No," Brody said. "This smells wrong because it is wrong. You're letting him dictate the outcome of a Sino-American war."

"I'm letting him prevent a Sino-American war."

Brody sighed and softened his tone.

"Something will go wrong. A nuke will land where it's not supposed to, someone will get pissed, and someone will fire back harder."

"I'm not risking American lives," Rickets said.

"It's a foregone conclusion. You can't let Taiwan go nuclear and expect to contain it. You're not controlling anything. You're opening Pandora's box."

"No!"

"Let me invade!" Brody

"Gentlemen!" Renard said.

Brody looked to the monitor and saw the Frenchman cradling a cigarette beside his cheek.

"What?" Brody asked.

"The Taiwanese Minister of Defense has given the patrol craft authorization to use tactical nuclear weapons. The decision is made, the order is given, and it is not yours to rescind."

"This is insanity," Brody said.

"Limited theater escalation is sane," Renard said. "This is a rational solution to a complex problem."

"God help us all when this goes awry," Brody said.

"We are all men of action," Renard said. "We accept and manage the gravest of risks."

"Don't try to compare me to you," Brody said.

He stood.

"Are we done here?" he asked.

"Yes," Rickets said.

"Excuse me."

Brody stormed out of the secretary's office, reflecting if he should resign his post or give the order to invade Taiwan before Rickets could stop him.

CHAPTER 9

Jake braced himself against a metal rail as the deck heeled underneath him. Henri stood by his side during the turn.

"There's no way they heard us," Jake said.

"What?" Henri asked.

In past challenges, Jake's comment would have been a catalyst for tactical interplay with Pierre Renard. Upon Henri's ears, useless. He missed Renard.

"Nothing," Jake said. "I'm trying to run behind the islet to shake the torpedo."

"Shall I relieve Jin?" Henri asked.

"Yeah," Jake said. "Jin, oversea the plot."

The Taiwanese officer stood and slid to the table in the room's center. Henri walked to the ship's control station and sat.

A piercing and repeating beep pelted Jake's head. He pointed to the active torpedo seeker alarm and yelled.

"Silence that damned thing!"

Jin twisted and reached over a Subtics monitor, and the beep subsided. He bent over the plot, absorbed the image, and looked up.

"Torpedo has passed our countermeasures," he said. "Impact in three minutes."

Jake turned his head toward a monitor framing a miniaturized rendition of the battle scene.

"Right," he said. "We're not getting away."

"We are dead, then?" Jin asked.

The omen from his brother Nick sliced Jake's mind.

"Prepare to abandon ship," he said. "Everyone gets off in two minutes. That's an order. No heroes."

Jin reached into the overhead for a microphone and extended its coiled cord towards his chin. He passed word on the ship's loudspeaker.

"Walk the ship and make sure everyone is getting off," Jake said.

Jin darted by Jake on his way aft.

"Henri," Jake said. "Prepare to surface."

Henri's eyes became black defiance.

"Use the hydrazine line," he said.

Jake tapped his memory for the concept of Henri's science project and found no tactical relevance.

"Trust me," Henri said. "I designed it for this very purpose, primarily."

"Torpedo defense?"

"Yes," Henri said. "In the Azores, the prototype line defeated a torpedo."

"No," Jake said. "I can get us off this thing."

"It will work, Jake. And you can still abandon ship if it doesn't."

Remy, earmuffs extending his wide head, announced that Jake's avenging weapon had discovered its target. The news was fleeting nihilistic justice drowned in his rising curiosity in Henri's invention.

"How do I use it?" he asked.

"Will you trust me to execute maneuver?" Henri asked as he stood. "For the sake of brevity."

"Yes," Jake said. "Attention in the control room. Henri has the conn. I retain the deck."

Henri traversed the small room and stepped up to Jake, who leaned back to yield a line of sight between the Frenchman and the monitor. A Taiwanese sailor wearing a life vest moved towards Henri's vacated station. Jake nodded and pointed, and the sailor sat.

"Right ten-degrees rudder," Henri said. "Steady course one-zero-five."

The deck shifted as Jake glanced at the monitor. A sharp green glow traced the *Hai Ming's* future path over the hydrazine line's eastern edge.

Jin returned wearing a life jacket and bearing word that the crew was stationed for a blitz exit. Remy updated Jake with an estimate of two minutes to torpedo impact.

"We've got to be on the surface in one minute to evacuate if this doesn't work," Jake said.

"We are shallow," Henri said.

"This has to work," Jake said.

"It will."

Seconds ticked through Jake's mind like a dirge. The thought of growing old with his wife glowed within him, mortal terror coaxing the concept's allure.

"All stop," Henri said.

"You're slowing?" Jake asked.

"To keep us near the activated section of the line."

The surreal grip of illogic tensed Jake's spine as he let a French mechanic retard his flight from a torpedo. His tactical intuition inverted, he sold out to Henri's plan.

"Does this work if we're surfaced?" he asked.

"Yes, of course," Henri said. "I see your point. We will slow more quickly."

Jake pointed to a seated Taiwanese sailor.

"Blow the main ballast tanks."

The sailor rotated two nobs upward. High-pressure air roared through wide pipes, and the deck pressed against his heels. The submarine surfaced and rocked.

Jake watched a green crosshair icon glide over the charted position of Henri's defense line. The Frenchman reached up and flipped a switch.

"Activating the hydrazine line," Henri said.

"That's it?" Jake asked.

"The fathometer is the system trigger."

"Using the backup fathometer frequency?"

"I knew you'd never use it intentionally."

Jake glanced to Remy and saw his toad-shaped head nod.

"He hears the gasses mixing," Henri said. "The line is activated. It's just a matter of seconds before the adequate pressure builds."

"Now it either protects us, or it doesn't," Jake said.

"Any second now," Henri said.

"Just in case…"

Jake reached for the microphone above, detached it, and moved it to his lips.

"All hands abandon ship. No life rafts. There's no time and no need. Get off the ship!"

"I'm staying," Henri said.

"Very well," Jake said. "Jin, lead the crew off."

"I will stay," Jin said.

"No," Jake said. "The men need a leader. Jump first so they follow you in."

The room expelled all inhabitants except for Jake and the Frenchmen. Before Jake could expel the sonar expert, thunder rumbled through his steel shell world, and a swath of acoustic fuzz etched itself on a monitor.

"Hydrazine and sodium azide are mixing," Henri said.

"So, we just wait and drift?"

"Yes," Henri said. "The torpedo should perish in the disruption above the line."

Jake turned his chin toward Remy.

"Do you hear anything?"

"A lot of hissing," Remy said. "But no torpedo."

Jake waited for the torpedo to reappear and end his life. Beside him, Henri appeared mesmerized in thoughts hewn between life and death. Jake remembered that talking helped deal with the slow moments of terror where fate unfolded its unavoidable mortal verdict.

"Henri?"

No response.

"Henri?"

The Frenchman turned his head and said nothing.

"How long does the hydrazine last?" Jake asked.

"As long as we need," Henri said.

He started to taper off. Jake engaged his companion's mind to keep it responsive.

"How long is that, Henri? Using the pumping system you designed, how long does the system work?"

"Only a subset of valves open near the location where we

crossed. It optimizes the gaseous distribution that way. We have at least three minutes."

"What happens to the torpedo?"

"It accelerates to penetrate through the noise, descends violently in the bubble curtain, and hopefully sustains damage to its sensors and guidance electronics as it hits the wall of water on the far end."

"Hopefully?"

"Probably. If not, the torpedo may be set wildly off course. In these shallow waters, it may also take on such a steep angle as to collide with the sea bottom."

Jake grunted.

"Remy, anything?"

"No, Jake. Just hissing."

"Would you hear an active seeker?"

"Yes, I think so. There's nothing."

Jake returned his attention to Henri.

"Can you turn the line off?" he asked.

"Five active pings in rapid succession will tell the operators in the pen to secure the pumps," Henri said. "They will hear it on the sonar arrays and recognize our sonar system."

Jake walked to the abandoned station beside Remy, tapped keys, and ordered the ship to render the sonar pings. As he returned to the chart, the crackling stopped, and he held his breath.

A phantom hiss toyed with his ears, and he knew that Remy strained through a similar auditory hallucination to discern the sea's true noises.

"Anything now?"

"Yes, Jake!" Remy said. "High-speed screws!"

"Damn it! Bearing rate?"

"Not changing."

Jake's heart sank, and he wondered if he could get off the *Hai Ming* in time.

"Wait, Jake. I hear Doppler shifting on the blades."

"It's turning?"

"Yes! In a tight circle."

Jake held his breath and waited for Remy to ratify his hopes. The Frenchman obliged with a howl.

"Incoming torpedo has shut down!"

"Keep listening for other weapons," Jake said.

"All I hear is ours, Jake," Remy said. "And it's about to impact!"

The control room boomed. Startled, Jake steadied himself with white knuckles on a polished rail. Sonic static sizzled, echoed, and tapered to silence.

"We just killed whoever shot at us," Remy said.

"I figured," Jake said. "What about incoming weapons?"

Remy pressed his muffs into his head.

"There's nothing Jake. We made it."

Jake clasped both hands on a polished rail, exhaled, and sagged his head between his shoulders. He felt Henri's hand pat his back. He straightened and grabbed the beaming Frenchman's shoulders.

"Holy shit, Henri. You did it!"

"The hydrazine line must have damaged the incoming torpedo and made it circle until it shut itself down on anti-circular run protection."

"Amazing, *mon ami*," Jake said.

"The crew?" Henri asked.

"Crap," Jake said. "I suppose it's too late to tell them not to jump."

"Indeed. We need to pick them up with haste."

A voice crackled from a loudspeaker.

"I will slow the ship."

Jake reached for a microphone and responded.

"Claude? I ordered you to abandon ship."

"I know," LaFontaine said. "But I assumed you needed control of your propulsion plant."

"You're a fool," Jake said.

"I was listening. I was ready to jump if you did."

"Give me a backing bell," Jake said. "We need to get the crew back on board and get the hell out of here."

CHAPTER 10

Translucent tracing paper crinkled as Lieutenant Commander Chan yawned and pressed his forearms on a table.

"How long has it been?" he asked.

The younger man with a rugged jaw turned his sharp nose towards a digital clock.

"Twenty minutes, sir," Lieutenant Huang Gao said.

Chan's eyes compared the penciled path his stolen submarine had taken against that of the South Korean destroyer that had followed him to the Chinese coast.

"They're still out there."

"Carbon dioxide is high," Gao said. "The soda lime beds can't clear it fast enough. We must snorkel."

"No," Chan said. "I suspect the diesel engines on this accursed submarine are too loud. We must be patient."

"The stench of the bodies. It's becoming unbearable."

Chan glanced to the deck at corpses stacked between electronic cabinets. He acknowledged the rising odor of rotting meat.

"We are near the kelp bed if we must hide," he said.

"You mean to snorkel, then, sir?"

"No. The risk is too great. We will instead run fans. Prepare to ventilate."

As Gao turned to execute the order, Chan stopped him.

"One more thing," he said. "Get a weapon ready with the tightest search parameters you can set. If I fire, I don't want to hit a friendly vessel."

Chan stepped back to the periscope well and flung a hydraulic control ring. A valve clanked, and a silvery cylinder rose. He unfolded two handles, pressed his orbital socket to the optics, and saw watery darkness.

"The ship is lined up to ventilate, sir," Gao said.

"Ascend to snorkel depth," Chan said.

The world remained dark as he walked the periscope in a circle. As his eyes adjusted, stars twinkled.

"Raytheon long-range radar, sir," Gao said. "Intermittent, low signal strength."

"I knew they were still out there," Chan said. "But they are fortunately distant. Raise the induction mast."

Hydraulic servo valves clunked while porting fluid to an actuator. As his vision steadied, Chan spied the green running light of a freighter steaming behind him.

"Induction mast is raised," Gao said.

"Ventilate," Chan said.

A fan whirred and breathed clean air into the hijacked North Korean vessel. Chan smelled the sea as he correlated two more ships in the transit lane against memorized bearings to sounds heard by the submarine's old but functional sonar system.

"Consider snorkeling now, sir?"

"No, Gao."

"Battery is at thirty percent," Gao said. "Ventilating with the fan is slow. Using the diesels would quicken our air purification."

"They've proven they can hear us," Chan said. "We would already be rid of that destroyer if this submarine weren't so damned loud."

"They may have been tracking us with active sonar."

Knowing the South Korean destroyer would be running dark without navigational lights, Chan twisted the periscope handle to allow high-power optics and identify a silhouette on the horizon. His eye followed the edge of a tanker's fantail and saw its white aft running light that had masqueraded as a star in low magnification.

"No, Gao," he said. "If they had achieved active return, they would have already prosecuted us. They have had only bearings to our noise, which is frustratingly high when making any speed on this worn down machine. They hear us intermittently, which is why they've been able to follow us loosely but not engage us with weaponry."

"Thales targeting radar!" Gao said. "High signal strength!"

"Damn!" Chan said. "Cease ventilating. Lower the induction

mast."

Chan flung the ring around the periscope and stepped back from the silvery metal slithering into its well.

"Increase speed to five knots," he said. "Dive to thirty meters."

Chan stepped to the chart and watched a mechanical plotter walk an incandescent crosshair toward a kelp bed. He noted the shallow water depth and recalculated.

"Make your depth twenty-seven meters," he said.

The steel plates below his rubber soles leveled as the submarine settled meters from the seafloor.

"All stop," he said.

"We're entering the kelp bed, sir," Gao said.

"Agreed. We should slow right within it. It's fortunate that we made it to our home waters. The Koreans don't even know it's here."

Chan looked to a speed indicator that told him the ship crawled below a knot through a tall undersea forest.

"Rig the ship for ultra-quiet. Walk the spaces to verify that every nonessential man is in bed and all equipment is off."

Chan eroded time by walking behind the small team of seated technicians, staring over shoulders at sonar displays and tactical plotting data. Something gnawed at him that he couldn't elucidate.

Gao returned to the control room, and Chan joined him at the central plotting table.

"No sonar activity from the destroyer, sir?"

"No," Chan said. "None. Either they didn't get a radar return from our masts, or they are changing their tactics."

"They must have had a return at that signal strength."

A cloud formed in Chan's mind.

"Rig for depth charge," he said. "They've deployed their helicopter."

Gao darted away, and a sonar operator called out that he heard chopping blades whipping the water. A loud splash then preceded the acoustic ping of a dipping sonar. Horrified faces looked at Chan.

"Be calm," he said. "The kelp will hide us."

Chan held his breath and thought he heard the South Korean helicopter's sonar with his naked ear. The sonic banging stopped, and Gao returned to his side.

"Helicopter," Chan said.

"Should we run?"

"No," Chan said. "We do exactly nothing."

Animated, the sonar operator warned of louder rotor sounds and a second immersion of the dipping sonar. Enemy hydrophones pushed sound through steel and into Chan's ears. Bodies tensed in his view.

"Trust the kelp," he said.

The sonic emanations rang three times and ceased. Chan glanced at the sonar operator who stated that all signs of the helicopter had vanished.

"I think we made it, sir."

"Keep awareness for that helicopter's next search."

"The current will push us from the kelp in approximately ten minutes," Gao said.

"Then we wait ten minutes," Chan said. "If we hear nothing, we evade to the south."

"We must charge our battery before daylight, sir."

"We will."

Chan pressed his forearms against trace paper and watched the incandescent crosshair slide to the charted edge of kelp. Other than a shrimp bed and passing merchant shipping, the water was silent.

"Helm," he said, "all ahead one third. Make turns for three knots."

As an hour passed, Chan labored against his tight chest to breathe, but the waters carried no acoustic threats. Gao returned from the engineering spaces, his face ghastly in the red light.

"We must snorkel, sir. Cells will invert soon."

"Agreed," Chan said. "We must take our chances."

Chan took the submarine shallow and viewed the night. The

red and green running lights of merchant ships dotted the lanes to the east, and the electromagnetic sensor atop his periscope sniffed commercial radars.

"Raise the induction mast," he said.

A hydraulic servo valve clicked, and rising steel rumbled in the tower above him. A sailor announced that the head valve had opened, and Chan ordered the diesels to life. The rhythmic clacking of their cylinders echoed, and Chan tasted the fresh sea air passing through the compartment en route to the hungry beasts.

"Raise the radio mast," he said.

A third mast rose above Chan, multiplying his vulnerability to searching radar waves.

"Message traffic!" Gao said.

"Can you read it?"

"It's encrypted, sir. I'll have to download it to a jump drive for the laptop and run it through decryption."

"Bring the laptop here," Chan said.

Chan heard the rustling of a dispatched sailor. As he felt the man brush by him, another called out a warning of a naval search radar.

"Lower the radio mast!" Chan said. "Identify the radar system!"

"It's ours, sir," Gao said. "Probable *Hainan*-class submarine hunter patrol vessel. There are several stationed in Qingdao."

Chan played hope against horror in his heart, wondering if his homeland helped or hunted him.

"Secure snorkeling," he said. "Lower the induction mast."

The diesel clacking quieted and the gentle reverberation of sliding metal rose and fell in the conning tower above. He kept his eye to the optics and scanned the horizon for the Chinese warship that he hoped recognized him as an ally.

"Tamir high-frequency sonar!" Gao said. "Why would the fleet search for us?"

"Note their signal-to-noise ratio and bearing."

"Their bearing is toward the kelp bed," Gao said. "The signal-to-noise ratio is appropriate for them searching at the range of the kelp bed. They're hunting for us."

"Be calm," Chan said. "Lowering the periscope."

He stepped back from the slithering cylinder and saw earnest faces.

"Any progress on the decryption?" he asked.

Gao bent over the shoulder of a man balancing a laptop on his knee. The sailor ran his finger over the screen, looked up, and smiled.

"The message from the fleet says that the South Koreans have left. The *Hainan* vessel is pretending to prosecute us with helicopter support and will employ depth charges at the kelp bed. The fleet will tell the Koreans we are destroyed. Our orders are to proceed undetected to the submarine base at Qingdao."

Relief spread through the room as Chan pressed his palms on the tracing paper, exhaled, and slumped his head between his shoulders.

Blind to his fate, he ordered the submarine west with ambitions of earning praise for delivering the mighty gift of a North Korean submarine to his country.

CHAPTER 11

Chan cringed as the ocean roared the thunderous rage of depth charges. Overlapping bursts curled his shoulders and squeezed air through his clenched teeth.

The final echo subsided, and, in his deafness, the odor of dirt specs lodged in inaccessible recesses rose through the familiar scent of rotting flesh and betrayed the submarine's age. Rubbing his ears, he looked across the plotting table.

"I pray that's the end of it," he said. "Pay attention for the sonar signaling frequency."

He watched Gao's lips move but heard a muffled drone. Barking, he repeated himself. Gao nodded and turned to a pair of sailors seated at sonar screens wearing earmuff headsets. His neck strained to vocalize audible words.

"We are listening," he said. "At these near distances, the signal will be obvious on the screen."

"Remind me of the frequency, Gao?"

Gao stiffened in defiance of the quiz.

"We are ordered to remain submerged and undetected with all masts and antennae unexposed until we hear the *Hainan*-class patrol vessel shift its Tamir sonar to its maximum thirty-kilohertz signal."

"And then what?" Chan asked.

Gao looked down.

"I am uncertain."

Chan had expected better from the eldest son of a ranking party official. Unlike himself, Gao had enjoyed privileges in education, guidance, and health. Chan checked his contempt and redoubled his effort to build his executive officer's confidence.

He waved his palm.

"Don't let the noise distract you," he said. "Review the orders and refresh your memory. We will discuss our next steps when you are ready."

Chan turned and lumbered by the periscope. He reached for

a foldout chair mounted on the after bulkhead, angled his buttocks toward its foamed seat, and slumped his weight onto its back. Expecting uneventful submerged drifting with his propeller stopped, he propped his elbow atop a semi-recessed metallic book cabinet and plopped his cheek against his palm.

The awkward posture surprised him with its comfort. His eyelids drooped, and his fatigue billowed. Squinting, he saw Gao with a renewed vigilance hovering over sailors, and he trusted his executive officer to remain alert. He allowed himself a nap.

He dreamt.

The adolescent Dao Chan slowed to gather his energy and allow the small lagging hand to reattach itself to his hip. Celebrating Lunar New Year, he picked the position in the game where he would chase the quickest child in the village, an older and faster boy.

Having reached the head of the dragon, Chan sought to catch that older child at its tail. He feigned fatigue, staring at his bare feet while monitoring his prey from his eye's corner. The elder boy's smile revealed the brash smugness of assumed invincibility.

His toes churning soft ground, Chan accelerated towards a target that frowned, bowed its head, and drove forward the smaller child in front of him. Chan lunged, but the boy whipped his hips aside. Stumbling, he recovered and let the lethargy of the dozen-child dragon spine slow his prey and create his second chance.

He leapt and tackled the boy. Violating understood game rules, he drove his shoulder into the boy's thigh. Numbness consumed his arm, and searing pain shot through his shoulder.

The world became white silence, and Chan awoke as the leg underneath his chest kicked free and scraped his neck. A cool puddle wetted his cheek, and the splattered mud on his tongue tasted fertile. A breeze carried a cooking fire's scent of burning wood across his face, and a stark epiphany struck him as he knelt and rubbed his aching arm.

Earth, water, wind, and fire. The foundational elements of life dictated his universe. Simple truths accepted, unquestioned, and even worshipped. He respected them, but his spirit craved more than plowing fields and growing wheat on his family's tiny farm.

Time slipped, and he stood before his smiling parents. For his mother, a woman with intelligence, a sharp tongue, and resentment for all life, the smile was an admission of defeat that someone else was entitled to happiness. For his father, a husky but downtrodden farmer, the smile was a plea for validation. Chan feared they had news that he would be obliged to appreciate.

"You've done well in your studies," his father said. "You've been chosen to have your high school tuition paid by a donation from a businessman who left our village long ago. We are very proud of you."

His subconscious mind embellished his memory, and his mother morphed into a dragon. She swallowed his father whole, and the beast spoke to Chan with his parents' synthesized gruesome voice.

"You should feel privileged. We never had such opportunities. If you earn your way to a university and to work in the city, you must send money to the village. We own you now by virtue of guilt. Why should you have advantages when the community does not? You have no right to succeed. You have no right to fail."

A sword appeared in Chan's hand, and he swung at the monster's belly. The blade tore through scales, and acid flowed from the wound, dissolving metal. Chan dropped the weapon and ran.

He turned his back to his parents, his siblings, his cousins, and the village. He ran to the east, toward the cities, seeking identity through survival.

Survival meant finding an alien world as far from a farming village as he could find, learning its foundational rules, and mastering them. Images of warships of the People's Liberation Army Navy danced through his sleeping memory, and his younger self knew that he would become an expert in naval warfare, if he were to exist at all.

A familiar voice returned his awareness to the hijacked North Korean *Romeo*-class submarine.

"The sonar signal, sir," Gao said. "The patrol craft is ordering us to snorkel depth."

Chan suppressed a yawn.

"Take us up," he said.

"It's dusk, sir," Gao said. "May I rig the room for red light? My eyes need to adjust."

"Rig the room for red light but don't hesitate. There's little of importance for you to see up there."

White bulbs faded, and a crimson glow turned gray metal black. Chan stayed seated and slanted his knees from the circumference Gao's trousers etched around the periscope. A sailor tore paper from a teletype printer and brought it to Chan. He dismissed the sailor and glanced at the curt instructions.

"Snorkel, Gao," he said. "Ventilate the ship, charge the batteries, and increase speed to five knots."

"Those are welcomed orders, sir."

"The Koreans are gone," Chan said. "And the patrol craft will escort us with safe passage to Qingdao.

*

Chan swiveled the periscope toward the rear of his submarine. Twisting the optics skyward, he watched the twinkling sky yield to fluorescent lights of the covered submarine pen.

"Are you lined up, Gao?"

"Lined up, sir."

"Very well," Chan said. "Surface the ship."

A low-pressure fan grumbled and blew air into the submarine's ballast tanks, and a depth indicator signaled the indiscernible rise.

"Shore support has just sent a message of tug boat assistance for our berthing," Gao said. "They've requested that line handlers report topside once we are surfaced."

"Very well," Chan said. "All stop, secure the engine room, and send line handlers topside."

*

Chan smelled diesel fuel and brackish water as he walked across the steel girder to the concrete pier. He saluted his squadron commodore, a pudgy man with beady eyes. He ignored the lackeys flanking his former boss.

The commodore hesitated and returned the salute. He talked through his nose.

"I had half expected to never see you again, Chan."

Chan thought the voice betrayed a mix of envy and pity.

"I'm here, sir. Do you know my orders from Beijing?"

"Of course not. You know I'm not privy to this pet project from headquarters. I answer to the North Sea Fleet Command and carry out meaningful operations with the rest of the ships in my squadron."

"I've just added one ship to the order of battle," Chan said. "I consider that meaningful."

"A gift offered by a traitor. The least capable crew in my squadron could have achieved as much. This is the only way you would have achieved command, such as it is."

Chan suppressed a smile. Risking command of the stolen *Romeo* became his only way to earn command after his commodore had proclaimed that a farmer's son would never lead a submarine in the North Sea Fleet.

"I sank a South Korean warship," Chan said. "To my knowledge, that makes me our only countryman to have done so."

"A North Korean crew that can barely stay submerged managed the same feat years ago. Hardly brag worthy. And you couldn't escape an inferior destroyer without assistance."

The veins in Chan's neck throbbed, but he remained silent.

"Very well," the commodore said. "Here are your orders."

He nodded to an assistant who extended a sealed envelope. Unwilling to give his commodore the satisfaction of a reaction,

Chan tucked it into his pocket.

"You have your orders," the commodore said. "And I have mine, which I will follow despite their absurdity. I've prepared the mess hall with a dinner for your entire crew. Alcohol is permitted, but no man may leave the waterfront. It is secured until you depart."

"And when is that, sir?"

Chan allowed himself petty delight in seeing the commodore's brow furrow.

"I assume your orders will say. I am obliged to give you top priority of all waterfront facilities until then."

"The irony, sir," Chan said, "is that you would deny a man of my abilities command in your squadron. But now that I report directly to fleet headquarters, I have a submarine of my own, full use of your facilities, and no requirement to do a damned thing you say."

"You will regret those words if you return from whatever mission you're undertaking."

Chan snorted.

"If I return, sir, I expect that I will do so in a body bag before I would risk reporting to you again. My crew?"

"The mess hall is ready," the commodore said. "You may send your entire crew there now. In fact, I recommend that you do. None of them want to see what's about to happen on that rusting relic of a submarine."

Chan returned to his *Romeo* and had Gao take the crew to the catered dinner. As the ship emptied and assumed an eerie silence, he walked into his stateroom.

He unfolded his desk and placed his buttocks on the leather cushion of his four-legged chair. Tearing open the envelope, he cut his finger and cursed.

The orders included a brief congratulations and an allowance to rest a day in port before taking station in the risky waters east of the Japanese Ryukyu Islands. No changes. No updates. No clarity on a target.

He picked up a wired phone handset and called the waterfront's operator.

"The mess hall, please," he said. "Any officer. This is their captain."

He heard the young and eager voice of a junior officer.

"Captain?"

"Tell Gao that tomorrow is a ship's holiday and that every man may indulge in food and drink tonight."

After the officer acknowledged the order, Chan left his stateroom to join his crew at dinner. He heard footsteps on ladder rungs, and a young uniformed officer greeted him.

"I'm doctor Lin," he said.

"You're here for the bodies?" Chan asked.

"Indeed. I'll store half of them in the torpedo room, half in the engineering spaces. Overflow will go wherever they fit. You've cleared room to stack them?"

"Yes. How long do you need?"

"My team is large. Three hours. This will be quick."

"Do you mind if I watch?" Chan asked.

"Of course not. But I assure you, you will be bored after watching the first body."

Chan sat in his foldout chair behind the periscope and watched men in lab coats and operating masks enter his ship with body bags. The first pair dragged a Korean corpse from the gap between two electric cabinets and rolled it onto the deck plates.

The body had a greenish blue hue, and its face seemed inhuman. The rotting scent of meat became pungent and repulsive again to Chan as he watched the men wrestle the body's Rigor Mortis. Straightening the limbs, the men slid a body bag over the shoes and wiggled it up the dead man's length. Once the plastic consumed the head, they zipped the bag closed.

Chan knew more was coming.

One man plugged an iron into an outlet while the other folded a plastic lip over the zipper. With impressive efficiency, one man ironed while the other walked plastic along the bag's length.

"That's a watertight seal?" Chan asked.

"Plastic welding," one man said. "Good to an atmosphere and a half. It's plenty, but we're leaving a few extra bags in case of leaks."

The other man moved to the ladder and waved his arm. A hose slithered down, and he pulled it down the ladder deeper into the control room. Satisfied with his slack, he returned to the bag and snapped the nozzle into a valve Chan had not noticed.

The man squeezed a handle, cocked his head to listen, and stopped. Then he grabbed with both hands and let the fluid flow. A minute later, the bag swelled.

"Formaldehyde?" Chan asked.

"Better," the man said. "But conceptually the same. The decay will cease, and the bodies will be at your disposal for whatever purpose. And despite what I might imagine, I have no desire to know what your purpose is."

Chan only half-knew his purpose, but he assured himself it was worthy.

CHAPTER 12

Jake Slate propped open the hatch, grabbed a railing, and hoisted himself atop the *Hai Ming's* conning tower sail. Disgusted and careless, he staggered in the shallow water swells and cursed as he braced himself against flat steel.

Sliding his hand into his parka, he groped for his waterproof global satellite phone. He withdrew it, tapped a button, and pressed it against his cheek.

As he awaited a response, he scanned the horizon and saw a solitary unnatural light in the moonlit darkness. Its radiance rose and fell with the rhythmic rotation of a navigation aid, and he recognized it as a navigation beacon on Yonaguni Island, the Japanese landmass closest to Taiwan.

His heart hit his throat at the sound of his wife's voice. She sounded elated.

"Hi, honey," Linda said.

He tried to feign coolness but knew he sounded giddy.

"Hey, honey," he said. "It's morning there, right?"

"Yeah. I miss you. Come home."

"Who's with you?"

"Your brother's been staying at the house," she said. "He's out getting coffee now. He's been great. The kids are with my mom tonight."

Jake credited what little calmness he discerned in his wife's voice to Nick. Despite his augury weirdness, his brother embodied compassion.

"No, I mean who else is there?" he asked.

"There's always a guy in a suit in the house. They work in shifts and they're supposedly here to protect me. They try to act polite, but they're creepy."

"They're not protecting you," he said. "They're policing you. They're listening to us talk, and they'll cut off this conversation if they don't like what we say."

"I hate this. I just want you to come home."

Priorities and loyalties became muddled in Jake's gut. Although accompanied by friends, twisted fate stranded him on an alien submarine fighting someone else's war.

"I can't," he said.

"I pray for you to come home every day. I want God to answer my prayers."

Nick's omen played in Jake's mind.

"He will. At least I think so. I don't know. I mean, nothing's certain."

"You say that Pierre has always said you're charmed. I don't know what that's supposed to mean. I'm scared."

"Pierre says a lot of things."

"I don't like him."

"You don't know him like I do," Jake said. "He saved my life. Granted what we did long ago was stupid, but I needed revenge, and he gave it to me."

"You talk like he rescued you."

"He did. I needed him."

"Yeah, well he needed you, too."

Jake squinted at the beacon and wondered if Renard needed him now. In his French friend's operation, he saw himself as a checker piece on a chessboard.

"Okay," he said. "I see your point."

"I've lost too much in my life," Linda said. "I can't lose you. I need you."

"I have something I need to do now."

"No! Don't go!"

"I'll call you back. I promise."

His eyes adjusted to the night, Jake made out the silhouette of the tiny island's sparse shoreline. He had set the submarine drifting as close to the shoals as he dared, and the beach seemed touchable.

He called Renard.

The Frenchman sounded fatigued, and, for the first time in Jake's reckoning, old.

"*Mon ami*," Renard said.

"You don't sound happy to hear from me," Jake said.

"Surprised. Cautious. I question why you are using your phone instead of the radio."

"It's encrypted, right?"

"Of course, but that is not my concern. It's your ability to use it. Where are you?"

"Japanese waters. Yonaguni Island. Right where I should be per plan. But I'm surfaced."

"Obviously, but dear God, man," Renard said. "Why?"

"I needed to talk to Linda."

"Call me a romantic, but I long for the days of wooden ships when men had no choice but to avoid such frivolous distractions."

"My wife needs me."

"Is there a crisis?"

Jake found Renard's question unsurprising but disliked the mistrustful strain in the Frenchman's voice.

"No," he said. "She just needs me."

"My wife needs me too. I understand that. But we picked strong women who accepted us for who we are."

"It's not your ass out here at risk," Jake said.

"Where's your courage, man? Where's your confidence? You're the best there's ever been."

"I just got my ass kicked, I barely survived an ambush, and I'd be dead right now along with the rest of the gang if it weren't for Henri."

"I've read your report. You made the right decision using the hydrazine line."

"Henri saved us. I'm supposed to be your genius protégé, but your mechanic saved us. I screwed up, and I can't figure out how. Something's wrong in this scenario."

"That was my fault. I unwittingly set you up for an ambush, but I also left you a defense as a mitigation. Give yourself credit for being smart enough to use it, even if Henri had to cajole you."

Jake remembered a pattern of hesitating in his past commitments to Renard. The Frenchman had always promised excitement, adventure, and purpose, and he had always delivered. But this operation torqued his guts.

Without warning, the answer hit Jake like a stomach punch. He was overkill in this one. Renard didn't need him.

The Frenchman had spent years advising the Taiwanese and had enjoyed the luxury of time and foresight to do what he did best–arm a nation per his plan. Jake digested the enormity of Renard's preparation. He had driven Taiwan to build the *Hai Ming*, to lay defensive hydrophones, and to equip its vessels for tactical nuclear combat.

"Pierre," Jake said. "You have this operation planned out like you never have before, at least not since I've known you."

"Perhaps. Yes, I've invested a good deal of time into this. It promises to be my most important accomplishment."

"Right. Your accomplishment. Not mine. This is your show, and you don't get me for free this time."

"I always pay you well, and I will for this operation. I know you trust me to make it worth your effort."

"That's not what I meant. For you and me, money hardly matters. I mean this time I have a home. I have something to lose. There's someone back there who loves me."

Jake noted a silence unlike any he'd shared with Renard. The Frenchman seemed struggling for words.

"Pierre? You still there?"

"Damn it, man," Renard said. "I love you."

"What?"

He heard Renard pause and sigh.

"I snapped as I said it, but I meant it," Renard said. "You are a son to me."

"You've run out of threats and prizes," Jake said. "Are you resorting to my softer emotions to manipulate me?"

"No, I think not."

"Then what the hell, Pierre? If you love me, why wait until now to tell me?"

"Because I'm proving it by letting you go."

Jake glanced at the beacon to assure himself the shoreline's proximity remained real.

"Really?" he asked. "You have a change of heart all of a sudden? On the doorstep of a battle?"

"I admit it to myself only now," Renard said. "I planned this operation to succeed without you. It wasn't until events unfolded and this became a reality that I felt compelled to garner your involvement. But in retrospect, I see it clearly. I'm only using you as an insurance policy."

Tension washed from Jake's body.

"Yeah," he said. "I get it now. That's what was bothering me. Maybe I wanted you to need me, but you really don't."

"And I'm sure this tastes bitter to you as it does now to me," Renard said. "I had no right, and I can hear it in your voice that your heart is not in this, nor should it be. I will let you go."

"Are you sure you can get by without me?"

Renard laughed. It was a mix of fatigue and emotional release.

"No, I would never dare say that my situation is better without you, but I trust that I've turned the odds enough in my favor to succeed."

"Can you get me off this thing?"

"I'm afraid there is insufficient time to send a boat to you," Renard said. "I can arrange transportation from the island to Tokyo for your flight home, but you'll have to make it to the island on your own."

"You're banking that I'm a strong swimmer."

"You're strong at everything, *mon ami*."

"So, that's it?"

"Give me a moment to speak to Henri first," Renard said. "I will contact him on the ship's radio."

Jake lowered the phone and took in the island's silhouette. It offered his exodus, but it threatened his longstanding bond of loyalty with Renard.

A voice from below startled him.

"Jake?"

"Henri?"

"I'm coming to the bridge," Henri said.

As Henri's soles thumped against metal ladder rungs, Jake

looked to his phone. Renard had hung up.

Henri's white hair emerged through the girder floor.

"I'm disappointed, but I understand," Henri said. "Pierre told me everything."

"I'm glad you understand."

"Here," Henri said. "For your phone or any other valuables you might have."

The Frenchman extended a small waterproof sack.

"Thank you," Jake said.

"Head below and exit from the sail door. You don't want to risk jumping from here. I will secure the bridge."

Through Henri's attempt at graciousness, Jake sensed his standoffishness. Abandoning a comrade prior to combat created discomfort.

Jake descended the ladder and placed his shoe on the lip of the pressure hull. He turned and opened the door. It creaked open. He ducked through it, closed it behind him, and crept around the sail to its far side where he paused to fulfill his promise of calling his wife.

Unwilling to specify the terms of his return home for fear of overpromising, he told her that he loved her but could make no commitment to a return date. She wanted more information, but he held his ground.

He put his phone into its bag, noted the direction to beacon, and leapt into the water.

CHAPTER 13

John Brody glared at Defense Secretary Rickets with the intent to gore him.

"Spit it out," he said. "You've been talking in circles for ten minutes. You already talk like a politician."

"Okay," Rickets said. "You're to withdraw all naval forces from the waters and airspaces of the Korean Peninsula, beginning immediately with a complete withdrawal in forty-eight hours. South Korea will defend itself."

"Of course," Brody said. "Now that the outcome is a known quantity, we back out and let our ally look strong in the finish. I get it."

Rickets shifted in his chair.

"I expected more emotion from you," he said. "And I expected you to ask if the president had already formally agreed, but instead you're acting like you foresaw this."

"I did," Brody said. "And I've ordered the fleet to prepare redeployment plans, and they're ready to execute at a moment's notice."

Rickets' face hardened.

"Redeployment plans? What are you up to?"

"You know damned well what I'm up to," Brody said. "Korea was a diversion. Chinese submarine operations in Japanese waters was just a distraction. I have capital warships that can converge on Taiwan in time to alter the outcome."

"Need I remind you, admiral, that taking action without consensus is unacceptable?"

"The Air Force and Marine Corps support me," Brody said. "You'll find the Army lukewarm to an invasion if you ask, but the general is unlikely to support you standing in my way. The chairman is abstaining from voicing his position, but he's just waiting for me to act before he gets on board. I know he will because he knows that kicking the Chinese off that island is the right thing to do."

Rickets stiffened in his chair as he pointed at Brody's nose.

"You accuse me of playing politics when I take a rational approach. Now you're rallying troops for your own glory at the risk of tens of thousands of lives. That's selfish warmongering, and I won't stand for it. Nor will the president."

"He will when he realizes he needs to in order to protect his legacy," Brody said. "He doesn't want to be the president remembered for cowering to China, and I'm not about to be the Chief of Naval Operations who let it happen."

"He doesn't want to be the president responsible for unnecessary mass casualties when a brokered and diplomatically sound peace is within reach."

Brody realized he was on the edge of his seat. He took a breath and pushed himself back.

"There's no peace within reach while the fleet remains out of striking distance," Brody said.

"Renard is taking care of that," Rickets said. "Or did you forget that Taiwan is taking matters into its own hands?"

The thought of Renard had taken root in Brody's mind. If nothing else, he realized, the Frenchman carried an encouraging charm. Needing a break from his anger, he exhaled and turned his attention to the monitor.

Rickets raised a remote from the arm of his chair, and speakers chirped. A dark screen presented the image of a Frenchman who portrayed newfound color and vigor.

"Good day gentlemen," Renard said.

"I hope the Taiwanese Navy shares your spirits today," Rickets said. "You look inspired."

"I am. And the fleet is ready, I assure you."

"Then everything is per plan, except our previously discussed exception about having only eighteen patrol craft available?" Rickets asked.

"There is one additional minor exception that has arisen, but for which I was well prepared," Renard said. "Mister Slate will no longer be involved."

"What's wrong?" Rickets asked.

"I let him go," Renard said. "I decided that I no longer needed him."

Brody considered the news a reprieve, a chance to confront Slate again. It also seemed a bittersweet opportunity that increased his chances of rescuing Taiwan by increasing the chances of Renard failing and needing his fleet's intervention.

"I delivered him to you because you told me you needed him," Rickets said. "I've made decisions assuming you would succeed based upon assumptions that you had him in your service. You would upset this balance at this late hour?"

"I agree that it sounds underhanded," Renard said. "But it was more of a realization."

"I'm all ears."

"Years ago I drafted a plan to allow Taiwan to stand against the mainland, and I eventually crafted a place for Slate within it. But my plan will survive contact with the enemy because I've had the luxury of time and resources to prepare an advantage. In the final analysis, Slate was only an insurance policy."

"You're not one to let your odds slip, even slightly," Rickets said. "There's something else at work here."

Renard inhaled from a Marlboro, sighed out the smoke, and returned his attention to the camera.

"Indeed," he said. "His heart is not in this. He doesn't feel any loyalty–at least no loyalty to me, my team, Taiwan, or anything else that I can see."

"We knew that going in," Rickets said. "That's why I applied pressure to get him there."

"There's more. I'm afraid the narrow escape from the submarine pen shook his confidence."

"We heard the explosions and an abnormally effective countermeasure system," Rickets said. "We assumed that was him, but I had no idea his escape was narrow."

"It indeed was," Renard said. "For the life of me, however, I cannot determine what mistake he might have made. I've heard the recordings from the islet's hydrophone systems and from the *Hai Ming* itself. I'll grant that the Chinese had reason to suspect the existence of our submarine pen, but it appears that a

Chinese submarine had divine guidance in knowing the exact location during Slate's departure."

Brody knew that no submarine commander could launch a weapon without targeting data. He shifted in his seat and prepared a line of questioning for Renard, but Rickets preempted him.

"I know what happened," Rickets said. "And I'll share it with you so you can make better decisions about using your submarine pen, and so that you can have a prayer of talking Slate into reuniting with you."

"Please," Renard said.

"It was his surface hump."

Renard squinted into the camera and absorbed the news as he inhaled from his cigarette.

"Damn," he said. "I might have guessed. I underestimated mainland satellite technology."

"Don't beat yourself up," Rickets said. "We had them pegged at three to five years away from having satellite radar systems good enough to identify submarine surface humps, but we now know that they accelerated the development."

"To track American submarines, I presume," Renard said, "until their drones heard Taiwanese submarine activity near the islet. Then they diverted the satellite to watch the pen."

"And positioned one of their least capable, most expendable submarines at the door at periscope depth to await targeting data from the satellite," Rickets said. "It was a turkey shoot. There was nothing Slate could do. I don't know how he managed to survive and even take out the attacking submarine."

"By escaping, even with help from my defensive hydrazine line designs, he has proven again that he is charmed," Renard said. "However, the *Hai Ming* is on station without him, and it's ready to support the operation. In fact, all is ready."

"Who's commanding the *Hai Ming*?" Rickets asked.

"I am, via telemetry," Renard said. "The ship will be in constant hardwired communications via surface support, using its drones to locate the enemy. This is how I had originally designed the operation prior to Slate's involvement. All is per plan, I assure you, even without him."

For the first time since the secretary had restrained him, Brody's cage gave way. Seeing daylight, he sprang with legerity and pointed at the monitor, flexing coiled muscles. Unsure if he should gore Renard, Rickets, or anything else in his reddened vision, he released a metered dose of bullish rage.

"Let me get this straight," he said. "The Chinese are surprising you with their technologies, they found your supposedly hidden submarine pen, and you're missing your ace commanding officer. You're only hope is launching the world's first tactical nuclear operation, and you're telling me to hold back the American fleet so you can take care of things."

The lingering silence lent gravitas to Brody's thrust.

"Have I made a valid point?" he asked.

"Indeed you have," Renard said. "And I cannot disagree with you. I can only ask that you trust me. Should I fail, I will have no choice but to join you in a new conversation about the involvement of the American fleet. But if I succeed, we will hold the tactical edge. Let me prove my merit to you before we entertain future scenarios."

Brody found the Frenchman smooth and confident, and he grasped how the man could have amassed a large and loyal international following.

He let glimpses of scenarios dance in his head that assumed Renard's success. Flashes of a chart showing boundaries where Taiwan used its stealth patrol craft to hold back Chinese submarines, giving free reign for American forces to steam toward Taiwan, enticed his imagination.

"Very well," Brody said. "We'll know the answer soon enough."

"I appreciate the opportunity, admiral," Renard said.

"I wish you luck, Renard," Brody said. "You'll need it."

CHAPTER 14

Lieutenant Commander Chan retraced the *Romeo's* path with his eye. With the South Korean Navy content that his countrymen had sunk the submarine that destroyed their corvette, he had driven his hijacked submarine eastward, unfettered by suspecting hunters, toward the Korean Peninsula.

He tapped Lieutenant Gao's forearm, nudging him from his boredom. The executive officer lifted his angular chin from his palms and stretched his arms while yawning. Chan noted the rapid onset of Gao's fatigue.

"Sorry, sir."

"You may rest soon, Gao," Chan said. "Check my judgment. Do you concur that it's time to turn south?"

Gao glanced at the chart and seemed to hesitate with the easy question. The illuminated cross-hair converged on the penciled line showing the path Chan had prescribed for the *Romeo*.

"Yes, sir. I concur."

"Good," Chan said. "Send one of the other officers here to relieve me of the deck. Then get my next radio reception to Park on a jump drive as soon as it's downloaded. After that, take three hours of rest."

Gao acknowledged the order and departed.

Chan ordered his *Romeo's* control room shifted to red lighting to let his irises dilate. He then ordered the ship southward and held a railing as the deck tilted. As the movement steadied, he gave the command to come shallow.

Reaching, he shifted a control ring, heard hydraulic servos clink, and watched the silvery periscope slither upward. He gave the order and placed his eye to the optics.

The night sky revealed empty water as he ordered the radio mast raised. Minutes passed as message traffic confirmed his shifted command structure from the North Sea Fleet to the East Sea Fleet.

Upon descending deeper and leveling the *Romeo*, he relinquished the deck to the officer Gao had sent to relieve him, and he read a printout of the message from his new command authority, the East Sea Fleet, verifying that his anticipated navigational track remained clear of interference from other fleet vessels.

Satisfied, he walked aft toward the engine room where he passed the whirring starboard propulsion motor as it drove sealed reduction gears. Further down the starboard shaft, he came to a pair of sailors seated on folding chairs and crouched over laptop computers.

Beside the sailors, duct tape bound a dozen more laptops to makeshift plywood shelves perched on hydraulic piping. Additional duct tape restrained extension cords and surge suppressors to the deck plates.

Chan crouched beside a strip of tape.

"Any luck, Park?" he asked.

The young sailor looked up, blinked, and rubbed his beady and bloodshot eyes.

"Sir?" Park asked.

Chan had selected Able Seaman Yueng-Ji Park to join his crew for his cryptologic prowess.

While examining a potential volunteer crew for his mission, Chan had sought radio technicians who scored high on entrance exams measuring technical aptitude but low in their exams in their primary rate of radio communications.

A man too smart for the training would be bored and would muddle through his radio training, Chan reasoned. Such a man might have other interests, such as hacking decrypting algorithms in otherwise secure message traffic.

When he discovered in Park's service dossier that the man's only disciplinary action had resulted from hacking into a naval personnel database to reduce his service obligation, he had found his man.

He promised Park early freedom from his military service in exchange for breaking into Chinese East Sea Fleet message traffic. Ignorant of his final mission and mistrustful of his final extraction from it, Chan wanted to know the orders his fleet gave to his surrounding assets.

He had dedicated the younger seaman seated beside Park to serve as his cryptologist apprentice. The seaman nodded and pointed at Park's screen.

"It looks like you found something," Chan said.

"Oh, that," Park said. "That was easy."

"What did you find?"

"Well, sir. First, I discovered that the East Sea Fleet shares nothing with the North Sea Fleet for encrypted orders. It's completely different."

"As you expected, correct?"

"Correct, sir. I also learned that all maritime patrol aircraft in the East Sea Fleet share the same encryption scheme. One of the messages we downloaded during our last snorkel operation was from Ningbo to all patrol craft."

"How do you know already?"

"I broke an earlier message from the East Sea Fleet that we picked up yesterday," Park said. "The message traffic had no specific orders for us yet, but I was still able to break the key for the patrol aircraft orders."

Chan hadn't asked Park to crack patrol aircraft codes, but he reasoned it was a good use of his time.

"Okay," he said. "So, how do you know there wasn't any specific message for a specific aircraft within the main message?"

"The message required only one decryption algorithm, and I decrypted most bits. The bits I couldn't decode were repetitive symbols serving as synchronizing characters, meaningless preamble if you will. Within the message, the text had specific information for each aircraft."

"That sounds like a vulnerability," Chan said.

"Not so much, sir. Patrol areas are vast. The orders are dull, such as aircraft one patrols a large box of sky, aircraft two patrols another. It's the sort of basics telling them not to fly into each other. Nothing risky if an adversary learns of it."

"And so you broke that scheme already?"

"It was a small key by modern standards and took only a few

hours running my decryption algorithms in parallel."

He waved his palm over the laptops.

"In parallel?"

"Yes, sir," Park said. "It's just bitwise mathematics. An encrypted message is the original message multiplied by a key of ones and zeroes. No encryption is perfect, but the more bits you use, the more times you have to attempt the multiplication to stumble upon the proper key."

"What does that mean in terms of time?"

Park glanced into the submarine's overhead piping and ran his index finger under his smooth chin while crafting a response.

"Well, you see, sir, it's a binary matter. If you need to multiply a message by a one-hundred and twenty-eight bit key, there are two to the power of that many permutations to attempt to break the code."

"That's a big number," Chan said.

"Of course, sir. With conventional computers, a brute force decryption would be impossible. But the computers you bought me have parallel field-programmable gate array cluster hardware. They are made for running decryption algorithms. It reduces the brute force hacking time significantly."

"How significantly?" Chan asked.

"For the encryption I expect to see from the fleet, a matter of decades."

Chan frowned.

"I'm not following. You said you had a good chance of decrypting all message traffic."

"Oh yes, sir. The biggest time savings is obviating the need for a brute force attack by identifying flaws in the supposed randomness of the encrypting computer."

"Go on."

"Perfect encryption assumes the generation of a perfect random number behind each encryption key, but I know that the fleet's cryptology computers are generating imperfect random numbers."

"That sounds like a flaw in fleet security."

"It is only for someone like me who already has access to de-crypted message traffic. Since I know how the cryptology com-puters attempt to create randomness for the once-encrypted general fleet updates plus the second-encrypted specific orders to our own ship, I can predict how they create randomness for other messages to other ships within the fleet. This reduces the complexity from impossible to just a modest challenge."

Park angled his nose to the monitor as if his conversation with Chan were an inconvenience.

"So, it's possible for a ship within the fleet to break the codes of another ship within the fleet?"

"It's quite possible," Park said. "The rationale is that it's not a threat. What does it matter if you know where another ship is steaming or what it's shooting at when we all take our orders from the same place? But for outsiders that have to break each general message once and then break it again for each ship's or-ders, it is statistically impossible."

Chan envisioned a bit stream of ones and zeroes in his mind to convince himself the report obeyed logic.

"Well done, Park," he said.

"This was easy. I expect a challenge for fighting or attack air-craft."

"And for surface vessels and submarines?" Chan asked.

"Yes, sir. That will be the biggest challenge, depending on the nature of the message traffic. I have something I can show you, for example."

Park's eyes remained on his laptop monitor as he tapped the keyboard. Chan commended himself for showing patience fa-cing the geek's quirkiness.

"What do you have?" he asked.

"Our last message telling us about our navigation area also included messages for other East Sea Fleet submarines that are probably nearby us."

"Let me see."

Park swiveled the computer on his lap, revealing a text file showing the *Romeo's* last navigational orders surrounded by data Chan had not seen when the message was printed for him. There were twelve character codes followed by bodies of text that appeared as gibberish.

"Why is this different than from my printouts in the control room?" he asked.

"The control room printer recognizes these header codes as information for other vessels and ignores them," Park said. "Otherwise the printer would just waste paper and ink."

"Do you know what the other vessels are?"

"No, sir. Not until I break their specific encryptions. I expect that each vessel has its own specific encryption code, as we do."

Although the fleet withheld his mission from him, Chan had been promised a safe return home after scuttling the submarine and escaping on a surface vessel dispatched to rescue his crew. But something in the way his mission materialized, piecemeal, in broken segments issued by various admirals, fed to him in suspicious scraps, roused his suspicions. He had recruited Park and equipped him with an army of computers to verify the orders to his rescuing vessel would be forthcoming.

"You'll report immediately if you break a code for any vessel," Chan said.

"Of course, sir," Park said.

"Keep it up, Park. Do you need anything from me? Something to drink? Food?"

Park had already lowered his nose to his monitor, tapping keys. His apprentice nudged him, and he responded without looking up.

"No, thank you, sir. We have plenty of tea."

He nodded toward plastic cups holding damp leaves on the deck plate beside a thermos of hot water.

Chan stood, turned, and walked away.

The image of an exhausted and caffeine-fueled geek drifted from his mind as he ambled forward to recheck the distance between his submarine and the Japanese Ryukyu Island chain.

Assuming quiet waters surrounding him, he would seek rest

and await news from Park about orders to a rescue ship that would lend comforting hope to his still-veiled fate.

CHAPTER 15

After slinking behind swing shift naval staff seated at monitors, Pierre Renard prowled to the central plotting table, rapped his claws against its plastic edge, and sniffed the regional waters.

The luminous dots and lines portrayed a quiet evening, and he stood and turned toward a vacant control station.

The junior admiral supervising the evening watch passed and forced a greeting so mundane that Renard realized he had become a fixture in the Keelung naval command center. He nodded and slipped into a seat.

His finger caressed a mouse wheel, bringing the screen to life. Having memorized the meaning of the icons beside Chinese characters, he clicked the one that directed an encrypted hailing signal to the western edge of the Philippine Sea.

Awaiting a response, he fumbled at his shirt pocket and crinkled cellophane. He twisted and looked over his shoulder, noticing a solitary smoker across the room. Free from others' fumes, he invoked willpower and released the Marlboros.

He clicked the icon again, and his nerves unraveled as he awaited confirmation of his hailing.

A voice speaking English startled him.

"Excuse me, Mister Renard," a staff translator said. "Admiral Ye asked me to check for you in the command center and offer my assistance."

"He suspected I'd be here, did he? Very well, I could use your help."

Renard pointed toward the screen, and the man crouched beside him.

"I suspect that one of these icons sets my hailing request onto an automated interval, every five minutes or longer, depending which icon I click. Does that agree with the writing?"

The man pointed.

"Yes, I think so. This icon mentions a one-minute interval. This one five. The next one fifteen. I assume this is what you mean."

Renard clicked the five-minute interval icon and saw a system response in Chinese characters.

"What is that?" he asked.

"Confirmation that you have indeed set the system up to send your hailing message every five minutes."

"Yes, thank you," Renard said.

The translator stood.

"Shall I stay and assist you?"

Renard groped for the Marlboros at his breast, thought better of it, and lowered his hand.

"No," he said. "Yes, wait. Can you find out who among tonight's staff is in communication with the fishing vessel?"

A blank look of confusion overtook the man.

"Of course," he said. "I will find out."

Renard silently cursed the East Asian inability to admit confusion, and he attempted to extract the truth without invoking shame.

"Before you depart, may I specify the fishing vessel with which I wish to communicate?"

"Yes, of course. Please."

"I will show you then," Renard said.

He stood, walked to the navigation chart, and pointed.

"Here," he said. "Two miles outside the twelve-mile national water boundary. This is the submarine with which I ultimately wish to communicate."

"I see," the translator said.

"A helicopter dispatched a dive team over the submarine to attach a cable to its external communications connection. The cable runs three miles to the fishing vessel here."

"The fishing vessel was fishing outside the minefield prior to the mainland laying it?"

"Indeed," Renard said. "And it has been pressed into service. The helicopter delivered electronics and radio equipment. It is through this connection that I will control the submarine–the submarine that I cannot hail despite the expected time for its response having passed twenty minutes ago."

"I understand," the translator said. "I will speak to the flag watch officer immediately."

Alone, Renard tormented himself with worst case scenarios. The communication line had severed, the fishing vessel had mutinied, or Henri had suffered defeat with the *Hai Ming* being lost at sea.

This time, the crinkling pack reached his mouth, and he wrapped his lips around a cigarette. His Zippo lighter approached the butt when a sound distracted him.

Henri's voice.

He stabbed the Marlboro into his breast pocket and darted for the console. A grainy image of his friend against the backdrop of the submarine's control room flickered. Renard fumbled for a boom microphone and headset and slid it over his silvery hair.

"Yes, Henri," he said. "I see you. Go ahead."

"I hear you, Pierre."

Henri's face was an unreadable ghostly rendering.

"How are you, my friend?"

"Say again, Pierre. Poor reception."

"I hear you rather well. Can you report a status?"

"I'm not sure what you're saying," Henri said. "I have contact with a hostile submarine. I need your guidance."

The news surprised Renard, but he rationalized it.

The Chinese had uncountable spies in Taiwan pointing telescopes and binoculars at the water. The Chinese must have noticed the migration of patrol craft from one naval base to another in preparation for the egress. He found the lurking hostile Chinese submarine presence logical.

"Henri," he said. "Tell me everything. Target range, target bearing, your true bearing. Your speed, target speed if you have it. Any identification of submarine class?"

Henri's face flickered as Renard heard the unintelligible static of his mutated voice. Then the screen turned black.

"Damn!" Renard said.

He whipped off his headset and tossed it on the keyboard.

Shifting in his seat, he lowered his head toward his knees and rubbed the bridge of his nose.

"Mister Renard," the translator said.

"Yes, man?"

"The commander in the console across the room is in communications with the fishing vessel. He has learned that the dive team had to be dispatched to tighten a loose connection at a cable interface. They expect communications with the submarine to be reestablished soon."

"Thank you," Renard said. "Please inform me of updates as you learn them. And tomorrow, have the console next to me staffed with the officer in charge of communicating with the fishing vessel."

"I will see to it."

"Also, let the watch admiral know that I am going to update the tactical scenario with the presence of an enemy submarine that the *Hai Ming* has detected."

Renard returned to the navigation chart, grabbed a touch pad, and wiggled his thumb across it. A red dot framed by an inverted semicircle appeared atop the blue semicircle of the *Hai Ming*. Renard slid his thumb, and a circle of uncertainty stretched from the red dot.

Considering that the *Hai Ming* had deployed drones into the edge of the minefield, Renard reshaped the enemy submarine's circle of uncertainty westward, morphing his circle into an oval.

On the chart's opposite side, the smallish man in a white one-star admiral's uniform clasped his hands behind his back and nodded.

Renard turned and paced an arc behind the backs of seated officers. Hoping for Henri's reappearance, he kept his dark monitor in sight.

A door to the antechamber opened, revealing a face puffy with sleep. Admiral Ye slid into the center, and the junior admiral sprang to him to offer a report. Ye bobbed his jaw up and down and then dismissed his underling.

He and Renard closed distance, and the Frenchman smelled the scent of halitosis and armpits.

"Mister Renard, I understand the *Hai Ming* has discovered a hostile submarine."

"Yes, my friend. But I have no data beyond the known presence. I await communications being reestablished to bring you better information."

"Do you intend to engage?"

"No. Not unless the hostile is a threat to the *Hai Ming*. I cannot even verify there is adequate targeting data or if the hostile is in range."

"I've been told you will have communications soon. If you decide to engage, wake me. Otherwise, I will rest. Tomorrow is a momentous day."

"Of course, my old friend. Get your rest."

"You, too, Renard. I need you alert, especially with the absence of Slate."

"I will get adequate rest, I assure you."

Ye departed, and Renard hovered over his console, urging it to life. As minutes gnawed at him, he yielded to the nicotine odor and reached for his unlit cigarette.

The officer at the console next to him stood, distracting him. The commander from across the room responsible for communicating with the fishing merchant appeared in his place, flanked by the translator.

"I've taken the liberty of shifting the fishing vessel communications here now," the translator said. "It will also be here tomorrow morning as you requested."

"Thank you. Any news?"

As Renard slid the cigarette back into his pocket, the seated commander fired urgent words in Mandarin into his headset microphone boom. After a rapid exchange, he updated the translator.

"The connection is repaired," he said. "You should have visual within seconds."

Renard curled his hips around his chair back and landed in the seat. Before he could slide on the headset, Henri's clear image appeared.

"Henri?"

"Much better, Pierre. I can hear you clearly, and I can see you this time."

"Excellent! Where am I situated?"

"I've taped a laptop with the webcam to the captain's chair," Henri said. "Right where you belong."

"Do I have a tactical feed?"

"Yes," Henri said. "Antoine saw to it with a pair of electricians. He said it was easy with the Subtics design. The user guide had a procedure for tapping into the central data. You can access any screen you want."

Renard looked at the blank monitor above his and then to the translator.

"Can I get a tactical feed from the *Hai Ming* displayed here?"

"I will see to it."

Renard looked to Henri's image.

"Is the hostile submarine close?"

"Antoine doesn't think so. We can't hear it now."

The news calmed Renard.

"That simplifies matters. How did you detect it?"

"The starboard drone. Lieutenant Commander Jin has proven his skill at deploying and using drones. It was a flawless swim two miles ahead and five miles abeam."

"I see," Renard said. "You've fully deployed the drones for tomorrow's exercise."

"Yes. We heard the hostile submarine bearing three-five-two from the starboard drone. The drone heard the submarine's blade rate, correlating to four knots, *Song* class, but the sound is now gone, over two hours ago. We're not hearing it on any shipboard intrinsic systems."

"Very well, then. It's unworthy of alarm, but a tactical advantage in knowing of the enemy's presence. Keep listening for other submarines. I hardly expect this fellow to be alone."

"I will, Pierre. I must also add that Antoine detected a hull popping transient from the hostile vessel about two hours ago, but it wasn't while the drone heard it."

"Hull popping? You're shallow?"

"Yes. Why?"

A technician, his face red with sleep, arrived at the console and gestured at the blank upper screen. Renard stood and stepped aside, his wired headset tethering him in orbit around the console.

"He went to snorkel depth, and his hull expanded with the lessening of sea pressure," he said. "The sound traveled in a duct of water near the surface. That's why you heard it on a ship's sonar and not the deeper drone."

"Pierre? Did I err?"

Frustrated, Renard imagined the outcome if Jake Slate had been in charge. Jake would have concluded that the drone and the hull popping were damning clues about the *Song*-class submarine.

His protégé would have connected the line between the drone and the *Song* with the one drawn from the *Hai Ming* to its target with a third line representing four knots of speed, a reasonable estimate for the hostile *Song*.

Though the solutions connecting these lines contained infinite iterations spanning fractional degrees, Jake would have boxed in their extremes, and he would have deduced that he had a high probability of destroying the *Song* with a torpedo targeted at the center of these bounds.

Jake would have considered the risks, calculated the gains, and fired a torpedo. That torpedo would have snuck up on the unsuspecting *Song* and destroyed it. Jake would have revealed the existence of the *Hai Ming* to the Chinese, but Renard would have preferred this over letting the capable *Song* remain in the upcoming engagement.

The sting of the leadership gap Jake's departure had opened hurt, but Renard rationalized that Henri had maintained the element of surprise by being too ignorant of his advantage to exploit it.

"No my friend," he said. "You did precisely as I had hoped you would."

The console's upper screen came to life with a sonar display from the *Hai Ming's* Subtics system.

"Ah," Renard said, "I see your sonar screen."

"Excellent," Henri said.

Renard looked to the translator.

"Ask the technician if I can control the screens."

Renard watched the translator inform the technician of his request. The technician toggled through screens, demonstrating that Renard could see each one from the *Hai Ming*. However, the technician made no attempt to control them. The scaling, the frequencies to observe, which torpedo's parameters to monitor... all of it out of reach, Renard concluded.

"Thank you, that's enough," he said. "You may dismiss the technician."

He sat and looked to the *Hai Ming's* control room.

"Henri," he said, "have a man at my disposal tomorrow who can serve as my hands on your consoles. I don't want it to be you because you will be busy relaying my orders."

"Of course, Pierre. It will be tight up here with the extra body, but we've been through worse."

Renard's adrenaline diminished, yielding to the swelling fatigue. He recognized that he had accomplished all he could for the night and had shaken out the kinks in the vital link to the *Hai Ming*.

He wished Henri a peaceful night, shutdown his console, and skulked to his quarters.

CHAPTER 16

Pierre Renard rolled from his bunk and pressed his feet against rough carpet. He bounded forward, a long nap and anticipation energizing him.

In his tiny quarters, he crept to the washbasin, met his gaze's reflection with eyes of blue steel, and examined himself. The mirror showed sharp features that, despite lines cutting into his face, retained a classic handsomeness under silver hair.

He brushed his teeth, spat, and rinsed his mouth. Glaring at day-old stubble, he decided that the patrol ship egress operation deserved a fresh shave. A razor buzzed as it grazed his chin. Slapping Versace aftershave against his jaw, he judged his image deserving of the man who would drive the day's victory.

He reached into the stall, rotated dials, and awaited the rise of steam. Registering hot water with his palm, he slid into the shower and rubbed a loofa over his lean physique. He shut off the flow, pranced to the towel rack, and rubbed fabric over cooling droplets.

Clothed in his trademark Chinos and white dress shirt under a gray blazer, he shut his chamber door and crept down a passageway. Oil-based brush strokes of Taiwan's seaborne military lineage sailed by, summoning his admiration from cherry wood frames. Empty wallpaper at the end of his pictorial time warp harkened future heroes, and Renard envisioned the *Hai Ming* and a stealth patrol craft challenging each other from opposing walls.

Reaching the cafeteria, he surprised the serving crew setting up the guest breakfast buffet. Aware that the only other guests at the command center were military journalists with no preparation required to chronicle the day from the control center's upper deck observatory, he expected to arrive first and eat alone. He gathered his breakfast, sat, and ate while cycling through his mental checklist of the egress mission's details.

He wiped his mouth and dropped his cloth napkin to the table. Coffee, oatmeal, and melon within him, he walked to an access point. He nodded to a uniformed guard, showed the badge dangling around his neck, and punched a key code into cipher lock. The door to the inner nerve of Taiwan's naval and air defense, staffed by its skeletal midnight crew, slid open. He slid through the doorframe and found his way to the central navigation chart.

Taiwanese defenses agreed with his expectations. Two blue triangles representing F-16 Fighting Falcon combat patrols flew in a northerly track on the island's contested western edge, defining a fuzzy battle boundary at the Straits of Taiwan. The other four covered the northeast and southeast edges of the island, defying Chinese surface and air assets to maneuver east into the Philippine Sea.

Renard considered the air patrols thin, but he respected the Taiwanese gambit to preserve fuel in favor of keeping a full scale vigil. The defenses had to both hold and endure.

He noted Suao Harbor, where eighteen interlaced blue semicircles represented the patrol vessels.

The flag watch officer, a man taller and more senior than the evening shift officer, slid beside him and spoke in respectable English.

"I will be off duty when you lead this operation, Mister Renard," he said. "But I will watch from the observatory. It will be a great achievement to reestablish undersea control of the Philippine Sea."

"This is but one step of many leading to the lasting independence for your countrymen."

The admiral's face darkened as he pressed his wireless earpiece against his cheek. He spoke with hoarse gravity, and moments later a soft siren whined, and pulsating red strobes bathed the control room.

"What is it?" Renard asked.

"Air attack," the admiral said.

"Where?"

"Southern quadrant. Please, give us room."

The Frenchman circled the navigation chart to its far side

and allowed officers to converge upon the admiral. The first to arrive wore a captain's uniform with glinting wings over his breast pocket that revealed him as the senior aviation expert on watch.

The meaningless Mandarin exchanges muted in his mind, Renard watched an unwelcome fire of six red triangles rise in the South China Sea. Long red lines foretold the future of the assailing jets, and he pursed his lips while contemplating their destination. A fuel depot seemed possible, but surface-to-air missile batteries rendered it impregnable.

Blue lines from the four nearest Taiwanese Falcons veered toward the Chinese jets, and four more lines came to life over runways, signaling the launch of ready alert aircraft. As minutes passed and the Taiwanese air defense shield faced the inbound invaders, Renard considered the attack impotent. He smelled a ruse.

He blinked, and as if queued by his suspicion, the scenario changed. The red lines reversed direction and new red triangles appeared from the southeast.

Recognizing the southern aircraft as decoys, Renard looked to a lone blue semicircle representing a secondhand American *Kidd*-class destroyer, defending its new Taiwanese owners as the *Ma Kong*. Stranded outside the minefield, the *Ma Kong* lent its arsenal of anti-air missiles to the island's weak eastern air defense net.

Grasping the intent of the encroaching hostile aircraft, Renard's tail bristled. Though miles upwind, his predatory instinct sniffed the movements of the hunt. He lifted his snout and barked a warning.

"I suspect their target," he said.

Mandarin murmurs fell, and the admiral looked up.

"Speak, Renard," he said.

"The *Ma Kong*."

The air officer shrugged, cocked his head, and nodded, providing tepid support to Renard's hypothesis.

"I acknowledge the possibility," the admiral said. "I am vectoring the Falcon aircraft to intercept the incoming attack, but there are at least eight intruders. If the target is indeed the *Ma Kong*, it will face a formidable force."

Renard calculated the munitions hail storm of eight attack jets against the twin dual-rail launchers and limited fire control radar systems of the *Ma Kong*. The numbers weighed upon him.

He teased himself with the fantasy that Taiwan owned an Aegis destroyer with ripple-launch ability from vertical missile cells and impregnable electronic tracking systems. Against an Aegis, the Chinese intruders would be on a suicide mission, but as reality reentered his mind, he lamented that the inbound aircraft would overrun the *Ma Kong*.

Officers, several picking crust from their tired eyes, flocked into the control center. Admiral Ye appeared beside the watch officer, who pointed at the chart while updating his leader.

While he spoke, two red triangles broke off from the Chinese squadron to engage the Taiwanese Falcons.

"Yes, of course!" Renard said. "Damn!"

As the alarms in the center subsided in response to being silenced, Admiral Ye shot the Frenchman a cold stare.

"Mister Renard, do you have insights?"

"They've sent two air-to-air fighters to engage your Falcons," Renard said. "That they only sent two tells me the rest of the aircraft intend to attack surface targets. Their two fighters are standoffs against your Falcons, opening the way for the other aircraft, probably bombers, to attack."

"Attack the *Ma Kong*?" Ye asked.

"As a first target only," Renard said. "They will attack the *Ma Kong* and then continue to the patrol convoy."

"The patrol convoy is their primary target?" Ye asked.

"Precisely," Renard said.

Ye barked in Mandarin, and a commander stationed at a console turned and announced his obeying of the order. The commander exchanged words with a distant officer via a headset and updated Ye.

"I've alerted the patrol craft," Ye said.

A hush overtook the circle of officers, followed by rapid fire exchanges as the red triangles split and multiplied like cells under a microscope. The Chinese raiders had doubled as the F-16 Falcons discriminated the radar signatures of the close-flying aircraft.

Renard realized he had expended his value in the air engagement, and his clients would have to prove the merit of their defense without his support.

He crept away from the navigation chart and escaped to the momentary refuge of his console to hail the *Hai Ming*.

Sliding his headset over his hair, he saw the crisp features of a young Taiwanese submarine officer.

"Lieutenant Pao, officer of the deck," he said.

"Good morning, lieutenant," Renard said. "How is the ship's status?"

"No hostile submarines noted. No regain of the *Song*."

"That is good," Renard said. "Remain alert, though. They will return. How are the ship's systems?"

"All systems normal. The battery is fully charged, and there are four drones deployed."

"Four?" Renard asked. "Is that possible?"

"For the standard operator, no, sir. But Lieutenant Commander Jin is exceptional. He deployed the two additional drones before retiring last night."

"Very well," Renard said. "I will trust him."

Renard let the thoughts of drones pass and considered the direct implications of the air attack on the *Hai Ming* submarine. There were none, but an indirect possibility of a coordinated air and undersea attack compelled him to roust the crew.

"Listen, lieutenant," he said. "There is a major air attack taking place to the north. I see no direct threat to the ship, but you must alert the crew and man battle stations."

The young officer raised his eyebrows and acknowledged the order. Renard fumbled for his cigarettes, teased himself with their scent under his nose, and admired his will power in returning them to his pocket.

Henri appeared in his camera's view, fatigue and concern carving shadowed recesses into his face.

"An attack already, Pierre?"

"Yes, my friend," Renard said. "For your sake, I trust there is nothing to fear, but you must be alert."

"Of course, Pierre."

"If you identify a hostile submarine within seven nautical miles, contact me," Renard said. "If you suspect one within five miles, shoot it."

"Where are you going?"

"I'm shutting down communications until this air attack is over. Let us not risk that an attacking jet gets a lucky sniff of radio traffic giving a clue to your location."

"I see," Henri said. "I know what to do."

Renard terminated the communications and noticed the prior evening's translator standing beside him.

"I came when the alarms sounded in the quarters."

"Good," Renard said. "Can you verify that the fishing vessel has ceased transmitting? It must remain in emissions control until I say otherwise."

The translator spoke with the navy commander seated at the console beside Renard. The officer nodded and verified the fishing ship's status.

Renard slid the headset to the keyboard and swiveled his chair to examine the battle. But instead of taking in the chart's tactical data, he looked up to a verbal exchange. Admiral Ye surprised him with the stern tone he directed towards one of his junior admirals.

Ye's junior flag officer appeared broken to the verge of tears, and the somber faces surrounding the room's solitary and one-way conversation reminded Renard of a dirge.

Ye finished his monologue and extended his arm toward the exit. The gesture struck Renard as a compassionate but irrefutable order as the junior admiral marched away.

Renard awaited a brief pause in the battle action to stalk Ye.

"May I be of service?" he asked.

"I don't think so," Ye said. "We are preparing to defend the second target of the attack, which appears to be the patrol craft at Suao, as you anticipated. I commend your foresight in arming them with Stinger air defense missiles. I question the efficacy of the missiles, even the updated variants you insisted upon, but you've at least given them hope of fighting back. You've done all you can."

"May I ask how the battle fares? I sense mixed emotions."

"The exchange is thus far costly for both sides," Ye said. "Two Falcons held the air-to-air fighters to a stalemate while the *Ma Kong* shot down half of the incoming aircraft, but the surviving aircraft overwhelmed it with missiles."

"Overwhelmed?" Renard asked. "Lost?"

"Destroyed, with few survivors expected."

"I am sorry."

"The admiral you saw me dismiss," Ye said, "is one of my best destroyer sailors."

"I had thought otherwise after observing your exchange with the man."

Renard noted compassion in Ye's eyes.

"His son was the executive officer on the *Ma Kong*," Ye said. "There are times to ignore human suffering, and there are times for grieving. I determined his son's death to be the latter case and relieved him."

"A bold but necessary decision," Renard said.

"This is now beyond scenarios foreseen in our doctrine," Ye said. "Bombers are attacking stealth patrol craft tied to their piers. There is no prescribed response. There has been no training."

"Indeed," Renard said. "This is the fog of war."

"Do you have any advice?"

Renard scanned his mental inventory of airborne weapons hardware and the tactics of using them, and the contradiction shot to his mind.

"They proved against the *Ma Kong* that they are employing weapons that inflict maximum damage to a solitary target, using a combination of radar and infrared seekers, I suspect," he said. "Set a blaze to your piers to conceal the craft behind fire. This will blind the infrared seekers. Also, burn nearby piers to disorient the pilots visually. You must have trucks available to spread fuel."

Ye curled his finger at a captain who jogged to his side. He relayed the order.

"It will be done," Ye said. "But this seems a partial solution. They will surely strike with a multitude of weapons."

"I suspect cluster bombs," Renard said. "The kind used against tanks. The bombers will want to damage as many patrol craft as possible in a single pass. They will use their remaining missiles, but then they will employ cluster bombs as well."

"I see," Ye said. "From their perspective, it is better to cripple two patrol craft than to sink one. They are stopping a mission."

"Precisely," Renard said. "And unfortunately, the best defense against cluster bombs is immediate deployment of the ships to sea in a scattered formation."

"Unfortunately, because they will have no protection from the infrared seekers of single-target missiles?"

"Correct," Renard said. "Your best defense is a combination of fire and chaff for ships that remain pier-side. For those that can get underway quickly, I recommend dispersing them far from each other to limit the effect of cluster bombs."

"I will relay the tactical insight to the squadron commander."

"I don't envy him his situation," Renard said. "But I pray that he is a leader ready to prove his merit."

"I selected him personally for the mission," Ye said. "If anyone can lead the squadron out of this mess, he is the one."

CHAPTER 17

Lieutenant Commander Yang Lei replayed visual echoes of pulsating platinum flashes, digesting them as missile explosions beyond the horizon. As he looked eastward through the bridge windows where the sea's opaqueness met the stars, a flaming orb from the sinking *Ma Kong* destroyer flickered, contracted, and yielded to the darkness.

He looked through the starboard bridge window at silhouetted sailors who unraveled nylon lines from the mooring cleats of patrol vessels, low shadows of stealth nestled beside concrete piers. The men moved with warranted urgency, but Lei found the noise of scared voices on the radio net cumbersome.

He impressed himself with his calm grit.

"This is Lei," he said. "Silence on the line."

Tickling his peripheral vision through the far bridge window, bands of fire sliced the sky. He slid behind members of his bridge team, brought dimension to his perspective, and watched missiles trace arcs seaward from their launch platforms high in the island's eastern mountains.

He recognized the Sky Bow missiles, the longest reach of the Taiwanese air net, retaliating against the airborne assailants that had eradicated the *Ma Kong*. Reckoning fewer rocket plumes than he hoped, he scowled, wanting for stronger shore-based defenses. Despite their supersonic speeds, he resigned to waiting a minute for fate, physics, and the skill of the targeted Chinese pilots to learn if the missiles would hit.

With Taiwan's focus west toward the mainland, Lei presumed that the Chinese had flown southerly and angled back to punch through a weakness in the air defense net. Having witnessed the fiery end of the destroyer buttressing that vector, he choked back his rising fear of a crushing raiding force and braced for battle.

A vocal cacophony lingered on his headset.

"I said silence on the line!"

Silence held.

"Patrol craft only," he said, "cast off all lines and make all engines ready. Frigates remain by the pier. Acknowledge via data link. Keep the voice line quiet except for urgent updates."

He watched his command console accumulate acknowledgments of the orders. Glancing at a nautical chart of Suao Harbor, he calculated how to disperse his ships from its dark morning waters.

"All patrol craft get underway and make top speed outbound," he said. "At channel marker bravo, I will turn Craft One on bearing of due north. Craft Two, steer bearing zero-one-zero. Three, steer bearing zero-two-zero. That's ten-degree increments per craft. Each craft acknowledge your outbound bearing via data link."

Data arrived on his console, each craft's commander proving he had selected his proper course. Lei appreciated his squadron's alertness.

"Get underway when capable," Lei said. "If you reach the minefield keep-out zone, stop. Keep all Stinger missile teams topside, weapons free to engage any aircraft."

The moonlit silvery wake of a patrol craft two piers away caught his eye, and he saw propeller wash as another ship accelerated past his beam. The silhouettes of two more craft converged in his view, appearing to merge as they crossed paths into the exit channel.

He tapped his executive officer on the shoulder.

"How long?" he asked.

"Twenty seconds, sir. The diesels are online, and the last mooring line is coming off."

"Stinger team?"

"Topside and ready, sir. On the fantail."

Lei watched his squadron in exodus slice wakes into the harbor's tormented waters, and he checked through the port window that the pier's cleats had released their hold on his ship.

"Now?" he asked.

"Yes!" the executive officer said.

"All ahead standard," Lei said. "Make turns for fifteen knots."

As his craft lurched, an inferno rose behind a fuel truck to the south, masking the frigate mated to the far pier. Lei watched the fuel truck sprint along the wharf to replicate the wall of fire beside the frigate at the northern pier, and as flames rose on a distant pier, Lei assumed a second truck contributed to the burning.

"Frigates light up all radars and anti-air defenses," he said. "Coordinate with shore-based surface-to-air missile batteries. Frigate *Cheng Kung* has command of all air defenses except Sky Bow. All other assets engage air targets at will. All air defense assets acknowledge via data link."

Acknowledgements arrived, and he tapped a button to shift his monitor to a tactical overview. Synthesized information from multiple radar systems confirmed his instinct. His squadron scattered under a sky ready to erupt with hell's fury.

Blue squares represented his eighteen fleeing patrol craft, and red triangles thirty miles away revealed a tight formation of incoming aircraft.

He grasped his executive officer's shoulder and spoke in his ear. Expecting to be rigid with the giving of orders, Lei surprised himself with a patriarchal calmness. Whether he believed it or not, he oozed an insider's confidence that he owned the morning.

He sent his executive officer below to the combat information center, the inner nerve where his second-in-command would oversee a tactical control team in the carrying out of his orders.

Sensing Lei's next move, his third-in-command, his navigation officer, looked up from a chart in the room's corner.

"Navigator?" Lei asked.

"Yes, sir."

"Take the conn."

"I have the conn," the navigator said.

"Get us out of here," Lei said.

He steadied himself against the console as the deck rolled and trembled. A glance at digital gauges satisfied him that his underling turned the ship to the correct heading and accelerated it to flank speed.

After twisting his boom microphone to his lips, he tapped buttons to hail the captain of the *Cheng Kung*.

"Yes, sir?" the *Cheng Kung's* captain asked.

"Why aren't you shooting yet?" Lei asked.

"I'm waiting for the Sky Bow missiles, sir. If I engage now, I could waste missiles on aircraft that are about to be shot down."

"Can't you redirect missiles in flight?"

"It is possible but not recommended. Our radars can lock and freeze while shifting targets."

Auburn semicircles riddled the horizon, and Lei deduced that Sky Bow missile warheads engaged low-flying targets. His monitor clarified the outcome–the defenses had thinned the incoming enemy horde to eight aircraft.

"Engage," Lei said.

Golden exhaust flashes from the single-arm launchers of the moored frigates illuminated the harbor, and Standard Medium Range missiles roared overhead. Stepping off the bridge and onto the superstructure, Lei looked over the fantail and squinted as yellowish plumes flaring from hillocks behind a weapons hangar lifted Hawk missiles after the Standards.

He slapped his palm against flat metal as the patrol craft rolled in the wake of a sister ship. His vessel felt solid and invulnerable to his hand but exposed and ephemeral against darkness' encroaching menace.

Brilliant bursts lit the shoreline, and he forced his eyes shut while turning his head. The shock wave of supersonic, kerosene-fueled ramjet engines screeched across the sky, compelling him to jam his moist palms into his ears. He blinked, looked to the hillocks, and saw smoke rising as moonlight-swallowing puffs.

The water reflected the chainsaw staccato of a frigate's Phalanx point defense system spitting desperate uranium sabots. Visible above the pier's diesel-fueled inferno, detonations danced atop a frigate. Ramjet shock waves pounded Lei's head again, and he crouched to the superstructure's nonskid to regain his lucidity.

Those were just the anti-radiation missiles, he thought. *Fast and small, homing on the radar systems to silence our defenses. The worst is yet to come.*

A damaged frigate electrically blinded and a Sky Hawk radar system silenced, Lei watched the harbor's halved air defenses flicker with each protective missile's outbound launch. Wanting to take action, he stepped aft and braced himself on his ship's anti-ship missile launchers, modified to manage nuclear-tipped anti-submarine weapons, but useless against the inbound jets.

On his darkened fantail below, he saw his two-man Stinger missile team scanning the sky through night vision.

They can't protect us, he thought. *The range is too limited and the targeting too manual.*

He stormed forward and reentered the bridge. The air felt dry and hot, and he smelled fearful sweat. Eyes turned to him for hope and guidance.

I must do something, he thought. *And there's only one thing I can do under an air attack–pop chaff.*

He labored to decide. Shooting chaff, tiny metallic shards, into the sky may cloud and confuse active missile seekers, he realized, but it may also call undue electronic attention to his otherwise stealthy vessel.

I must do something, he thought. *Doing nothing is doing something when it's the right decision.*

He knew that his squadron would need chaff in the open ocean–if it survived this attack and the ensuing trek across a hostile minefield–and it may not have time to replenish its canisters if expended now.

I must do something, he thought. *I pray we can reload chaff quickly if we survive this attack.*

A vessel that pops chaff and drives away from the metallic cloud gains no defense, he reasoned, and he noticed that his ships were too close together to stop running. They couldn't pop chaff and stop.

I must do something.

Chaff is useless against heat-seeking weapons, useless against cluster munitions, he reflected.

I must do something.

He stood at his command console and pressed a button to talk to his ships' captains.

"All patrol craft," he said, "this is Lei. Pop one chaff canister immediately. Then pop one more canister when you stop at the keep-out zone."

He looked to his navigator.

"Pop chaff, one canister only," he said.

The thump reverberated through the soles of his boots, and he looked to his console.

Hazy clouds littered the sky over his fleeing patrol craft. He also noticed eight incoming triangles, confirmed by Keelung as Chinese JH-7 Flying Leopard fighter/bombers, slowing to subsonic speeds to launch their crushing blows.

A swarm of overlapping scarlet triangles, too numerous for Lei to count, signaled incoming anti-ship weapons. Speed leaders from the blue triangles of Standard and Sky Hawk missiles tickled the red menaces, but the complexity and uncertainty of defensive missiles knocking down hostile missiles at rates of closure four times the speed of sound, left him anxious. Ship-killers, inbound vampires from the sky, would slip through the defense.

Lei stepped to the starboard bridge window and grabbed a pair of night vision binoculars from a cradle. He placed the optics to his face, scanned high in the greenish night, and followed bright arcs behind the exhausts of the outbound missiles.

He looked southeast, hoping to glimpse the Chinese Eagle Strike missiles. The inbound ship-killers flew low, concealed below his horizon.

He lowered the optics, clenched his jaw, and prepared to meet his encroaching fate.

CHAPTER 18

Bright orbs on the horizon caught Lei's eye as they swelled to a crescendo of pulsating light, flared, and died into darkness.

He checked his monitor in hopes that the harbor's air defenses had eradicated the saturation attack, but red speed leaders showed surviving hostile missiles. He feared one would to veer towards his ship, mock his puny air defenses, and engulf his crew in a sinking blaze.

The navigator's shrill voice startled him.

"Five hundred yards from the minefield keep-out zone."

"Stop the ship," Lei said. "Pop chaff."

The ship shuddered with a backing bell, and thunder clapped to the south. He glanced at his monitor before racing off the bridge to the aft superstructure and noticed that three incoming missiles had fanned across the harbor entrance, over the escaping patrol craft.

Beyond his fantail, firecracker strobes peppered the water, and wave tops echoed their anger. Lei recognized the explosions as anti-tank rounds jettisoned from flying warheads, designed to pierce armor and damage multiple dispersed small targets.

He dared to hope that every round would hit water until an ominous beacon carved a semicircle in the blackness. Dark plumes wafted from the silhouette of a patrol craft that rode low in the water.

The air felt moist as his ship slowed, and a thunderclap signaled that another craft absorbed a hit.

"Damage reports, all vessels," he said. "Report in order."

Before anyone responded, anti-tank munitions pelted the burning piers, and the blinded frigate to the north erupted under the barrage of two huge anti-ship warheads.

The maelstrom of noise died, and Lei heard his executive officer reporting that his ship had been spared.

"One, no damage."

The next craft chimed in.

"Two, no damage."

Lei heard controlled terror in the voice of the next man to speak.

"This is Craft Three. We took a round in our combat control center. Approximately ten casualties, but we have back up combat capabilities and full propulsion."

"Very well," Lei said. "Do you need assistance?"

"Negative. The fires are contained."

Lei swallowed the guilt and sadness of his dead warriors and sought the condition of the rest of his team.

The fourth through sixth ships confirmed they were unscathed, but silence filled the gap where Lei expected to hear from the seventh.

"Go ahead, Seven," he said.

"One, this is Eight. Seven is burning. I think they took a round in their fuel tanks. It's bad."

"Very well," Lei said. "Six and Eight, head toward Seven to spray water and pick up survivors."

Golden exhaust flashes from a single-arm launcher outshone the burning harbor, and Lei heard Standard Medium Range missiles roaring overhead.

He watched the surviving frigate, the pier's dancing flames revealing smoke rising from its multiple wounds, prove it remained in the fight.

Damn it, Lei thought. *I forgot the remaining aircraft.*

He depressed a button on his headset, switching to his ship's internal voice circuit.

"Navigator, receive the remaining data reports. I want to know if anyone else has been hit."

"Aye, sir."

"Executive officer," Lei said. "What's still out there identified as a threat?" he asked.

"All eight remaining enemy aircraft vectored north and are now heading back south at low altitude. The *Cheng Kung* is engaging them with Standard missiles, but they are too many. I believe they mean to strafe our ranks!"

Lei refocused on the remaining threat. Eight aircraft–minus whatever the frigate could eliminate–were overrunning his squadron. And his ship stood first in line for the beating.

"Navigator," he said. "I want the Stinger team and the twenty-millimeter gun to bear against the incoming aircraft. Do you understand?"

"Yes, sir."

"Bring us to a full bell, turn us away from the minefield, and show the intruder a quarter bow aspect."

Lei's thighs stabilized him as the ship rolled. He shifted his voice circuit to all ships.

"All units, this is Lei. We are being strafed from the north. All units engage with Stingers and twenty-millimeter guns. Evade in random directions at random speeds. Be unpredictable. Force them to maneuver and adjust fire. Pop chaff and throw off their radar."

His executive officer told him that the frigate's Standard missiles had eliminated three of the enemy. Of the survivors, four held their formation while the fifth skimmed the wave tops and vectored toward his ship.

"Range to target?" Lei asked.

"Three miles," the executive officer said.

Lei stepped to the superstructure's railing and looked to the Stinger missile team on the fantail. Legs spread, one sailor pressed his eye to launcher optics while holding the weapon on his shoulder. His partner crouched below him, balancing a reload against his thigh.

Lei muted his mouthpiece and screamed.

"Shoot! Damn it! Shoot!"

Light sliced the sky and sketched a curve toward the inbound jet. Lei heard rapid gunfire echoing off wave tops and saw his ship's gun's tracer rounds. Retaliatory muzzle flashes popped in the sky, followed by chirps and splashes.

As the splashes became discordant clanging, Lei dropped his belly to the nonskid. As the bullets fell silent, he craned his neck and saw the Stinger missile fall in a ballistic death-dive. He crawled to his knees and saw his Stinger team flattened.

He jumped to the ladder and slid down to the fantail. He darted to his reload man and found him lying motionless with dark holes across his torso. Beside him, his launcher man writhed on the deck, clutching his shin.

A blood-speckled white shard extended through severed skin, and Lei recognized a future amputee. He grabbed the man's jaw and crouched over his face.

"Can you shoot?" Lei asked.

The man winced and ignored him. Lei released him and grabbed the launcher. He found the reload round, fumbled with it, and then inhaled to clear his mind. The missile slid into the launcher, and he hoisted it over his shoulder as he knelt by his sailor.

"I need you to shoot! Get up!"

Lei curled the sailor forward and stuck his head under his shoulder.

"Up!"

Lei lifted, and the man howled as he stood and dangled mangled flesh. Lei reached for the strap and extended the launcher in front of his partner.

"Take it and shoot!" he said. "Lean on me for support."

"Yes, captain."

The man balanced the weapon over his shoulder and pushed his eyes into the optics. Lei heard a violent swoosh and braced against a mild kickback. Rocket exhaust illuminated a trail of smoke.

Lei heard his ship's gun belching bullets, and he heard new chirps and splashes as his assailant adjusted its flight and targeting. Bullets punctured his ship again, and he dragged his injured sailor to the deck.

Engines whined as the formation of four mainland jets sought the rest of Lei's squadron. He learned the fate of the fifth jet as he rolled to his side and saw its fiery fuselage plummeting.

He rolled to his hip and adjusted his earpiece.

"Executive officer," he said. "What's going on?"

"Sir, the Stinger missile took down the inbound bandit!"

"Excellent," Lei said. "We can do this!"

"No, sir! Friendly Fighting Falcon aircraft have arrived. They've ordered us weapons tight."

"So be it," Lei said.

He shifted his frequency.

"All units, this is Lei. Friendly aircraft inbound. Weapons tight! Weapons tight!"

He shifted his frequency once more and asked the executive officer to send the medic to the injured Stinger operator.

He unbuttoned his shirt and twisted it tight while walking to his injured sailor. Wrapping the fabric into a tourniquet, he heard enemy aircraft climb and run from incoming Fighting Falcons. Friendly jets rumbled to the south as they chased away the remnants of the menace.

The sailor looked to Lei.

"What happened, sir? Did we get him?"

"Make no mistake," Lei said. "You hit him. You fought through your pain and performed your duty with honor. No matter the outcome of this campaign, and whether or not you need a prosthetic to walk again, you will recover in your hospital bed knowing that you are a hero."

A smile beamed behind a grimace, and the man lay back.

"We can triumph, can we not, sir?"

Lei considered his injured squadron and its mission. The hardest challenges lay ahead, and he disliked his odds.

But he knew men fought beside him with courage and resolve, and he embraced his faith in both the human spirit and a higher power.

"All things are possible," he said. "We may indeed triumph."

CHAPTER 19

Jake Slate had expected sleep in the reclined luxury of first class flight over the Pacific Ocean, but a nagging thought pricked at him from Tokyo to Chicago.

He deplaned and marched through the United Airlines terminal to his connecting gate, but his fuzzy mind sought a resolution to the nagging.

Planning to surprise his wife Linda with his return to Michigan, he realized he had the freedom to take a detour.

Having removed the number of his ex-girlfriend from his phone, he scoured his memory for it. He dialed his best guess, heard an unfamiliar voice, and apologized for the misdial. He tried again and stopped breathing when he heard CIA agent Olivia McDonald.

"Olivia?" he asked.

"Jake? Wow. What's it been? Three years?"

"Something like that."

"So," she asked. "How are you? You're married, right?"

"Yeah. It's awesome. I mean, I'm a totally different person. Linda is the center of my life, except, when I'm, well, you know."

"Doing clandestine things?"

"Yeah. I don't suppose you know what I'm up to anymore. No more need to know?"

"No more need to know."

Jake's stomach tightened as he groped for a segue to his request. He backed into a plastic chair and sat.

"Roger and I just got engaged," she said.

"Roger?"

"The naval intelligence officer I met while, well, doing clandestine things you don't need to know about."

"I remember you mentioning him," Jake said. "That's great. You sound happy."

"I am."

Chains fell from his shoulders as her words released him from the subconscious lingering responsibility he had internalized for her well-being.

"What's going on?" she asked.

"I wanted to know if you can get me time with one of your subjects."

"I have many subjects," she said. "You'll have to be more specific."

"We would agree that this is your most interesting and challenging subject."

"You can't be talking about... really?"

"Yes."

"Why? You can't possibly understand him better than the army of psychologists that's dissecting him."

"I'm not trying to understand him," he said.

"Then what?"

"I'm trying to understand myself."

Tension rose in her voice.

"I can't just let you see him for fun. There are rules, protocols. I stake my reputation and career on every person I let near him."

"This isn't for fun," he said. "I'm not even sure I want to."

"Make up your mind," she said. "I would need to pull strings–especially for you since you're supposed to be–"

"Dead," Jake said. "I'm supposed to be dead. But I'm not. I'm alive, and talking to him will help me make sense of things."

He heard her exasperated sigh.

"Since when did you become a philosopher?" she asked.

"Since I got tired of living to cheat death."

"Interesting," she said. "I'll get you in front of him."

*

Deep in an underground floor of a federal building, a guard escorted Jake down a long corridor of cells holding prisoners behind clear plastic walls.

At the end of the hallway, the guard stopped.

"Here he is. Return to the guard post when you're through. You've dealt with him before, and you know the rules."

Jake turned to the glass and compared the handsome, lean

man seated behind it against his memory. He recognized Hana al-Salem.

Salem lowered his tablet computer to a table, rose from his chair, and walked to the glass.

"You look familiar," he said. "Have we met?"

"Yeah," Jake said. "I almost killed you. Had the chance. Didn't bother."

Salem's face lit up.

"I remember you. You and your French friend. You visited me soon after I had been incarcerated here."

"That's right," Jake said.

"You didn't mention that you were a commando, although I see now that you have the physique and you carry yourself like one."

"I'm not."

Salem squinted and studied Jake's face.

"If I remember our last visit correctly, you took credit for having saved the *Bainbridge*," Salem said. "Now you say you almost killed me. That suggests that you were among the commando team that infiltrated my submarine to take it from me. I am confused."

"It wasn't your submarine. It belonged to the Israelis."

"Perhaps we should avoid arguing about the proper stewardship of submarines gifted through guilt by the Germans to a race of people who stole land from its proper inhabitants."

Jake sat in a plastic visitor's chair.

"I didn't come here to argue history."

"Do you mind if I sit as well?" Salem asked.

"Go ahead," Jake said. "It's your cell."

Salem reclined in a chair that appeared comfortable by Jake's expectation of prison standards, and his voice came clearly through the ventilation holes in the glass.

"I assume you came here to ask me questions," Salem said, "but would you be so gracious as to explain how you almost killed me?"

"I was in another submarine with a torpedo headed for you.

I shut the weapon off when I realized my friend and the commandos had taken the *Leviathan* back from you."

"I see. I hadn't realized how extensively my good fortune ran that day. First, a commando's bullet is targeted to wound but spare me, and then you spare the submarine because your friend is aboard it."

"That's why I didn't bother to kill you."

"I'm glad you didn't."

Jake leaned forward, placed his elbows on his knees, and rested his chin in his palms. He cast his gaze to the tile floor and realized he didn't know what to say.

He felt Salem watching him and sensed his curiosity. Jake blurted out his first thought.

"I don't get it," he said. "You hit the world harder than I did, but you couldn't have been half as pissed off as I was for revenge."

"In all my interviews with countless experts," he said, "you are the first to volunteer a personal comparison to my life."

"I'll be blunt," Jake said. "I'm not here to learn about you. I'm here to learn about me."

Salem's knuckles turned white on his armrests.

"Fascinating," he said. "I don't even know your name."

"Call me Jake."

"You will tell me your story then, Jake?" Salem asked.

"Most of it will be cryptic, but you'll get the point. I only ask that you volunteer the truth in return."

"Of course," Salem said, "assuming that you don't ask me to identify the names of people I've already refused to identify. I've been pressed for this information many times, and threats to extract it from me by torture have proven idle."

"I don't care about any of that," Jake said.

"What do you care about then?"

Jake pressed his back into the chair as he recognized his jealousy.

"I care about why I fell short trying to do exactly what you did," he said.

"You certainly didn't attempt to disable the United States with an electromagnetic pulse attack, did you?"

"No," Jake said. "But I did steal something powerful, just like you did when you stole the *Leviathan*. I also intended to do something epic with it."

"Epic?" Salem said. "You see my actions from my perspective and without disdain. And you do this naturally. I can tell when a psychologist is forcing an effort to gain my perspective, such as the redheaded lady who has been attempting to dissect me."

"She told you I was coming?"

"Yes. She's brilliant. I almost find myself willing to trust her, but a deeper part of me knows better."

Jake shifted in his seat.

"You'll trust me," he said.

"Because you have no agenda other than learning about yourself?" Salem asked.

"You're starting to understand why I'm here."

"Perhaps. You said you intended something epic. Did you fail?"

"I stopped at the last minute," Jake said.

"I see. You seem the type of person to succeed when committed. I assume then that you lost your motivation."

In a flash, doubts of his visit's appropriateness evaporated. Salem understood him. Better than Renard. Better than anyone. The feeling excited and sickened him.

"I was angry... vengeful... even proud," he said. "Then I realized that these reasons didn't justify my actions."

"I see immediate differences between us," Salem said, his face darkening. "My motivation was selfless. I sought to shock a nation for the greater sake of the world, and I didn't care if I lived or died. Because of this, my motivation was solid as bedrock."

"You're saying I'm selfish?" Jake asked.

"The evidence supports it, based upon what you have shared with me."

Jake swallowed the concept as truth.

"So, I was selfish," he said. "Maybe I still am. But I don't see why I should risk my life for strangers."

"The most noble purposes involve serving others," Salem said. "Whether you know them or not is irrelevant. You are the only interviewer I expect to understand why this was the inspiration for my deeds."

"You called it divine inspiration when I was here last time," Jake said. "Now you're calling it servitude."

Salem stood and approached the glass. His glare surprised Jake and clutched his soul.

"When you can see that these are one in the same, Jake, you will have resolved your inner dilemma."

CHAPTER 20

John Brody stormed into Secretary Rickets' office and slammed the door.

"It's over," he said.

Rickets slouched in his chair behind a thick mahogany desk. He appeared wounded but resilient.

"It's not over," Rickets said.

"Suao Harbor is on fire. Two frigates are damaged–one a mission kill, the destroyer *Ma Kong* is on the bottom, and God knows how many patrol craft survived, if any."

"I know," Rickets said. "Renard just texted me."

"You're making national security decisions based upon an unsecure text from an international criminal?"

"There's plenty of security protecting my cell phone," Rickets said. "And he texted me all I need to know with cryptic information."

Rickets stood and walked around his desk.

"Well?" Brody asked.

"Fourteen or fifteen. Proceeding," Rickets said.

"That's it? That's all he texted?"

"I assume it's the number of patrol craft that survived the air attack and are available for the egress."

"Why are we speculating?"

"We don't have to," Rickets said. "I just got another text from him. He's asking for a teleconference."

Rickets sat in his chair and turned on the monitor.

"Are you going to sit?" he asked.

"I'll stand," Brody said.

The screen brought the Frenchman's visage into form.

"Gentlemen," Renard said.

"What the hell's going on?" Brody asked.

"The Chinese launched a surprise anti-shipping attack from the air, but the convoy survived."

"Define 'survived'," Brody said.

"Fourteen vessels are untouched or sustained minor strafing

damage. A fifteenth is operational on one diesel engine and will continue on the mission. Two are damaged beyond use without major repairs, and one was sadly lost."

"Fourteen or fifteen," Brody said. "Your ranks are dwindling, and you haven't even started yet."

"The convoy will survive the minefield with enough integrity to provide anti-submarine coverage at the choke points."

"You can't assure that," Brody said.

"No," Renard said, "But within a matter of hours I expect to share with you news of our success."

Brody judged a matter of hours too long for the Seventh Fleet to wait. He excused himself, and as he closed the door to Rickets' office, he decided to lower his head, charge, and impale his enemy.

He marched through the hallway to give the order to mobilize a strike group in Hawaii to begin steaming towards Taiwan.

*

Renard swallowed saliva, accentuating his hunger. The Chinese interruption threatened his hunt, but his resolve remained. He would adapt his tactics to the changing wind, redirect his tracks, and outfox his prey.

"Admiral Brody remains pessimistic," he said.

Rickets' image moved with slight latency across the laptop monitor.

"His opinion doesn't matter," Rickets said. "All that matters is that you succeed."

"He had an air about him of quiet defiance."

"I'll keep Brody in check."

"Please do. I fear he may send American ships to places where they could only complicate matters."

Renard inhaled the calming taste of his cigarette.

"Other than the loss of patrol craft," Rickets asked, "have you made any adjustments to your plans?"

"Timing has slipped forty minutes as the surviving ships assess damage and regroup, but this is hardly a concern as we have forfeited any element of surprise. The Chinese learned of our egress and have certainly already dedicated every asset to it they see fit."

"Submarines," Rickets said.

Renard exhaled smoke into a cloud that rose into the Keelung command center's high ceiling.

"That's all they have left other than the aircraft they've already expended and the mines they've already dropped. Taking a skewed perspective, the Chinese air attack at least proves that they fear the patrol crafts' capabilities."

"You can do this without Slate?"

"I've planned for it all along."

Renard glanced over his shoulder at the empty seat from which he would command the *Hai Ming* submarine. Duty called, and he looked back at the webcam.

"Secretary Rickets," he said, "I have business to which I must attend."

"Get it done, Renard. I'll be watching."

Renard logged off the laptop and stamped out his Marlboro in a tray.

He brushed by the Taiwanese flag that served as his teleconference backdrop, bringing the panorama of the buzzing control center into view.

Adrenaline carried him across the carpet, and he stopped to look over shoulders at the navigation chart.

Outside Suao Harbor, a complete squadron of F-16 aircraft protected the sky against a potential second wave of assailants.

Fourteen patrol craft formed two columns of seven, their beams separated by a quarter mile with a half mile separating their sterns and bows. A fifteenth, the lead vessel, drifted in front. It pointed toward the minefield, represented by slashed red lines four miles wide inside the twelve-mile territorial boundary.

Within the center of the screen's focus, a narrow corridor showed green hashes interlaced between the minefield's lines of red. Renard recognized it as the route the patrol crafts would run.

He recalled that sled-carrying helicopters had cleansed the route with multiple counter-mining runs, but the water remained lethal due to the imperfections of minesweeping and the ability of mines to ignore a preset number of targets before exploding.

The helicopters had fooled five mines into harmless suicides, but he knew that surviving mines may have inched closer to their detonation count with each helicopter pass, while others may have escaped their sleds' influence.

Based upon the expected density of mines Chinese aircraft had dropped, Renard calculated that four mines remained to threaten the patrol craft. An unknown mix of mines—some lurking below the surface but tethered to the seafloor to prevent drifting to international waters and others resting on the bottom to launch torpedoes—threatened the convoy.

He walked around bodies to his seat. Contemplating restraint, he smelled the room's thick clouds of cigarette smoke and yielded to his life-threatening habit. He puffed the Marlboro's tip into an amber glow with an instinctive flick of his gold Zippo lighter.

His finger caressed a mouse wheel, bringing the screen to life. He clicked the memorized Chinese icon that directed an encrypted hailing signal to the western edge of the Philippine Sea.

Awaiting a connection through the fishing vessel to the *Hai Ming* submarine, he stirred. His translator appeared from nowhere, proving his prowess in finding Renard with impeccable timing.

"Good morning, Mister Renard," he said.

"Good morning," Renard said. "Do you have a technician standing by? I doubt I'll need him, but this is not the moment to be without him."

"Of course."

The translator lifted his arm and extended his fingers toward a corner of the command center. The white creases in his crisp white uniform moved with his lithe figure.

Renard stood and noticed four men with technical manuals and electronic diagnostic equipment in the corner.

"I see," he said. "Out of the way, but ready."

"Correct."

Renard turned to his screen and saw Henri's image looking back at him from the *Hai Ming's* control room.

"Can you hear me, Pierre?" Henri said.

"Yes," Renard said. "Status please."

"Battery is eighty-five percent. Four drones deployed. I believe you have telemetry data on our location and those of the drones. We track no submerged contacts."

Renard looked at his console's upper screen which displayed sonar data from the *Hai Ming's* Subtics system.

"I see," Renard said. "I expect this is the calm before the storm."

"There already was an air storm," Henri said. "We heard much of it. I'm encouraged that most of the patrol craft survived, but it is a pity for those we've lost."

"A pity indeed," Renard said. "Let's keep alive those who have survived."

"I intend to, Pierre."

Renard leaned into his screen.

"Remember one thing, my friend," he said. "I need data immediately. This is atypical submarine warfare. This is a rapid reaction to the first verification of a hostile vessel. You are an information service. Your torpedoes are all but useless."

"But they are ready, if needed."

"I'm sure," Renard said. "I expect that your first and only piece of targeting data may be launch transients and hostile torpedoes aimed at the convoy. Make sure Antoine distinguishes one torpedo from another and one launching submarine from another. The bearing rates on the torpedoes may be sufficient targeting data, and bearings to launch transients will confirm. Make sure you share your immediate acquisition data on the tactical net."

"I will, Pierre," Henri said. "And I have a man set up with a headset to press buttons for you at a dedicated console. We are ready."

Renard puffed from his cigarette and leaned back. He heard a commotion behind him, glanced over his shoulder, and sensed history being set in motion behind him.

"I know you are, my friend," he said. "Keep the line open, but excuse me."

He slid his headset off, stood, and faced the navigation chart.

An aura of power and destiny enveloped the small form of Admiral Ye, his radiating cheeks lighting the room. He raised a finger, the room fell silent, and he uttered a command to an officer seated meters from the chart. His words carried restrained power, and the seated officer stirred under Ye's will.

Lights flashed, a klaxon blared, and pneumatic actuators drove shut every door to the center. Ye barked another order, and an Air Force general beside him announced what Renard assumed was part of a memorized code to authorize the use of nuclear weapons. Three officers, huddled around a console, scribbled as the general spoke. Admiral Ye then vocalized his half of the authorization.

An officer tapped a sequence into a keyboard, informing Taiwan's armed forces that were authorized to use nuclear weapons within predefined offshore coordinates.

Renard noticed a commander flanked by four armed sentries slide a briefcase–handcuffed to his wrist–onto a flat surface before Ye. Ye stepped aside for the general to punch in his half of the case's combination, and then he stepped in to finish the sequence.

Ye stared with wonder, hesitated, and then withdrew a sealed, laminated card. He tore it open and let the general read it. The general announced characters followed by a memorized phrase that Renard estimated served as his formal command to launch nuclear weapons. Then Ye spoke, his words crafting a replay of the general's effort.

A final man in a black suit seemed to slip from shadows and emerge next to the general. Renard recognized him as the Minister of Defense, his face dark under a furrowed brow. The Minister read the characters aloud and declared his concurrence of his nation's order to use nuclear weapons.

An officer tapped a new sequence into a keyboard, broadcasting unlock codes to the patrol craft.

Renard felt a spark rise within him as the room held its collective breath. The pseudo-nation of Taiwan had just granted the young commander of the patrol craft squadron the trigger to nuclear arms. In the silence, Ye extended his palm toward the chart and uttered a single word.

Renard knew scant words in Mandarin, but he grasped the admiral's utterance as if it were his native tongue.

He had said 'begin'.

CHAPTER 21

Strafing bullets had punctured Lieutenant Commander Lei's ship, but they missed sensitive equipment, passing through the keel or ricocheting off a steel reduction gear case. His crew had shored up the slow leaks, and welding teams were reinforcing the major wounds.

Through the bridge window, moonlight danced on the glowering wave tops of the Philippine Sea. His grieving for fallen comrades postponed, Lei turned his attention to the dangers of the looming minefield.

As he lowered his chin, the helmet strap under his communications headset tickled his neck, and the monitor's useless illusion of calmness irked him. Blue triangles patrolled the sky, blue squares filed behind his craft, and inverted triangles marked the *Hai Ming* submarine and its drones. But unseen perils prowled below the swells.

He tapped a button on his headset.

"All craft, this is Lei," he said. "It's time. God protect us. All craft, all ahead flank."

The ship lurched, and glimmering silver sea spray shot over the bow. While a bridge full of eyes scanned the water through binoculars, Lei focused on his monitor's overhead rendering of his vessel sprinting toward a minefield's invisible boundary.

Isolating Lei's home island, the mainland had dropped mines along the ten-mile curve, leaving a margin of error to prevent stray mines landing outside the twelve-mile international waters limit. The screen showed an additional two miles of landward margin, and he respected the eight-mile curve as his keep-out zone.

He intended to slow at the edge of danger–unless torpedoes forced a desperate evasion. Mainland submarines could reach across the minefield, and he would be blind to the subsurface menaces save for input from a solitary friendly submarine.

He glared at the screen, praying for the *Hai Ming* to provide him adequate warning.

Via data link, the *Hai Ming* answered his silent plea and begat his waking nightmare.

Startling him, an inverted red triangle appeared to the northeast. Blood coursed through him, turning fear into action. A second torpedo appeared, and he expected more.

He studied the red lines that predicted the future locations of moving bodies, shifted his weight over the pitching deck, and spoke into his boom microphone.

"Incoming torpedoes to the northeast," he said. "Crafts One through Three maintain prescribed course and speed. Crafts Four through Nine are at risk. Turn starboard and circle back to the end of the column. Ten and higher maintain course and speed."

Four more torpedoes appeared, completing a six-torpedo salvo from a hidden mainland submarine.

Is that your full volley? Lei thought. *When will the* Hai Ming *expose you to my wrath?*

The deck rumbled through his bones during an otherwise silent sprint.

Where are you? he thought.

His eyes burned, and he blinked moisture into them.

Where are you!

An inverted red triangle appeared on the far side of the minefield.

Thank you, Hai Ming. *My turn!*

He switched his circuit to his executive officer below in the combat information center.

"Hostile submarine!"

"I see it, sir. Designating submarine as Sierra One. Targeting with Tube One."

The kill zone for the predicted salvo of nuclear warheads appeared on Lei's screen, centering on the hostile submarine but tickling the *Hai Ming*.

"Set warheads three and four to half yield," he said. "They are threats to the *Hai Ming*."

"Setting warheads three and four to half yield, sir."

The arcs of destruction surrounding two of the missile's eight warheads shrank, retracting the kill zone.

"Prepare to launch Tube One at Sierra One," Lei said.

"Tube One is warmed and ready, sir."

"Shooting Tube One," Lei said.

He flipped a plastic guard and depressed a button.

A swooshing roar bellowed behind him and reverberated throughout the bridge. Through the side window, a rocket plume sliced the darkness, climbed, and veered north.

He lowered his gaze to see his missile, but new red threats, torpedoes from the southeast, burned onto the console. With crafts four through nine reversing course, a dozen of his ships steamed into the new weapons' paths.

Another salvo from the north appeared, and Lei recognized a triangulated attack. He had expected a surgical strike, but the mainland had revealed its shotgun approach. Amid the chaos, he changed his plan and ordered a tactical retreat.

"Crafts four through fifteen," he said, "return to the harbor, flank speed! Race for cover behind the breakwaters! Crafts one through three, continue through the minefield."

The red character representing the submarine behind the second salvo materialized on his screen.

"Craft three," he said, "designate the submarine to the south as Sierra Two. Engage Sierra Two with one missile."

Time stopped for Lei during an eerie quasi-silence where nothing seemed to be happening. He noticed his pulse throbbing through his neck as rocket exhaust lit the night off his starboard beam.

Nuclear weapons in flight, he returned his attention to his overhead tactical view. The screen showed his ship entering the keep-out zone, and he slowed to five knots. As the decelerating deck tipped him forward, he kept his gaze on the monitor.

A blue icon representing the first warhead in ballistic free fall separated from his ship's missile and etched an X in the display. The flying weapon dived and turned to draw its entrapping octagon around its target. Numbers beside the diving missile ticked downward with altitude.

The executive officer's voice in his headset confirmed the first warhead's release.

"Tube One, first warhead deployed."

A counter on his screen reeled off seconds as the warhead descended. Lei trusted that the missile would release the next seven warheads at lower altitudes so that the points of the inescapable death octagon would detonate at similar times as they reached the preset depth of five hundred feet.

Since the seafloor dropped east of Suao, Lei choose five hundred feet to concentrate the jolting blows and oscillating fireballs upon the submarines while delivering minimal energy to his surfaced crafts. But unavoidable shock waves would ride up the underwater mountain that shouldered Taiwan, and they would hit his small ship.

Preparing for waterborne punches, he optimized his bearing for his ship and the two that flanked him through the minefield.

"Crafts one through three," he said, "turn to course zero-three-zero."

He also needed to protect the ships against incoming airborne shock waves and the contamination that the southerly winds would soon carry.

"All ships," he said, "rig for shock waves and contamination."

His craft rolled through the turn, and an explosion startled him. He raced to his port window and saw an arcing rainfall of moonlit glistening silver.

Water whipped white by expanding gases cut the blackness and marked the point where a mine had severed Craft Two. The vessel's sinking silhouetted halves twisted in opposing directions.

As Lei internalized the loss of his comrades, a steel shutter rolled closed outside the window, protecting the bridge from airborne shock and radioactive contaminants. Absent moonlight, the bridge became ghastly red.

Another explosion, distant, thundered. He slid back to his console for understanding, and the dizzying array of crisscrossinglines held no conclusions.

But his executive officer clarified the truth.

"Sir, Ten just reported. Fifteen took a torpedo. Fifteen is lost. They couldn't evade."

I ordered Fifteen to continue on this mission, hindered in speed with one diesel offline, Lei thought. *I doomed them.*

A glance below his chin revealed that his ship's missile had released all its warheads prior to tumbling into the sea. As the counter tracking the sinking of enriched plutonium reached ten seconds to estimated detonation, he allowed himself a final view of the world prior to entering the tactical nuclear age.

He depressed a button, and his screen showed the view from an infrared camera pointing aft.

The green hue near the harbor showed wakes hitting wakes, suggesting that the bulk of his squadron had evaded torpedoes behind the jetties. Unable to see evidence of the ill-fated Craft Fifteen, he nudged a joystick on his console in search of survivors from Craft Two, less than half a mile behind him, but the sea had swallowed the mine's victim.

He shifted his view to a forward camera with savage hopes of watching his underwater nuclear attack. The sea appeared calm, but as the seconds reached zero, he sat in a shock-mounted chair, grasped its handrails, and braced for nuclear fury.

CHAPTER 22

His knuckles white on his chair's arms, Lei saw the first warhead lift the sea's surface in the greenish hue of his monitor. The watery protrusion of the sub-kiloton blast impressed him with it smallness, but the shock wave caught him off guard.

Coming from below, the direct-path shock lifted the bow. His chair pitched, its solitary base leg dampening the axial and lateral blow. He had left his mouth open, and the impact shut it. He clenched his teeth to stifle a curse as the wave's reflection off the steep seafloor jolted his ship sideways.

Seven more warheads detonated, and Lei clamped himself to the chair with a death grip. As the last shock passed, he felt catatonic, and he stared at the monitor showing the darkened outside world.

The camera revealed the foggy base surges as shreds of blast energy escaped the water's surface, rose in hot mist, and expanded outward.

Unsure how a commanding officer should react to self-inflicted blows, he heard himself addressing his bridge crew through his mental mist.

"Any injuries?" he asked.

As heads shook in silence, Lei remembered that the warheads of a second missile would soon explode. He ordered his ship and the flanking Craft Three to turn. Facing south, Lei rode eight more shock waves and their reflections.

When he gathered his thoughts, he realized that the third submarine had appeared on his screen, and he took action.

"Craft Four," he said, "can you hear me?"

"Yes, sir. This is Craft Four."

The response confirmed Lei's expectations that the seawater had absorbed the electromagnetic pulses. Shipboard electronic communications remained robust.

"Craft Four," he said, "designate the submarine to the far north as Sierra Three. Engage Sierra Three with one missile, but remain behind the breakwaters while launching. There may still be torpedoes in the water."

"Craft Three," he said, "follow me out of this accursed mine-field. Course zero-eight-zero. All ahead standard."

Text acknowledgements appeared on his screen from his ships, keeping his voice line clear for his commands.

"Crafts Four through Fourteen, remain behind the break-waters until the *Hai Ming* can give confirmation that hostile tor-pedoes are no longer running."

His executive officer spoke with urgency.

"Sir, Keelung demands to speak with you."

Now? Lei thought.

"Patch them through," Lei said.

"Lieutenant Commander Lei, this is Admiral Ye."

"Sir?"

"The hostile submarine to the north, the one you've desig-nated as Sierra Three, is surfacing and assumed to be in distress. I've taken the liberty of standing down Craft Four's missile attack on Sierra Three."

Lei glanced at his monitor and noted Craft Four's aborted launch sequence.

"I see, sir. What are your orders?"

"You and Craft Three are to take station on Sierra Three. You are to prevent her from raising a communication mast, and you are to prevent her from submerging."

Lei found himself dumbfounded but hesitated before asking the admiral how to carry out the orders.

"Yes, sir," he said. "I understand my orders."

"If she raises a mast, shoot it down," Ye said. "If she opens her ballast tank vents and you see sea spray, shoot holes in her pres-sure hull."

Lei exhaled in relief of the admiral's clarifications.

"I will see to it, sir."

"If she takes no hostile action, keep your weapons tight," Ye said. "The mainland is listening, and we don't want them to know what we're about to accomplish."

"What do you need me to accomplish, sir?"

"Not you," Ye said. "Helicopters are en route to the submarine. We will board her. Just keep her from submerging or communicating."

"I understand, sir."

"You'll have to pass through the radioactive cloud of mist to reach the submarine quickly."

Lei glanced at his screen, realized he was clear of the minefield, and agreed with Ye that the southerly wind would blow the radioactivity into his path.

"We're rigged for contamination, sir," he said. "I am concerned, however, that our cannons may be unable to penetrate submarine steel."

"Based upon reports from the *Hai Ming*," Ye said, "I doubt you will have to find out. I expect that we will find very few survivors, and I expect that the ones we find will be begging for medical assistance."

"Craft Three and I are en route now," Lei said.

"The *Hai Ming* has confirmed that your warheads have sunk the other two hostile submarines," Ye said. "And all hostile torpedoes have stopped running. Send the remainder of your squadron through the minefield."

*

The blast-created mist appeared gentle as Lei watched his bow cut through the water at flank speed, but he grasped its man-made danger.

"Do you have radiation levels yet?" he asked.

"Calculating initial levels, sir," his executive officer said. "They appear to be hazardous for long-term exposure. We will require a salt water spray down."

As the last contaminated wisp rolled over his bow, he swiveled his camera towards the expected location of the surfaced submarine and saw darkness.

"Train the starboard camera on Sierra Three," he said.

"Training," the executive officer said. "We have multiple eyes seeking it."

Lei scanned the bridge and noted three other sailors looking for the submarine in their monitors.

"Remember that the *Hai Ming's* estimate of the submarine's location is imperfect. It could be off by more than a mile. Submarines work with acoustic data that creates such uncertainty."

"Shall I illuminate our surface search radar, sir?"

"Restrict your radiation to within thirty degrees relative to the bow. Radiate."

Lei flipped from his camera view to his radar and saw the return he wanted.

"That's her," he said. "Secure radiating."

He adjusted course five degrees to point toward the submarine, and he flipped his monitor back to its forward camera view. The dark square of a submarine's sail appeared. As his target grew larger, he noted a bow wake.

"What do you think," he asked. "They're not trying to run from us, are they?"

"I doubt it, sir," his executive officer said. "But I can't tell you why they are making way."

Lei approached, and the submarine became clearer.

"That's a *Kilo* class, isn't it?"

"Probably, sir. We'll know for certain after the boarding parties arrive. They're five minutes out."

Lei stationed his ship off the submarine's beam and matched its course and speed. He kept his twenty-millimeter cannon trained on the sail, but no masts rose.

Instead, the first sign of life came from the forward hatch. It flipped open, and for an eternity, nothing happened. Then a human head appeared, followed by a torso that fell to the deck. Another human figure appeared, pulled itself over the first, and slithered forward, dragging useless legs.

A Blackhawk helicopter appeared from above and hovered over the open hatch. A soldier wearing a forced-air anti-contamination suit and carrying a rifle rappelled from the helicopter. He inspected the crippled mainland sailors for weapons as three soldiers followed him to the steel.

The fire team disappeared into the submarine.

Four more soldiers descended from the helicopter, followed by unarmed men carrying waterproof bags. The second wave of infiltrators slid through the hatch, their weapons over their shoulders.

A second Blackhawk replaced the first and released additional men to the deck. Lei noted that each remained unarmed, and he thought he saw a medical kit.

The bow wake subsided, and Lei swiveled his camera to check that the submarine's propeller had stopped. Shifting his camera back to the conning tower, he heard welcomed news from his executive officer.

"It's done, sir. They've taken the submarine. We are ordered to clear the area and continue on our primary mission."

"That seemed too easy," Lei said.

"We now know what happens when a submerged vessel takes the shock wave broadsides from less than two miles, sir. Even though they were outside the octagon, warhead number two was close enough to do this."

"Any insight about the possibility of being able to salvage the submarine?"

"Not yet, sir."

"Perhaps that's a question that we would be wise to remain ignorant about."

"Agreed, sir."

Lei checked his monitor. The remainder of his squadron had cleared the minefield. He shifted his voice to his entire squadron.

"Congratulations on a victorious egress operation," he said. "We have lost many comrades, and for them we shall mourn at the appropriate time. But now, we must complete our mission and guard the straits."

He double-checked the numbers in his head.

"Crafts Ten through Fourteen, you are now the Luzon Task Force. Craft Fourteen, you have command of the Luzon Task

Force. Head south and patrol the Luzon Strait. All other vessels follow me east."

Lei tapped a button on his console to bring up a view of the Japanese Ryukyu Island chain. The line showing his nation's undersea hydrophone array gave him hope.

He faced a challenge covering all mainland submarine passages between the islands, but he expected that his squadron would succeed in placing the Philippine Sea under his navy's control and making it safe for the merchant shipping his nation would need to endure.

CHAPTER 23

The base at Qingdao a days-old memory, Dao Chan sniffed the stolen North Korean *Romeo's* cramped confines. His recollection of the East China Sea's moist salted aroma had yielded to the dry metallic taste of carbon dust from rotating electrical machines.

His executive officer ducked through the forward door, brushed by seated sailors, and overpowered the staleness with the stench of rancid meat and formaldehyde.

"A bag is leaking in the torpedo room," he said. "I've already ordered the body moved to a spare bag."

"That's the proper action, Gao," Chan said. "Have you yet determined if the leak was due to a failure in the bag or by an accidental tearing?"

"I've not yet made that determination, sir."

Chan doubted that Gao had recognized the importance of the distinction.

"If the bags are failing due to a design flaw," Chan said, "then we face a problem of limited replacement bags and preservation fluid. If a sailor tore the bag by accident, we must seek a better way to stack the bodies out of the way."

"Yes, sir."

Gao appeared defeated. Chan dismissed him with a nod and a stern index finger toward the door.

He turned his gaze to the chart and watched the lighted crosshair walk under translucent tracing paper. His ship appeared alone in the sea, but he realized that maintaining his ten-knot pace kept him deaf to his surroundings. If a capable submarine were trailing him, it did so as a ghost.

As he approached the Ryukyu Islands, penciled arcs proclaiming Japan's twelve-mile national water boundaries pinched down on him. He checked his ship's bearing to verify that he drove between Yakushima to the north and Kuchinoshima to the south. He intended to grab another satellite fix to assure his location prior to violating a sovereign nation's water.

A line paralleling the island chain represented the expected location of a Taiwanese undersea surveillance array. The system's sensitivity remained an unknown since the Taiwanese had restrained their reaction to detections of any submarines, but Chan expected the system to be online and listening, and the lack of orders warning him to slow while passing over the hydrophones concerned him.

Either his faceless masters assumed the Taiwanese system to be offline, his stolen *Romeo* its hopeless victim at any speed, or worse. He entertained thoughts of being expendable–perhaps a decoy for a larger operation.

He quelled defeatist thoughts by reminding himself of an evacuation plan that included leaving the submarine burning on the surface with its former crew's charred corpses aboard. Planted evidence of North Korean misdeeds, he assumed.

Plus he had drafted the son of a ranking party member to his team. Gao, despite his mediocrity, shielded him from expendability.

Startling him, his executive officer appeared.

"Sir," Gao said. "The torn body bag resulted from a sailor slicing it with wire wrap. He confessed to dragging the wire accidentally across the bag while he was en route to locking a valve stem. He said he inspected the bag and didn't notice any leaks, but he must have weakened the bag to begin a slow leak."

"Or he was in too great a hurry to correctly assess the damage," Chan said. "He was certainly in too much a hurry to properly carry his wire wrap."

"I shall see that he is disciplined," Gao said.

"Better yet," Chan said, "let him explain his errors to the entire crew so that they recognize the hazards of careless haste."

Gao's eyes widened.

"The shame," he said.

"See to it, Gao," Chan said. "My methods are effective. Each sailor will think twice before compromising what little capability this submarine has."

"Yes, sir."

Gao departed, and Chan returned his attention to the chart.

Running his finger between the Japanese islands and over the Taiwanese hydrophone array, he considered his speed options.

He could slow and try to sneak over the arrays unnoticed, or he could concede being heard and attempt to pass at high speed to the eastern side of the islands. A flash of inspiration told him to go as fast as his submerged *Romeo* would take him–an anemic thirteen knots–and put the issue behind him.

*

His grip tight around the handles, Chan staggered and arched back from the periscope. Swells bucked the *Romeo* to the side, and the submarine plummeted.

"The head valve has shut," Gao said. "The diesel engines have secured."

Chan looked down to his executive officer who braced for balance by the navigation chart.

"Get us back up," Chan said. "One meter shallower than before."

"You're risking exposure of our conning tower, sir."

Chan suppressed an impulse to chastise Gao for challenging him and welcomed his underling's courage to voice an independent thought.

"You're right, Gao," he said. "But that's a risk I must take. We need air, we need to charge our battery, and we need a geographic fix. Get us up."

*

The *Romeo's* battery charged and its air clean, Chan felt the rocking subside as the deck angled downward. He slid by a polished railing to join Gao by the navigation chart.

At the narrowest point of the strait, the twelve-mile curves surrounding the Japanese islands crossed. He realized that his would be the first Chinese crew to violate Japanese sovereignty during the campaign to reclaim the renegade Taiwanese province.

Projecting battery depletion curves in his mind's eye, he

jabbed one end of dividers into the trace paper and spread the other across the track he would drive through the Tokashi Strait. He grunted as he lifted spread pointers and placed them on the scale to measure the distance to the island chain's far side and the Pacific Ocean's Philippine Sea.

"Our battery won't support it," he said. "Not at maximum speed. Not even at twelve knots."

"Sir?" Gao asked. "I think the battery curves would support twelve knots."

"You're correct, assuming a clean hull and new battery cells. But we've seen that we perform less than optimum in both areas. We must get closer to the center of the strait before accelerating."

"Perhaps we should just remain slow throughout the transit to avoid detection," Gao said.

"No, Gao. I understand the trade-offs, but I desire to violate Japanese waters for the smallest amount of time as possible. We stay at four knots for the next hour. Then, we accelerate and take our chances."

*

An hour later, Chan checked his chart.

"All ahead flank," he said. "Make turns for twelve knots."

The submarine shook while laboring. Human noise ebbed in the control room, save for an occasional cough and clearing of a throat while the *Romeo* passed over the suspected Taiwanese hydrophone array.

As the crosshair passed over the array's line, Chan noticed the tight, arc-sided triangular intersection between the Japanese territory boundaries and the Taiwanese hydrophone system. For a moment, he violated one neighbor's waters while exposing his acoustic presence to the hostile renegade province.

His fears chided him into speculating that he undertook a suicide mission. Though he conceived no strategic value in his demise, a skilled politician may have arranged the sinking of his North Korean submarine in Japanese waters to forward an agenda beyond Chan's sight.

He swallowed as the submarine reentered international waters and slipped into the Pacific Ocean. As he reached his desired distance from the strait, he relaxed his grip on the navigation table.

"Slow to four knots," he said.

"We have thirty percent battery, sir," Gao said.

"Excellent. Take us to snorkel depth and charge the battery. Get a fix and seek new radio traffic. I'll be in the engineering spaces."

Chan walked aft toward the engine room and passed a whirring propulsion motor, sealed reduction gears, and the length of the starboard shaft. Surrounded by duct tape, extension cords, and laptops on plywood shelves, a lone sailor crouched over a computer.

Chan crouched beside his cryptology ace.

"How's your progress?" he asked.

Color flush in his cheeks, the sailor looked up.

"Good news, sir," Park said.

"You see evidence of our rescue ship?"

"That's not what I meant, sir, but I am breaking the codes to the seven ships you thought might be serving as our rescue ship. I expect to start reading their messages in about eighteen hours, on average, as I break each code. I can go faster on select ships if you let me work my algorithms in parallel."

"No," Chan said. "That's fine."

A younger sailor walked to Chan.

"Sir, the executive officer reports no new message traffic and requests permission to descend from snorkel depth when the batteries are charged."

"Permission granted," Chan said.

The sailor departed.

"This leaves you with no new data," Chan said.

"That's okay, sir," Park said. "That's the good news. I'm confident I can predict the behavior of the random-number-generating algorithms used by the computers behind the broadcast messages we're interested in."

"You're certain?"

"Just minutes ago, I cracked the code for an East Sea Fleet *Kilo* submarine, hull three-six-six."

"Show me."

Park twirled his laptop, and Chan devoured a secret message intended for his compatriot. The news astounded him.

"The *Kilo* is also heading to the eastern side of the Japanese islands."

"I didn't recognize the numbers as coordinates, sir."

"That's what they are," Chan said. "Whatever our mission, we are part of something greater. We are not alone."

"That's encouraging. Right, sir?"

"Yes, Park," Chan said. "Can you break more of these, for other submarines?"

"Of course. It's just a matter of time."

"What about that garbled text?"

Chan pointed at the screen.

"It's a third layer of encryption. Probably a brief note for just the commanding officer."

"Can you break it?"

"That would exhaust my resources," Park said.

"Can you break the second layer for the East Sea Fleet submarines first and then break the third layer for the one that will be stationed closest to us?"

"I can, sir, if you let me know which one will be the closest to us."

"Consider it done, Park," Chan said, "as soon as I know."

As he walked forward, he thought he heard an unfamiliar low-frequency drone. The sound perplexed him, and he flagged his memory to ask his executive officer to check the ship for a sound short. There would be disciplinary action if a sailor had left a tool connecting a loud machine to the hull, bypassing sound isolation mounting.

His eyes wide, Gao met him at the navigation chart.

"Sir, active intercept, two hundred hertz."

"No ship uses a sonar frequency that low," Chan said.

"I know, sir."

"Do you have a bearing?"

"It's vague, sir. At best within ten degrees, it's roughly coming from the west. We're also catching reflections from the south-west at lower power."

"Reflections from what, Gao?"

"That's the problem, sir. There's nothing out there for the sound to reflect from, unless there's a nearby submarine."

"Draw the bearings on the chart, Gao. Include the reflections."

Chan watched his underling brush a pencil over trace paper. An idea formed in his mind, but he hesitated to vocalize it–until he heard the active broadcast again.

"There it is again, sir," Gao said.

"Same bearings?"

"Same bearings, sir."

"Secure snorkeling and take us deep," Chan said.

Chan tapped his fingers on the chart, pondered the incoming sounds, and waited for Gao to reappear.

As the deck leveled, he grabbed a pencil and drew hard lines over the Taiwanese hydrophone system.

"What are those, sir?" Gao asked.

"These are my best estimates," Chan said, "of the newly dis-covered Taiwanese active-emission sonar hydrophone array."

"Active-emission, sir? You think that we've not only verified the existence of the Taiwanese hydrophone array, but we've learned that it includes an active transmission?"

"Yes, making secret passage over its length nearly impos-sible," Chan said. "And this also implicates the Japanese beyond doubt as providing a power source."

"What do we do, now, sir?"

Chan stepped up to the conning platform and sat in his fold-out captain's chair.

"We clear out of here, pray nobody follows us, and share what we know with the fleet if we survive long enough to do so."

CHAPTER 24

For the first time, Pierre Renard wished he had been aboard a surface combatant instead of a submarine. He had built the consensus, drafted the plans, and brokered the weapons transactions, but young men on small patrol craft had faced the mortal danger in carrying out his vision, and they had prevailed.

His adrenaline had spiked and then fallen after feeding the egressing squadron the spying *Hai Ming's* undersea information. Lifting an unlit cigarette to his lips, he glanced at his console to verify his visual connection with Henri. Crouched in his seat, his countryman rested his sweaty hair in his hands awaiting orders from Keelung.

Renard left Henri unperturbed and stepped to the navigation chart to learn progress aboard the captured mainland *Kilo* submarine. Admiral Ye's staff buzzed around the command center churning stolen encryption codes into cracked intercepted mainland message traffic. As an officer rendered his report to Ye and departed, Renard approached his client.

"What have you learned, my friend?" he asked.

"Not as much as I would hope," Ye said. "We've taken their radio modules for inspection, and the photographs and videos show what we would expect from a *Kilo* submarine. The cryptology data lets us read East Sea Fleet message traffic, but there's at least one more layer of encryption required to learn the location of their ships."

"But with focused hacking," Renard said, "and if the mainland doesn't know the fate of its submarine for days..."

Ye raised his palm.

"I know what you're thinking, but I'm afraid the *Kilo* sustained too much damage. We cannot take it for our own use, and we cannot keep it afloat much longer. I've ordered it to be scuttled within thirty minutes."

"Before dawn," Renard said. "Before the sun burns away cloud cover and exposes the submarine to the mainland's surveillance by reconnaissance aircraft and military satellite."

"Yes," Ye said. "Not to mention civilian spies on our coast. Military police patrol the highest floors of buildings near Suao, and helicopters search the nearby mountains to verify nobody is watching, even now to thwart those who would spy with night vision."

An officer approached, and Renard stepped away. As the officer departed, he moved back to Ye.

"You seem perplexed," he said.

"We've received a download of their tactical system," Ye said. "Four of their reload weapons are North Korean."

"You mean of a design they would export to North Korea?" Renard asked.

"No," Ye said. "North Korean. They are from North Korea, including North Korean inscriptions and manufacturing data. The infiltration team verified this in the torpedo room."

"Good God, man," Renard said. "I could only begin to speculate the implications."

"Hold on," Ye said.

He barked in Mandarin, and an officer nodded and scurried to a table where analysts sifted through incoming screens of data from the captured submarine.

"I told him to expedite the review of the contents of the captain's safe," Ye said. "They blew it open for a reason. There's bound to be something insightful inside."

"I should hope so," Renard said.

His phone vibrated, surprising him. He withdrew it from his blazer and checked the caller identification.

"Of all people," he said. "Excuse me, admiral."

Renard placed the phone to his ear as he walked toward the solitude of his webcam and laptop in the corner of the command center.

"Yes, Jake," he said. "It's good to hear from you."

"You, too, Pierre," Jake said. "Is now a good time?"

"Why not? We've just entered the tactical nuclear age, and my plans are proving bulletproof! I doubt you've called to let me boast, but if you'll allow it..."

"Go ahead," Jake said. "It would help my guilt."

"I wish I could," Renard said. "But on second thought, you're calling from your unsecure line."

"Yeah. Right. Well, I didn't call to say much. I just wanted to apologize."

"I don't think you owe me such a gesture."

"I've been selfish," Jake said.

Renard pondered the years he had known his conflicted protégé.

"I think you had your requisite opportunity for personal growth stolen from you in your early adulthood, and you're just late to reach a developmental crossroads. Your behavior is normal. But if you feel that you've wronged me, I forgive you."

"I left you when you needed me," Jake said. "I need to make it up to you."

"Very well," Renard said. "I disagree with your harsh self-assessment, but I accept that you feel an obligation. I therefore promise to recruit you for my next opportunity. You know there will be one."

"Well, sure. Thanks, Pierre."

"Why don't you head home and–"

The air moved, and Renard felt a presence. He turned and saw an eager expression on his translator.

"Mister Renard. Alarming news."

Renard covered the phone.

"Yes?"

"The mainland means to attack an incoming American aircraft carrier with a wolf pack of submarines."

"You jest. There's no incoming American carrier."

"The mainland seems to know more than we do about such a movement."

"Even if a carrier were coming," Renard said, "mainland diesel submarines are too slow to give chase. They'd need to know the carrier's path well in advance."

The translator lifted his nose and appeared agitated for the first time in Renard's memory.

"I will complete a written translation of the *Kilo* captain's patrol orders for you, but you will have to trust me in the meantime that this is an accurate summary."

"Very well," Renard said. "I shall take it on faith while you translate and while Admiral Ye's staff verifies the accuracy of the documents. They could be a ruse to protect against this sort of captured vessel situation."

"I doubt it, Mister Renard."

"Why?"

"The attack will be made to appear as if the North Koreans were responsible."

"This all sounds preposterous. There must be a better explanation for the *Kilo* captain's orders and for the Korean weapons on board."

"The *Kilo's* captain did not survive. Very few sailors did, and no officers. There is nobody worth questioning."

"Then what more evidence is there?" Renard asked.

"There's a possible North Korean submarine involved."

"The *Romeo* that crossed the hydrophone array from the north?" Renard asked. "The loud one we thought was from the mainland's North Sea Fleet being sent to the Philippine Sea as a distraction?"

"Yes. Very likely. We're reviewing the acoustic data, now that there is increased interest."

"Thank you," Renard said. "Will you excuse me?"

As the translator nodded and turned, Renard's scheming mind entered hyper-drive. He placed his phone to his cheek.

"Jake, please find your way to an airport and prepare to make for Tokyo."

"Seriously? What's going on?"

"Perhaps nothing. But there's a chance I may need you much sooner than I could have anticipated."

His protégé sounded relieved and eager.

"I'm on it," Jake said.

Renard returned his phone to his pocket and reached for his lighter. He released it and congratulated himself for invoking willpower. Gathering what thoughts he could, he turned the corner and headed for Admiral Ye.

As he rounded the navigation chart, Ye surprised him with an invitation that felt like an order.

"Will you join me in my office?"

*

Renard judged Ye's office on the second floor of the center austere by Asian standards, but he appreciated that Ye would dedicate the space to function at the expense of flair.

Small stacks of papers cut sharp lines behind the admiral on a maple bureau. A model of the *Hai Lang* submarine, the admiral's last command at sea, stood as the sole attempt to personalize the room. Ye lifted a porcelain teacup from his desk, sipped from it, and lowered it.

"Tea, Mister Renard?"

"Yes. Thank you."

Ye reached for a pot and poured as steam rose. When finished, he slid the silver platter to the Frenchman. Renard sipped warm bitterness.

"We have an issue with Admiral Brody," Ye said.

"It appears there is conjecture about an incoming American aircraft carrier, a mainland submarine ambush, and a North Korean angle to complicate matters."

"It's more than conjecture," Ye said. "Unless we're victims of an elaborate hoax, we've stumbled upon an intelligence coup. We can't prove that all of it is true, but we can verify the first major assumption."

"The aircraft carrier?"

"Yes."

"If he's indeed sending a carrier," Renard said, "then that will lend credence to the speculation that the mainland is preparing to ambush it."

"I've requested an audience with him. We'll be connected soon."

Ye aimed his fingers at a monitor on his wall.

"How much of your newfound data are you willing to share with him?" Renard asked.

"It will depend on his demeanor," Ye said. "If he is candid, I will be candid."

"What's the status of the *Kilo*?"

"Scuttled. Prior to sunrise."

"Silently?"

"All doors and hatches were open on the way down," Ye said. "So, it was done as quietly as such a thing can be."

"Have you sent a bogus signal to the mainland pretending to come from the *Kilo*?"

"Yes," Ye said. "We sent a situational report stating that the other two ships–a *Song* and a *Ming*–were destroyed by tactical nuclear warheads and that only two patrol craft had been sunk."

"You sent the message from the doomed *Kilo* itself?"

"Yes, and we received a standard reply. We later intercepted orders telling the *Kilo* to continue on its mission with respect to the American carrier."

As Renard's mind teased him with scenarios based upon knowing the mainland's plans, one of Admiral Ye's staff appeared on the monitor. After Ye held a brief exchange of words, Admiral Brody appeared.

"Good evening Admiral Brody," Ye said.

"Good morning Admiral Ye," Brody said. "I see you've ushered in the tactical nuclear age."

"As promised."

"How is the fallout?"

"Minimal and confined to the sea, as expected."

"You requested my time, Admiral Ye," Brody said. "What can I do for you?"

"I'm curious about your plans of sending your naval power near my homeland."

"I always share my plans with you as a courtesy," Brody said. "At least when I deem it relevant."

"Would you deem it relevant to tell me if you were sending the *Reagan* strike group from Hawaii?"

Brody frowned.

"I can send the *Reagan* strike group anywhere I want without telling anyone, as long as I honor international boundaries. But you didn't call me to discuss hypotheticals, Admiral Ye. What are you getting at?"

"There's a lot of water between Hawaii and my homeland," Ye said. "You may think you can move a carrier strike group in secrecy, and normally you can. However, you've been defeated in areas where you didn't know you had vulnerabilities."

"I'm not following."

"The mainland has studied your personality and your tendencies," Ye said. "They believed with enough fervor that you would be an aggressor, no matter what policy the president or his cabinet chose. They predicted that you would send major resources to the region."

"Even if they were right, how is that a defeat?"

"They're defeating you in cyberspace," Ye said. "They have access to your communication network, and they know that you're sending the *Reagan* strike group here, along with an amphibious landing force."

"If your intent is to make accusations, we have little else to discuss."

Ye stood, withdrew a note card from his breast pocket, and walked to the monitor. He raised the card to the camera eye.

"I have intercepted intelligence from the mainland that the *Reagan* is roughly here, at these coordinates."

"This would prove nothing, even if it were accurate."

Ye moved to his desk, lifted a pile of papers, and returned to the monitor.

"Then perhaps this does," he said.

As he raised the papers, Brody's face became ashen.

"Those are my orders to the *Reagan* strike group. Where the hell did you get those?"

"We forced a mainland *Kilo*-class submarine to surface," Ye said. "This came from the commanding officer's safe. Also on that submarine was a plan for a multi-submarine wolf pack attack against the *Reagan*."

"They wouldn't succeed. They wouldn't risk an act of open war."

"Submarines only, Admiral Brody," Ye said. "Plausible denial of participation."

"Plausible denial? Who else would possibly be held accountable?"

"North Korea. We found North Korean weapons on the *Kilo*, and a North Korean submarine is involved."

"We tracked a surfaced *Romeo*-class submarine through the East China Sea," Brody said.

"We heard it pass over our hydrophone array," Ye said.

"So, are you suggesting that I back off and let you stick with your plan of securing the Philippine Sea with an underwater hydrophone system and a squadron of nuclear-armed patrol craft? Just because of a few submarines and cyber-hackers."

"Yes," Ye said.

"No!" Renard said.

Ye returned to his desk, sat, and appeared quizzical.

"I was wondering why you were so quiet," Brody said.

"Now that we've established an understanding, I thought we may now discuss how to make use of this knowledge from the captured *Kilo*."

"I'm listening, Renard," Brody said.

"The mainland doesn't know that we have this information, and they don't know yet that they've lost their *Kilo*. Nor to do they know the *Hai Ming* survived the attack at its submarine pen. I recommend that the *Hai Ming* masquerade as the *Kilo* and continue on the mission per the mainland's plans."

"You would use the *Reagan* as bait?" Brody asked.

"Why not?" Renard said. "We have every advantage, and its fate in absence of this conversation would be no better than any plan I can concoct. Better to be bait in an encounter of our own design than to be the unwitting victim of an ambush."

"I could use a different form of communications to send the *Reagan* a different way," Brody said. "But, if I continue with the status quo, what's the upside?"

Brody's interest encouraged Renard. He sensed appreciation for having exposed the ambush.

"You will use disinformation that resembles the truth enough to set a believable trap but differs from the truth enough to protect your assets."

"I get it," Brody said. "There are many ways we could go with that approach."

"If you will permit me to run my thoughts by Admrial Ye, we will soon share with you a plan to destroy every mainland submarine east of Taiwan, set the Chinese fleet back ten years, sanitize the Philippine Sea for the American fleet to steam at will, and take a towering upper hand for negotiating cessation of these hostilities."

Brody nodded.

"That's interesting," he said. "But what if I'm hesitant to risk the *Reagan*?"

"Don't worry, Admiral Brody," Renard said. "My plans will address that concern, and I'm apparently on a run of good luck in this region of the world."

CHAPTER 25

As he deplaned in Los Angeles International Airport, Jake questioned his haste in seeking redemption with Renard. He selected Los Angeles for its direct flights to Tokyo, and the terminal served as his purgatory pending sentencing from his French judge.

He sauntered to a sports bar and ordered a Miller Lite. When his phone chimed, he snatched it from his pocket in hopes of learning his fate, but the caller identification surprised him with his brother's name.

"Nick?" he asked.

"Hello, Jake."

"How'd you know I'd be available?"

"It just felt like the right time to call you."

Jake lifted the phone and scanned his call log. This call marked Nick's first attempt at contact since he had left Michigan. He returned the phone to his ear.

"Jake?"

"Yeah, sorry," Jake said. "I was just checking something. Where do you think I am?"

"Far away, but closer to home. I've felt you moving around a lot."

"Well, damn, you're good," Jake said. "You caught me. I'm on dry land."

"But you're not coming home now, are you?"

Jake extended the phone again and checked the time. He wanted Renard to call.

"I don't know. You won't tell Linda I'm not on a submarine will, you?"

"No. It would only scare her. You've escaped a life-threatening risk–the one I felt before you left–but you're still in danger."

"Still in danger," Jake said. "You know how to cheer a guy up. What the heck am I supposed to do with that?"

"You have split loyalties."

"That's not an answer."

"But it matters."

"You're saying I should come home? I'm not sure I can. I just made a commitment."

"To Pierre?"

"To Pierre," Jake said.

"Part of you wants to come home to Linda, but someone far away needs you. I think it's him."

A waitress poured a Miller Lite into a clear mug, and Jake forced a smile.

"Let's say Pierre needs me," he said. "Don't I owe him? I mean, if it weren't for him, I'd be doing God knows what in some dismal failed life. Thanks to him, I've got tons of cash, I live adventures most people couldn't dream of, and I get to make a difference in the world. Why shouldn't I be his servant? It's selfish of me to think otherwise."

"Are you trying to convince me or yourself?"

"Fuck you."

Jake bowed his head.

"Sorry," he said. "I didn't mean that."

"I know you didn't."

"What are you getting at?" Jake asked.

"I didn't mean split loyalties to people. I meant split loyalties to principles. I meant you're torn between life and death."

"Well, shit, Nick. Isn't everybody? You're slipping into useless metaphysical mode again."

"No, I'm being specific. It hit me after your latest danger slipped into your past. You think you're free and clear of your anger, your hatred, and your vengeance, but you're not. You still have deep, unresolved wounds, and it's driving you to kill."

Jake reflected on the malice inflicted upon him when a scared man, in an attempt to protect his career, infected him with HIV after an accident on an American naval submarine. The bottle of antiretroviral pills rattled in his pocket as he shifted his weight over the bar stool.

"Yeah," he said. "So what? I've got a right to be angry. I deal with it."

"I don't think you deal with it. I believe that you distract yourself from it by killing, and you justify the killing by labeling your victims as an unjust enemy."

"Come on, Nick! I took down a guy that was going to launch a nuclear bomb, I've taken down Chinese submarines that were out to kill Taiwanese sailors, and I didn't even kill the guy who wanted to cripple every electrical device in America! I don't see what's wrong with any of this!"

"You keep seeking out situations that let you vent your anger. I'm afraid that your anger will backfire and get you killed."

"No," Jake said. "I've been through that. When it comes to pulling the trigger, I get real calm, real quick."

"I'm not concerned about your demeanor when in combat. I'm concerned that you'll let anger and bloodlust push you into combat when killing should be far from your mind."

Jake heard a beep and moved the phone to his face.

"Hold on Nick. I need to take another call."

Jake switched to the incoming call from Renard.

"Pierre?"

"Yes, my friend. How are you?"

"That depends on what you're about to say."

"I have an opportunity for you that promises to be–"

"I'm in," Jake said. "There's a plane leaving for Tokyo in two hours I can still make."

"I haven't even finished stating my case."

Jake guzzled half his beer and plopped the glass on the counter.

"Do you need me?"

"This is a serendipitous opportunity, but it incurs uncertainty. I require a level of expertise, intuition, and delicacy that few men possess. You are the only one who is capable and familiar with the team and assets."

"No sales pitch needed, Pierre. Do you need me?"

"Yes."

"Then let me get to Tokyo," Jake said. "I'll trust you to get me transportation from there to wherever I need to go, and I'll study whatever material you send me."

"So be it, my friend. I appreciate your support."

Jake wiggled his thumb across the capacitive touchscreen and pushed the phone against his cheek.

"Nick?"

"Yes. I'm here."

"You know what you were saying about the killing? Did you consider that I need to help Pierre out of selflessness? Maybe I need to appreciate what he's done for me despite the danger."

"I'm concerned that you're going too far."

"Too far or not," Jake said, "I'm off to kill again."

*

Jake remembered taking a sleeping pill and a shot of whiskey before reclining into a deep sleep in a first class chair. When he deplaned in Tokyo, a uniformed Japanese colonel greeted him in flawless English and escorted him to a military jet.

As Jake's solitary companion in the cabin, the colonel let him fall in and out of sleep. After a nasty bump in turbulence, he asked the man where he'd learned English.

"The University of Washington," he said.

"You're a Husky," Jake said.

"I am."

"You've been ordered to not ask me questions about where I'm going or what I'm doing, haven't you?"

"Of course. But I do know, however, that you will be taking a helicopter from Minamidaito Island to meet with a surfaced Taiwanese submarine in the Philippine Sea. I must know this to translate with our helicopter crew and the submarine crew to help you get safely aboard."

"So, you speak Mandarin too?" Jake asked.

"I studied it while I was a Husky."

Jake shifted in his seat and looked out the window at endless water.

"What do you think about the hydrophone array the Taiwanese have strung between your islands?"

"Like most of my compatriots, I find it to be a great shared asset. Our allies from Taiwan provide the design, monitoring, and upkeep. We merely provide the communications connections and electrical power from generators on inhabited islands. And Chinese submarines are no longer free to pass into the open ocean undetected."

Jake said little else before landing on a tiny speck. He deplaned, and a humid afternoon breeze brought the taste of the sea. From a small team of Japanese rescue divers, a wetsuit appeared in his hands, and his translator escort asked him to don it. A radioed helmet followed, and after ambling through unmoving time, he realized he crouched in a thumping helicopter seat.

The island became a distant bright dot in glimmering darkness. His bones shaking, he extended his leg and stretched it. A crewman stood, offered him a winch harness, and helped him strap it on.

The nylon chaffed his groin and pinched his scrotum, but he wiggled into a position where the apparatus could support his weight without disemboweling him. He waited within the shaking cabin, running through the *Hai Ming's* acceleration numbers in his head to distract himself from the flight's discomfort.

As the crewman slid open the door, the world appeared as a void. The helicopter surprised Jake by slowing and descending since the *Hai Ming* eluded his surveying of the water through his visor.

Through his helmet, he heard his translator.

"We will lower you in three minutes."

Time slipped without reckoning, and the crewman signaled to Jake to step over the ledge. He slid his feet backwards into the nothingness, placed gloved hands on the deck, and sank his weight over the side. His winch cable became taut, and it held him. Then it lowered him into the rotor wash.

Jake panicked when he looked down and saw nothing. As he spun, the surfaced submarine's black sail came into view and then slipped behind him. It circled into his sights again as he felt a hook yank his cable and pull him laterally. His translator's voice in his ear startled him.

"Prepare for release to the deck."

Not knowing if the gesture mattered, Jake gave a thumbs up. He tensed his thighs, and the submarine's deck hit his boots. He collapsed to the steel, his palms smacking nonskid. He felt hands grabbing his harness, freeing him from the cable, and helping him stand.

Two Taiwanese sailors led him through a hatch, and he climbed down ladder rungs. Moist air yielded to the dusty aroma of a submarine's innards. His soles reached the deck plates, and he felt at home.

He once again would command a submarine.

CHAPTER 26

Lieutenant Commander Lei watched the crouched sailor extinguish his torch and lift his visor.

"How's it look?" he asked.

"That should hold until we get back to port, sir."

Lei dropped to his knee and studied weld lines that cut into the fantail's nonskid surface and held metallic planks over aircraft-delivered bullet holes.

"Spray seawater over it for five minutes while someone inspects for leaks below," Lei said.

He patted the nodding sailor on the shoulder and turned toward the superstructure. Ascending the ladder rung by rung, he glanced into the clear sky. His wish for clouded obscurity remained unanswered, and he prayed that the ocean's vastness would conceal his small stealthy craft from mainland surveillance.

The door's latch felt moist as he pulled, and the climate- controlled air on the bridge felt cool and dry. Electronic humming called his attention to his console's display.

Red triangles showed bothersome patrolling aircraft on the mainland's side of the Japanese Ryukyu islands. Their spying radar systems sought him, but on-board sensors assured him that his ship's skin absorbed and deflected their invasive electromagnetic energy.

Blue triangles on the eastern side of the islands showed friendly combat aircraft which, combined with the mainland's respect for Japanese airspace, kept his airborne chasers at bay.

The narrow gap south of Okinawa presented the only path north of Taiwan for mainland aircraft to enter the Pacific Ocean via international airspace. The frigate *Cheng Kung*, seaworthy and lethal despite missile hits during the aerial assault at Suao, plugged that gap.

Raiding the damaged *Kilo* submarine had yielded the cryptology keys to predict the locations of mainland submarines east of Taiwan. The adversary's submerged armada pointed east toward the incoming American aircraft carrier, freeing Taiwanese minesweeping vessels to sanitize the egress route Lei's squadron had blazed.

Wondering if the mainland would respect the détente established across the elongated hydrophone-bolstered Ryukyu Island choke point, Lei entertained thoughts of a quiet dinner with his officers.

The general quarters alarm startled him.

A glance at his shrugging, youngest officer who managed the bridge confirmed that the combat information center had raised the alarm.

Caressing his cheek, he remembered he had left his headset at his console. He turned and darted down the ladder to the ship's tactical nerve. As his eyes adjusted to the fluorescent lighting, his navigator stood from the room's central armchair.

"Submerged contact confirmed, sir."

"Where?" Lei asked.

Calculations ran through his mind as he crouched beside the navigator at a monitor. After the hydrophone array gained a positive contact on a submerged submarine, Lei expected that it would transmit active every minute while hearing reflections off its victim's hull.

Lei's squadron needed to launch a missile while the targeting data remained fresh and relevant.

"Here, sir. Northeast of Takarajima Island."

"Craft Four is the closest," Lei said.

The navigator tapped buttons and rolled a track ball. Attack arcs from ships in Lei's squadron converged on the mainland submarine, proving that Craft Four had the ideal shot by ten miles over Craft Five.

Hesitating a second to convince himself fate called upon him to exercise his launch authority, Lei took one deep breath.

"Instruct Craft Four to engage the submerged contact with one missile."

Lei watched his navigator lift a receiver to his ear to relay the order.

"Craft Four acknowledges, sir. Estimated launch time is in thirty seconds. Final targeting coordinates to follow the next active return from the hydrophone system."

"Draft a message for Keelung and for the Japan Maritime Self-Defense Force. Feed them the targeting coordinates, launch time, and expected detonation times directly from our tactical feed."

"Yes, sir."

Calmness overtook Lei, and he felt weightless as he climbed the stairs.

"Where are you going, sir?"

He looked over his shoulder to his confused navigator.

"Outside," he said. "Secure general quarters."

"I don't understand, sir."

"This will be the first and last mainland submarine to test our defenses," he said. "The wind will carry the fallout safely away from us, and I thought I'd enjoy the sunset."

*

Dumbfounded, Admiral John Brody closed the door and stood in the hallway while pondering the report that had confirmed his irrelevance as the Chief of Naval Operations. One tiny Taiwanese warship had delivered the blow, sinking a Chinese submarine and proclaiming a defensive barrier he had considered impossible.

Masterminded by a presumptuous Frenchman, equipped with weapons-grade fuel by Rickets, and determined to scratch out an optimum endurance strategy, Taiwan had established a détente against the mainland. His navy–the strongest fleet since the dawn of mankind–had contributed nothing.

The best analysts in his navy confirmed his worthlessness. The tactical nuclear arsenal aboard stealthy patrol craft provided an anti-submarine Maginot Line. Complemented by air defenses, the line drew a zone of safe passage through the Philippine Sea.

Unfettered, minesweepers swept, naval escorts returned to

port for reloads and repairs, and sea lines of communication promised a renewed waterborne economy. The bravest commercial fleets were negotiating shipping rates with Taipei to revitalize the island nation.

The final sticking point for guaranteeing the vitality of trade–the Chinese submarines remaining on the wrong side of the line. Time and secrecy mattered, and the Frenchman–with his unimaginable mélange of brilliance, reputation, and luck–had been gifted the makings of a trap to ensnare all the submarines at once.

His bullish pride bleeding from a picador's lances, Brody lowered his head as he lumbered towards Rickets' office.

He found the door open and saw the secretary seated at his desk. Rickets waved him in and lowered his phone conversation as a smug smile crept across his face.

"What can I do for you, admiral?"

"I imagine you've heard about the Taiwanese sinking a Chinese submarine with a tactical nuclear missile?"

"Just confirmed by Keelung," Rickets said.

Thinking that he faced the next Republican presidential candidate, Brody looked to the carpet.

Having been wrong in every assumption about the Chinese campaign, he accepted Renard's support and would capitalize upon it. Irony pulsated through him as he realized that years ago Renard and Slate had nearly killed him when he commanded a submarine, and then he had spared their lives. Now, allies.

He blurted out his thoughts.

"You were right," he said. "I owe you an apology. Renard and Taiwan had a great plan. I was wrong to doubt it and challenge you. I apologize."

Rickets stood and approached him, extending his hand. Brody shook it.

"I don't think you owe me an apology for a difference of opinion," Rickets said. "But we're good."

Rickets stepped back into his teleconference chair and gestured for Brody to sit beside him.

"I still have work to do for you," Brody said.

"Agreed," Rickets said. "You protected our allies in Korea and demonstrated a presence beside our allies in Japan. Now you can divert your forces toward sinking the Chinese submarines remaining in the Philippine Sea."

"How much time do I have?" Brody asked.

"Ideally, three weeks. Although a few shipping companies will take the risk before you sanitize the water, it won't be enough capacity to sustain Taiwan. Food shortages are already starting in remote parts of the island, and their jet fuel reserves are four weeks away from drying up, assuming the first risk-tolerant tankers get through."

"What if they don't get through?" Brody asked.

"Three weeks. Either way, Taiwan is close to losing air superiority over the Philippine Sea due to lack of fuel," Rickets said.

"And if that happens, it's a free-for-all for Chinese surface combatants. They take over the Philippine Sea, they block incoming shipping, and they take out the patrol crafts to open up the sea again to their submarines."

Something sat wrong with Brody. He looked at the darkened monitor, half-wishing Renard would appear to clarify his doubts.

As if inspired by the Frenchman, he grasped his concern.

"I can't just attack Chinese submarines in international water," he said. "Technically, they haven't done anything."

"Right. You'll have to escort commercial shipping and catch them in the act of aggression. It's difficult, and it's going to put you in compromised positions. There will be casualties, unfortunately, and it will be a race against time to account for every hostile submarine, but I have faith that your unit commanders can pull it off."

Brody chewed on Rickets' ugly option and then thought of the opportunity Renard had created using the *Reagan* as bait. He chuckled, and Rickets raised his eyebrows.

"What's so funny?"

"Well, shit," Brody said. "I think I've got a trick up my sleeve to get out of this jam by the end of the week and with zero American lives lost."

"How?"

"With my newfound respect and alliance with Renard."

CHAPTER 27

Jake stepped out of his wetsuit while sailors locked the hatch above them. They scurried away with a haste that caught Jake off guard.

Expecting a greeting party from the front, Jake had to hit an about face to see who cleared his throat from the engineering spaces.

"Hello, Jake."

"Claude. It's good to see you, my friend."

Sweat covered the cotton shirt draped over the lean frame of the French engineer. Jake noticed Claude LaFontaine's stand-offish body language and stood fast.

"What's going on, Claude?"

"I won't speak for myself because I'm honestly undecided how I feel about it. But there's a bit of resentment among the crew."

"Resentment?" Jake asked. "For me?"

"You left us, we went to battle without you, and now Pierre has put you back in charge."

Jake choked on a surge of anger, swallowed it, and forced himself to see the crew's perspective.

"Yeah," he said. "I get it. I've been selfish recently. I guess I need to repair some relationships."

"It's good that you realize it. You have work to do, and little time to do it."

"Can you help me understand, Claude? What's the tone? What are the expectations? I'm getting everything one-sided from Pierre, but I see he and I both missed this issue."

"Regaining Henri's confidence is your best option. Antoine will follow his lead, as will Lieutenant Commander Jin. The rest of the crew will fall in line behind them, including myself."

"Where is Henri?" Jake asked.

"Judging by our down angle, I imagine he's submerging us at the moment."

Jake took note of the tension as his calf muscles balanced him against the decline.

"Can you give me advice, Claude?" he asked. "This isn't the sort of thing I'm good at."

LaFontaine turned toward the engineering spaces. As he stepped away, he offered advice over his shoulder.

"Move cautiously."

Alone, Jake rolled his wetsuit and stuffed it under his arm. He walked forward, crouched through a door, and paused in the berthing area. The vessel's formal commander, Lieutenant Commander Yangi Jin, had ceded the senior stateroom to Jake, and he hoped to find that Henri had showed no signs of having used it during his absence.

As he slipped forward to the captain's personal space, Jake felt relieved to see crisp sheets and no sign of Henri's presence. He hung his wetsuit on a door hook, sat on a foldout chair, and reached for a phone. He dialed the engineering spaces.

He heard an unfamiliar voice with a Mandarin accent. He asked for LaFontaine and waited.

"Yes, Jake?"

"Claude, can you have someone bring me a tablet computer? I need to prepare a tactical briefing."

"I could, but–"

"I know it's not your job," Jake said. "But I don't want to bother the others while they're submerging."

"I will see to it, Jake."

"Will you also do me one more favor?" Jake asked. "Please ask Henri to come by my stateroom at his convenience."

"I'm uncertain that such a move is cautious."

"Emphasize the part where it's at his convenience," Jake said. "But I want him to come to me."

"I'm no diplomat, but I will do my best and let you know what he says."

Jake hung up. Minutes later a Taiwanese sailor brought him a computer, and he began crafting a tactical engagement on an electronic chart. He blended knowledge of the *Reagan's* approach to the Philippine Sea with the Chinese submarine wolf pack's reaction to that knowledge.

The phone rang.

"Jake."

"It's Claude. Henri said he would see you shortly after settling the ship on depth."

Jake glanced at the depth gauge and noted that it had been steady at one hundred meters for ten minutes. Henri delayed his visit, as he expected.

"Thank you, Claude."

Jake hung up and returned his attention to his navigation chart. Time flew as he updated his briefing, and two knocks on his door startled him.

"Come in!"

The door clicked open.

"You summoned?" Henri asked.

"We needed to have a conversation."

"I'm here."

"Fine," Jake said. "You led a perfect mission while I was gone, but I'm taking command of this submarine at noon. If that bothers you, now is the time to speak."

"Pierre led the mission from Keelung."

"You led the crew in every aspect except tactical decisions," Jake said. "In my absence, they follow you."

"It's your absence that bothered me."

"I was gone for less than three days, and I left because the mission parameters were so concise that you didn't need me. Now you need me."

Jake replayed his words in his head and admitted that they sounded brash.

"That remains to be seen," Henri said.

"Whether or not I need to make a tough decision, I need to be here in case something unexpected happens."

"I understand that you have the experience and intuition," Henri said. "But let's be candid about recent history. This ship and crew have been through two tight combat situations. We survived one without you, and we survived the other because I told you what to do."

"That's a dangerous perspective. There's no hydrazine line out there, and you won't be in connection with Pierre. I understand that you and the others may think I abandoned you, and I agree that there was a degree of selfishness on my part. But in the ultimate judgment, I left when I was unnecessary, and I'm back now when you need me. If you don't see that, you're going to be a liability."

Jake sensed he had cracked through the Frenchman's indignation, but nagging doubts lingered. Henri seemed stoic at best.

"I'm no liability," Henri said. "I will have Jin announce your command at noon."

"Very well."

"Will you excuse me?"

"Of course."

The door closed behind Henri, and Jake turned to his digital chart. Minutes unfurled as he sketched and assessed the Chinese ambush on the *Reagan* that he would sabotage.

The ship's speaker system crackled, and he heard the voice of the formal Taiwanese commanding officer.

"Attention. This is Lieutenant Commander Jin. I retain formal command of the *Hai Ming*, but as of this moment, I grant advisory command to Mister Slate. I order each member of this crew to join me in following his orders as if he were your commanding officer. I will now repeat this in Mandarin."

Jake waited for Jin to repeat himself and then picked up the phone and summoned a sailor. When the sailor arrived at his door, he handed him a jump drive from his computer.

"Have this uploaded into Subtics and schedule a tactical briefing for all officers and Subtics operators in two hours. Have someone wake me fifteen minutes before the briefing."

Jake locked the door, stripped out of his clothes, and slid into his bunk.

Hours later, he awoke with the rapping at his door, and he sought the shower. Revitalizing himself with the hot water and steam, he washed away a day's worth of travel.

He dressed and headed forward to the control room where he found familiar figures stooped over a charting table. As he anticipated, the tactical data overpowered his return to the ship in capturing his men's interest. It also gave him a chance to greet them with authority.

"Let me verify the data," he said.

Bodies shifted, creating a gap for him to press his palms on the table. Five upside down red semicircles represented a hostile submarine wolf pack. Blue squares marked the *Reagan* and its escorts.

"Looks good," he said.

He pointed at the square of the aircraft carrier.

"The Chinese have hacked into a communications network that the Seventh Fleet uses to communicate with the *Reagan* strike group. The *Reagan* has leeway to maneuver to complicate torpedo targeting from potential submarine threats, but the general course and speed is established by the Seventh Fleet. And the Chinese know it. We learned this from the damaged *Kilo* submarine."

Jake shifted his finger to an inverted red semicircle.

"This submarine was North Korean when it left port two weeks ago," he said. "But thanks to data taken from the damaged *Kilo*, we know it's now under Chinese control. It's over a hundred miles from us now."

He tapped the screen to advance time into the future.

"But it will be stationed five miles from us when the Chinese submarines form this funnel to trap the *Reagan*. There are two *Songs* with a wider spread, and then two *Yuans* with an even wider spread. The *Songs* and *Yuans* have air independent propulsion and can cover ground submerged."

Jake ran his finger in a V shape over the chart.

"Per the Chinese plan, the *Yuans* are designed to box-in the *Reagan*," he said. "If the *Reagan* veers far enough from the center of its projected course, one of the *Yuans* will have a shot at it. If not, the *Reagan* will steam right between both *Songs*, deeper in the funnel. If it turns, it's going to run into one of the *Songs*. And if the *Reagan* blows through the center of it all, that leaves us and the *Romeo* to strike it first."

Jake welcomed his first question from Antoine Remy, his sonar ace.

"The Chinese then expect to encircle the *Reagan* after the first torpedo hits?"

"Yes," Jake said. "They know one or even two torpedoes may not cripple the carrier. They've designed their mission to send it to the bottom."

"And that explains the Korean *Romeo* and Korean weapons on the Chinese submarines? So that even the acoustic evidence suggests Korean weapons?"

"Yes. We don't have all the details, but we know they're going to let the *Romeo* be found, whether on the surface or on the bottom. It's too risky politically for China to attack an American carrier in international waters. America would at least retaliate in Taiwan, ruining everything they've worked for. But if they can plant evidence that a North Korean submarine got lucky, well, then they've kicked our asses and made us look stupid."

"So, what's our plan?" Remy asked.

Jake tapped the screen, working through menus to bring up a new chart.

"The real scenario will be slightly different from the Chinese plan. It begins with our charade as the *Kilo*. They believe they sank the *Hai Ming* outside our underground pen, and they also now believe we are their sunken *Kilo*. Isn't that right, Henri?"

Respecting caution, Jake pulled the Frenchman into the conversation with the simplest question. Henri had no choice but to answer or reveal hostility.

"That's correct. We've sent two messages to the Chinese East Sea Fleet headquarters using the *Kilo's* radio equipment, and we have received standard responses. We've also confirmed that the captain of that *Kilo* was the senior officer in this wolf pack and in charge of the attack on the *Reagan*."

"Excellent," Jake said. "Just as Pierre had reported. The plan now is to continue the charade until the point of attack. But instead of shooting at the *Reagan*, we will be shooting at a helicopter-dragged acoustic broadcast of the *Reagan's* sound signature, as will our Chinese victims."

Bodies around the plot stood straight, and sailors exchanged knowing glances.

"Well that answers one thing that didn't make sense until now," Remy said.

"Right," Jake said. "The real *Reagan* will lag thirty miles behind its recording so that its anti-submarine aircraft can still have the flight range to engage the *Songs* and the *Yuans*. We will also have P-3 Orion anti-submarine aircraft support from airstrips in Japan."

"Sitting ducks," Remy said.

"That's the plan," Jake said.

"What about the carrier escorts?" Remy asked. "Destroyers, cruisers, frigates?"

"The Chinese hope to avoid them and get to the prize in the center. Our plan is for the escorts to avoid the Chinese submarines to allow the illusion of this hope coming to fruition. Same thing with the *Reagan's* escort submarines. The Chinese will think themselves lucky in having avoided the escort ships until death strikes them from above from aircraft."

"That's why the North Korean *Romeo* is last in the line," Remy said. "So, it's likely to survive and be found."

"That's probable."

Jake felt appreciation for the plan growing around the table in the animated gestures of the French and Taiwanese crew.

"Then what about sinking the *Romeo*?" Remy asked.

"For some reason, the Chinese wanted their *Kilo* to be close to that *Romeo*. So, that means we have to be close to it–too close to have an aircraft attack it for risk of friendly fire hitting us."

"Then what, Jake?"

Jake looked up to make sure everyone at the table knew why he had returned to command them.

"Because this will be open-ocean warfare with another submarine," he said. "We'll have to take the *Romeo* down ourselves."

CHAPTER 28

Lieutenant Commander Dao Chan extended the printout from East Sea Fleet headquarters.

"Come see this, Gao."

His executive officer slid around the navigation table and read the message.

"I understand your excitement, sir."

"This is our call to action," Chan said. "It's the call for every submarine within reach of the *Reagan*. Each of us is ordered to take station and loiter in wait of the American carrier. Each of us has permission to launch weapons. This is magnificent!"

"Agreed, sir. Shall I set a course to our loiter area?"

Chan checked the chart and crunched numbers in his mind. His stolen ship could reach its destination in the allotted thirty-six hours.

"Plan for eight knots average speed, south, to reach our loiter area. Take us there, Gao."

Gao acknowledged, and Chan walked aft with a jump drive carrying the latest radio traffic his *Romeo* had sniffed while snorkeling.

When he arrived in the engineering spaces, he found his cryptology expert with puffiness around his eyes.

"How's your energy?" Chan asked. "Are you rested?"

"I'm fine, sir," Park said. "I have the engine room team wake me whenever we go to snorkel depth just in case you have a download for me."

"Excellent. Where's your assistant?"

"He's coming, sir."

"What's the status of finding our potential rescue ship? Any luck?"

"Nothing, sir. I'm breaking the encryption schemes of the ones you tell me to look at, but nothing's coming up."

"The fleet is notorious for withholding orders until the final hour," Chan said. "That's prudent, and I'm probably being paranoid by asking you to do this."

Chan realized he had uttered his assuring words for himself more so than for Park.

"Perhaps, sir, but I'm happy to keep looking."

"I appreciate it."

Chan started walking away.

"Oh, sir? I have some insight into the other submarines in our area."

"Yes? Go ahead."

"The only one with a third layer of encryption is *Kilo* hull three-six-six. The others don't include a third layer, at least not in the messages you've given me."

"Really? Have you deciphered the *Kilo's* message?"

"Yes, I have. But there was nothing to report because it was empty, like a placeholder. Just a message header, a long string of zeros, probably to retain a minimal or predetermined message length, followed by a cyclic redundancy check on the backend."

"What does that mean?"

"It means there's a communications channel for the fleet to send something private to someone on the *Kilo*, but they're not using it. At least not yet."

Chan frowned and stroked his jaw.

"The commanding officer aboard the *Kilo* is the senior officer among those in the Philippine Sea. He may be privy to privileged data."

"Will he also be the closest to us? You once asked me to prioritize my third-layer encryption hacking by geographic proximity. Given that the *Kilo* is the only one using a third-layer, I'll focus on it, but I'll also see if the fleet invokes a third layer on the others as we intercept message traffic."

"Agreed," Chan said. "The closest is in fact the *Kilo*, hull three-six-six. The next closet is *Song* hull three-two-two, then *Song* hull three-two-four."

"Thank you, sir."

"Keep up the good work, Park, and I'll have you out of the navy within days of our triumphant return."

A sardonic grin overtook the young sailor's face.

"That's all I ever wanted."

A day later, Chan felt assured. Mere hours separated him from his starting position in his legendary ambush. Uncaring that the Taiwanese had established an impassable line between him and his home, he trusted that carrying out his mission would earn him both a safe return and recognition.

After returning from snorkel depth, he paid another visit to his encryption ace in the engineering spaces. He watched Park study computer screens as decryption algorithms unraveled messages sent from the East Sea Fleet to nearly two dozen surface vessels in the Philippine Sea.

"Nothing yet, sir." Park said.

"I'd be lying if I said I wasn't disappointed," Chan said. "But we must keep our faith. The rescue ship could be any vessel in the area. In fact, there could be multiple potential rescue ships, and the fleet may be awaiting the outcome of the battle to determine which one will meet us."

"It's all possible, sir."

"I may be able to get you one more download before we begin our mission."

"That might help, sir."

"I'm going to get some sleep, Park," Chan said. "I recommend you do the same."

In his chamber, Chan dreamt.

His mind's eye hopped between parallel simultaneous realities. In one dimension, Chan commanded his stolen submarine, evaluating data on the navigation chart. In the other dimension, he watched the *Reagan* shape-shift from formed metal to a living dragon.

The dragon shot across the water's surface, outpacing torpedoes in its wake. Fireballs shot from its mouth and plunged into the water. Seeing the world again from the navigation chart, Chan watched the dragon's belched fury transform into supercavitating torpedoes, inverted triangles of red with speed-leader lines targeting the other submarines of his wolf pack.

Time blinked, and the blitzing torpedoes eradicated his comrades. Alone against the dragon, he launched his ship's weapons toward it.

As he prayed for success against the supernatural, he heard alarms announce incoming weapons. A glance at the chart confirmed a betrayal. Instead of retaliating against the enemy dragon, every ship in his team had shot their weapons at him.

He ordered his lethargic submarine to escape, but his perspective returned to the parallel dimension above the *Reagan*. The monster opened its mouth and inhaled water, swallowing the sea with infinite power and capacity. Despite its pathetic flank-speed fleeing, Chan's *Romeo* flowed backwards in the current.

Alarms ringing in his head in the control room, he watched the inverted red triangles of his comrades' torpedoes converge on him. A lucid slip across dimensions showed hurricane forces whipping salt spray and the sea into the dragon's mouth, and he watched his submarine's puny hull slip towards a devouring demon-leviathan orifice.

Alarms-orifice. Alarms-orifice. Alarms-orifice.

Alarm. Alarm. Alarm.

His eyes popped open, and the *Romeo's* general alarm snapped his awareness to waking reality.

He rolled to his feet, pulled his jumpsuit from a hook on his stateroom door, and zipped his uniform. Jamming his thumb behind his heel as he crouched into his sneakers, he twisted into the tight hallway.

As the alarm subsided, he darted to the control room and into Gao's concerned face.

"Active sonar, bearing zero-five-one," Gao said.

Chan slid to a nearby sailor's monitor and verified the data over a sonar operator's shoulder. The frequency appeared familiar, matching his studies of the *Reagan* strike force's escort vessels.

"Adjusting for Doppler," he said, "I expect it's a *Burke*-class destroyer."

Sailors who huddled over a codex manual exchanged banter and nodded agreement.

"We can't estimate the target's speed," Gao said. "They can adjust their system's frequency to mask the Doppler effect. But it correlates with a *Burke*. Probably an escort for the *Reagan*."

"Agreed," Chan said. "Warm up a weapon."

"Our orders are to avoid the escorts, sir. This mission is exclusively about the carrier."

"I have no intention of shooting," Chan said. "But only a fool would be unready to do so. Warm it up."

"Yes, sir. Should I also slow and rig the ship for ultra-quiet running?"

Chan realized he had already answered the question subconsciously by letting it slip from his mind.

"No, Gao. We need speed to verify that the *Burke* is indeed, as I hope, moving faster than thirty knots and doing so from far away. If we retain eight knots of speed and the bearing remains the same, we can be confident it is distant."

"They may hear us, sir."

"If they are distant and moving fast, they will not."

"And if they are close?"

"Then they will discover us regardless of our speed."

As his submarine drove geometry relative to the enemy sonar, Chan watched the bearing to the *Burke's* periodic active pulses stay constant. Five minutes flew by, and he exhaled.

"No change in bearing," he said. "They must be far."

"That may explain why we don't hear their ship's noise," Gao said.

"I hope so," Chan said. "Power down the weapon."

"Done, sir."

"Slow to four knots," Chan said. "And rig us for ultra-quiet running. Now that we know the *Burke* is distant, I am concerned about its helicopters."

Ten minutes passed, and the bearings to the *Burke* walked westerly.

"That's normal," Chan said. "Even at distances of tens of miles, our ship's motion and theirs will change the bearings over time. What's your solution, Gao?"

Gao stood from his crouch beside a seated sailor.

"We've got a good estimate, sir. Eighteen miles away, speed thirty-two knots. Course one-nine-five."

Chan heard a sailor announce a course change for the *Burke*. Gao leaned forward to analyze it.

"Take two full minutes, Gao," he said. "At this distance, there's time to get it right. Remember that destroyers stay alive by changing direction frequently."

He let Gao assess the *Burke's* new course.

"Same speed," Gao said. "New course is due west."

"Logical," Chan said. "The average course between their prior leg and this one aims them between Kikaijima Island and Kita-Daito Island. This is the expected path the *Reagan* strike force will take towards Taiwan, and the *Burke's* passage signals that our trap's victim will arrive soon."

CHAPTER 29

While the *Hai Ming* sought the *Romeo*, Jake locked himself in his stateroom to strangle his rising rage.

Bitterness of his victimization when he was a naval officer had simmered for years, even after lashing out by stealing a Trident missile submarine. Opportunities to seek redemption, build wealth, and create a private life had held the anger in check. But it lingered, like a fault line, awaiting a stressor to unleash its destruction.

He needed privacy to vent it, but solitude let it oscillate unchecked, driving his hardened innards to fracture. It rose, and he bent over, trying to dissipate it in his flexed muscles.

Internal conflict fueled it. To feel complete, he wanted to be home with his wife. But without his submarine comrades, guilt and avoidance of danger's thrill hobbled him. Forcing himself back into the submarine brought him unexpected resistance as reward for separating himself from his wife and risking his life for someone else's cause.

Fate damned him if he sought a private life. It damned him if he imperiled himself for others.

An incarcerated terrorist had preached selflessness, and it stuck. But as Jake tried to apply the lesson, it backfired. He couldn't swallow the role of sacrificing himself, and his perspective failed. He had nothing, saw no hope for a future, and felt nothing but anger.

Redness framed his blurred vision, and his ears shut out sounds. His chest tightened and burned. A right cross to a cabinet door avulsed his knuckles, and he heard his echoing scream.

Blood pounding through his neck, he sat, sucked the blood from his torn skin, and swallowed. He sensed the submarine rocking at snorkel depth and realized the motion had thrown off his punch.

"You stupid shit," he said.

He remembered angrier times when his rage would surge for hours. Once confident that he had matured to overcome his anger, he now questioned if it only flared less frequently because it had exhausted his life's energy. He wondered if age wore him down.

"Living for others," he said. "Bullshit. Ayn Rand was right. Selfish. Do shit for me. Screw everyone else."

Then he thought of his wife. Something angelic about her penetrated his psychological fog, and she reminded him of Christianity's virtues.

"Charity," he said. "Giving of myself to a community."

The rage redoubled and lifted him to his feet. Another venting punch against the cabinet swelled in his gut. He hissed through his teeth to calm himself.

"How the fuck can I give to people who reject me, to help people who don't appreciate me, to pay a debt I don't owe?"

Conscious of the avulsion risk as his vision tunneled again, he sent his palm into the cabinet. The door thumped open, and Jake sank back into the chair, cradling a sprained wrist.

"Just give me a sign, for fuck sake!"

He heard a knock on his door.

"Come in!"

Henri's white hair appeared, followed by a face filled with wonder.

"What's wrong?" Jake asked.

"Orders from China's East Sea Fleet," Henri said. "You won't believe it."

"Go on."

"After the assault against the *Reagan* is complete, we are to sink the *Romeo*."

"No shit?" Jake asked.

"No shit, as you say."

Jake questioned if a supernatural force had brought the news but pushed the speculation from his thoughts to clear his mind.

"Technically," he said, "that doesn't change anything. It's just a set of orders from a different master to complete our mission."

"But odd that they'd kill their own crew."

"Maybe not," Jake said. "Sounds like they convinced a crew to hijack the North Korean submarine just to set them up for a secret kill. Some guy in Beijing is going to carry that guilt to the grave, but it still might be a sound strategic move, depending on your assumptions."

"Shall I call the officers together? To discuss those assumptions, perhaps?"

"No, not yet. Let me brood over this. Since nothing has changed in our mission, let's let this sink in. We've got time to digest this, and I plan to use it."

*

Chan ran his finger over the navigation chart. The path the *Burke* destroyer had carved into the sea irked him. He considered asking Gao's opinion, but he judged his thoughts too radical to share.

He wondered if any of the other officers had noted the peculiarity. If they had, he realized, they would avoid sharing their observation for fear of ridicule. And Chan ridiculed himself as wonderment took root in his mind and drove the peculiar concept to fruition.

The *Burke* had driven the perfect path to avoid Chan's *Romeo* and the closest *Song* submarine to the northeast. Like Ulysses bisecting Scylla and Charybdis, the *Burke* had split equal distances between the Chinese submarines.

He questioned if coincidence had allowed this avoidance of conflict, or if a will beyond his reckoning had spared the destroyer and submarines from mutual discovery.

Keeping his speculation silent, he shuddered when Park appeared at the chart.

"Park? What are you doing here? Did you find our rescue ship?"

Terrified, Park looked misplaced among a room of warriors preparing for a nautical ambush. He uttered a demonic mantra that Chan strained to hear and understand.

"I know I'm right. I know I'm right."

Chan shook his shoulders.

"What are you right about, Park?"

"I know I'm right, sir."

"Of course you are, Park. Go ahead. Tell me."

Park swallowed and glared into Chan's eyes with horror. His voice fell to a hoarse whisper

"*Kilo* three-six-six has orders to kill us."

*

Jake sought Lieutenant Commander Jin's perspective.

"I'm trying to make sense of this," he said. "I'm trying to think about what this would look like if the United States Navy were doing it. It's almost unthinkable but not quite."

"A suicide mission?" Jin asked.

"Americans have done suicide missions," Jake said. "But I don't know that an entire crew would be willing. It's possible, but it's a long shot."

"It's more likely in Eastern cultures," Jin said. "Being part of a community and placing the self behind the good of the common people is respected. The peer pressure would be a strong factor if leaders among the *Romeo's* crew agreed that making the ultimate sacrifice was necessary."

The concept of a volunteer Chinese crew hijacking a North Korean *Romeo* submarine and expecting to die aboard it settled in Jake's mind.

"If this is a suicide mission for the *Romeo's* crew, why not just scuttle the ship and go down with it?" he asked. "If they signed up for a suicide mission, why go to the trouble of having another submarine sink them?"

"Assurance," Jin said. "Inevitability. The *Romeo's* crew is more likely to scuttle the ship by their own hands if they know a torpedo is pointed at them."

"Fair enough," Jake said. "But wouldn't you give the *Kilo* the order before it started the mission?"

"You may not," Jin said. "It would create unnecessary tension for the *Kilo's* crew–or at least its commanding officer–to carry that burden until the last minute. Mainland warriors are human, too, despite their adherence to a flawed regime."

"Okay," Jake said. "Draft a note to the East Sea Fleet acknowledging the order."

As Jin departed, fatigue crept up Jake's torso. He turned to Henri.

"Head to snorkel depth and make sure Pierre knows about this order," he said. "Maybe he has insights."

Henri agreed, and Jake retreated to his stateroom. Expecting to be within reach of the *Romeo* in four hours, Jake slid into his bunk to refresh himself.

As he drifted to sleep, an incongruity pricked at him. An idea sprouted, grew into something concrete, but diffused into a mist before he could grasp it.

*

Refreshed from his nap, Jake ran his fingers through his hair, waiting, and staring at the navigation chart in hopes of making the *Romeo* appear.

From the corner of his eye, he saw ear muffs on Remy's toad-shaped head roll forward. Jake had seen the body language dozens of times, and he held his breath, watching Remy's ritual unfold.

Fingers turned white as they pressed the muffs to a head. Even on profile, the sonar expert's scrunching face revealed an agony that Jake recognized as the pain of yearning. He had watched Remy discover many hostile submarines, and pain drove his French friend more than any other motivator. Only knowledge would liberate him–knowledge of his target submarine.

Jake felt anticipation rising with the drama playing out in Remy's head. His adrenaline surged when the Frenchman twisted, pulled the left muff behind his ear, and opened his mouth to announce his findings.

"*Romeo*-class submarine, bearing zero-five-nine," Remy said. "I have blade-rate correlating to three and a half knots on twin shafts."

"What sensor?" Jake asked.

"Hull array."

"Can you get a low-frequency tonal on the towed array at this range?" Jake asked.

"I'm trying," Remy said. "Integrators are processing. Give me ninety seconds."

"Very well. If you don't get it, I'm turning to drive bearing rate."

"I think I can get something from their propulsion system since I know where to listen."

Jake resisted the temptation to huddle over Remy's shoulder. He noted the time and toggled his gaze between his sonar expert and the seconds ticking on a digital readout.

"I have it," Remy said. "Fifty-hertz electrical system, bearing zero-five-two on the towed array. I'm confirming in Subtics."

Jake pointed his nose to the chart and watched lines of incoming sounds cross inside the *Romeo's* loiter area.

"It may be old," Jake said. "But it's quieter than you might think. It's only thirteen thousand yards away."

"If it has sonar equipment worth a damn," Remy said, "this may not exactly be the turkey shoot we hoped for."

"Easy, Antoine," he said. "We hold every conceivable advantage over it, and everyone in the world wants us to sink this thing. Fate has already ordained the outcome."

Jake inhaled as he pondered and then ignored the warning from his brother about redirecting his anger into senseless slaughter.

"It's a done deal," he said. "We're putting this thing on the bottom."

CHAPTER 30

Focusing on information flow instead of letting fear consume him, Chan scanned the control room to verify nobody else had heard Park.

"Are you sure?" he asked.

"I know I'm right," Park said. "It's impossible to break their encryption and produce the words I did."

"Let me see, Park. And stay quiet about this."

Scenarios of betrayal plagued Chan's imagination as he followed Park to the engineering spaces. No treacherous scenarios materialized during his conjecturing, and Park's news remained surreal as he reached the laptop, awaited a printout, and then read it.

"See!" Park said.

Chan fought back the rising fear and anger.

"It certainly tells them to sink us," he said. "This is sent by the East Sea Fleet to *Kilo* three-six-six?"

"Yes!"

"Could it be someone else simulating the East Sea Fleet?"

"No! I'm cracking these messages because I know the random-number-generating biases on their computers. Remember? This is real!"

"And no sign of a rescue ship?"

"That's the primary reason you brought me here, and I look at every message to every ship you download, but no rescue ship. Why would they send one if they're going to kill us?"

"Easy, Park. You're jumping to a conclusion."

"What more do you want, sir? We need to run!"

"Let's dissect the evidence."

He noted that Park's terror subsided with the focus on logic. Calmness begat calmness, and Chan found mental clarity that had eluded him since hearing the news.

"We've already accepted that the orders to a rescue ship may not come until after the attack. So, let's remove that from the evidence that the East Sea Fleet wants us dead. They could have just as easily ordered a rescue ship in our direction if they wanted us dead, right?"

"I suppose so, sir."

"So, the presence or lack of a rescue ship is meaningless with regards to this message. Let's analyze it on its own merits. Perhaps it's a ruse."

"To fool whom, sir? It's a secret message for one man, encrypted within layers."

"Perhaps the fleet suspects that the encryption has been compromised and is testing any would-be listeners. For example, these orders would tempt an American submarine to take abnormal interest in the affairs of *Kilo* three-six-six. Note that it didn't mention the *Reagan* or an attack on a carrier specifically. It mentioned taking action after today's mission was complete, which is generic. Perhaps this is a trap."

"You mean that the commanding officer of *Kilo* three-six-six was told that he would receive this order but that he was to ignore it?"

"Quite possible, Park. And why all the trouble with giving us body bags to carry this ship's proper crew aboard? We are indeed going to finish this mission, lay the bodies where we found them, and burn the inner guts of this submarine to unrecognizable charred remains."

The scared, scrunched features of Park's face relaxed.

"I understand, sir. A message itself doesn't mean anything. It's the context and larger possibilities."

"Exactly, Park," Chan said. "Keep your hopes up."

Chan patted Park on the shoulder and departed with a confident stride, but his swagger drained from his extremities as he lumbered forward. Doubts ate at him, and he sought his trump card in the control room.

"Gao," he said.

"Yes, sir?"

"Join me in my stateroom."

Chan led his executive officer to his room, sat, and gestured for Gao to close the door.

"Sit, Gao."

Gao unfolded a chair and obeyed.

"You seem concerned, sir."

Chan withdrew the printout from his pocket and handed it to Gao.

"What sort of reassurance might you give me that this note to the commanding officer of *Kilo* three-six-six is something more complex than it appears?"

Chan watched Gao's eyes widen as he read.

"Sir? How did you get this?"

"I've had Park decrypting tactical message traffic in his free time while not searching for our rescue ship. Now answer my question."

"I… I have nothing."

Chan's fear gave way to anger.

"What?"

"I have nothing, sir. I mean I could speculate and concoct hopeful scenarios, but it would be a fool's folly. This is terrible news. The fleet has abandoned us. Worse, they're hunting us. Why?"

"Damn it, Gao! I expected you as the firstborn son of a ranking party member to tell me why we are safe."

Gao's gaze fell to his shoes. A hot spike of fear careened through Chan, piercing his anger like lava as he watched his trump card ooze into gelatin.

"A year ago," Gao said, "I made a mistake. I became careless and impregnated one of my father's wait staff. When my son was born in secrecy, my father disowned me. He couldn't have his inheritance aimed at a bastard commoner firstborn grandson."

"Go on."

"My father now considers my younger brother as his firstborn. He kept this news private to avoid embarrassment, but those in my father's inner circle within the party had to know, to groom my brother for his future responsibilities."

"You imbecile! You didn't think to tell me this when I specifically sought you for this mission?"

"You didn't tell me you were recruiting me as insurance against betrayal! How could I have known you were using me?"

Chan stood and lifted his arm to backhand the wretched mistake, but as he hesitated in doubt of the act's correctness, his stateroom phone distracted him. He reached for the handset, identified himself, and heard the voice of his youngest officer.

"Sir, the encounter with the *Reagan* has begun!"

"It's at least twenty minutes earlier than anticipated," Chan said. "What evidence do you have?"

"Distant explosion bearing zero-four-three."

The sickening combination of betrayal's fear wrapped around hope resonated within Chan.

"Did one of our wolf pack already strike the *Reagan*?"

"I don't know, sir. I called you as soon as we heard the explosion."

"You did the right thing. I'll be right there."

Chan moved by Gao and opened the door.

"Can you keep your mouth shut about this message to *Kilo* three-six-six?"

"Yes, sir."

"Good. If you can pull yourself together, get your miserable soul involved with the resolution of this mess. You're not a complete idiot, and I may need you before this is done."

Chan marched to the control room and ducked through its door. Faces of seated sailors looked to him to validate hopes that one of their countrymen had struck a blow against the *Reagan*. He forced his features to freeze for fear of fostering false hopes.

"Has anyone bothered to discern if that was a heavyweight Korean warhead or some other sort of weapon?"

After the young officer manning the control room explained that the analysis was taking place, Chan slid by him to a monitor and reviewed the direction to the noise.

"The bearing to this explosion intersects with the loiter area of our western *Yuan* submarine," he said.

Gao appeared, his face revealing either confidence or resignation. Chan couldn't tell, but he didn't care. He welcomed the company of someone capable of digesting his thoughts.

"I agree, sir," Gao said.

"Do you understand why I fear this is bad news?"

Gao squinted while ascertaining possibilities.

"I am afraid I do, sir. If a weapon had impacted the *Reagan*, we would expect to hear it on a different bearing, at least ten degrees more to the east."

"Exactly," Chan said. "Unless the *Reagan* happened to flee to the west after being positioned far to the west to begin with, this looks like an attack upon the *Yuan*. At best, it's an attack by the *Yuan* on a carrier escort, which would cause the *Reagan* to flee and jeopardize our mission."

"At least we know we're in battle, sir. Shall I rig the ship for battle stations?"

"Silently. Spread the word without an audible alarm."

Chan tried to make sense of the information overloading his frontal lobe. He wanted time to think, but the battle had reached him. Then Gao brought him the next piece of condemning news.

"Sir, the sonar team has analyzed the explosion. It was a lightweight torpedo. Probably air dropped."

"But no sign of a sinking ship?" Chan asked.

As if proving the folly of questioning reality, a sonar technician announced that he heard creaking metal on the bearing of the explosion.

Chan found no option but to set people into motion. Activity would prevent imaginations from spinning. He projected his voice throughout the room.

"Very well," he said. "The Americans have killed our comrades. But five of our submarines remain to carry out this mission, and we will make ourselves ready to fight. Warm up two torpedoes with presets to attack a surfaced target."

Shocked faces began to reveal conviction.

"Also," Chan said. "Warm up all the other weapons for submerged targets."

Confusion contorted faces in the room.

"This is battle, gentlemen," Chan said. "You've already proven your mettle in extreme danger, and I trust you to continue doing so. I am proud of you all, and I would select no better crew for our fight. But we must be ready for all foes, known and unknown, surfaced, submerged, or worse."

Chan sensed pride rising as he spoke.

"Warm up the weapons, remain alert, and forget that you are aboard the least capable vessel in this engagement. History is filled with examples of great men defeating lesser foes who were better equipped. You are on a vessel that is capable enough, and you will prove that you are a better crew than any adversary."

CHAPTER 31

"What blew up?" Jake asked.

"Air dropped torpedo, American Mark Fifty-Four," Remy said. "It hit the *Yuan* to the north."

"Did the *Yuan* get off a torpedo?"

"No. I don't hear anything."

"Damn," Jake said. "When you know where a submarine is hiding, it's not really hiding. Easy pickings for aircraft. It's not even fair."

From a seated perch at his control panel, Henri glanced over his shoulder and caught Jake's eye.

"I believe it's time to maneuver in closer to the *Romeo* to align a kill shot," Henri said.

"Hold on," Jake said. "That *Romeo* knows that something is going wrong. It heard the same explosion we did. There's a commanding officer on it with an itchy trigger finger."

"All the more reason to end this quickly," Henri said.

"I'll end it when I end it. Firing point procedures on the *Romeo*, tube one. Set a slow-speed search on the torpedo."

"Slow speed? Why?" Henri asked.

"I want the wire to stay attached so we can steer it, and I want its fuel to last in case our target runs. Any more questions, or can I shoot this damned torpedo?"

Henri sighed, shook his head, and faced his panel. Jake kept his eyes on the mechanic's white hair while turning his head toward Jin. Holding a détente with the Frenchman, he shifted his eyes to the seated Taiwanese officer.

"Commander Jin?" he asked. "Are you ready to go to firing point procedures?"

"I'm setting the parameters in tube one for the *Romeo* based upon the present Subtics solution."

"Very well," Jake said.

As Jin tapped his screen two seats away from Remy, the sonar technician announced the continuance of the fray.

"Torpedoes in the water! Multiple bearings. Multiple

sources."

"Anything coming at us?" Jake asked.

"I can't tell yet," Remy said.

"Anything from the *Romeo*?"

"No," Remy said. "It's the only thing quiet out there. All three of the other Chinese submarines have launched torpedoes at the *Reagan* decoy."

Jake looked to the chart. The helicopter-dragged hydrophone array blaring sounds simulating the *Reagan* slid through water twenty miles away.

From the corner of his eye, he watched the fingers of Remy and a Taiwanese companion beside him fly across two consoles, confirming acoustic data in the Subtics system. Enemy torpedo locations and movements faded in to illuminated life on the chart.

"Are you seeing the bearing rate to support this?" Jake asked. "Or are you just guessing that they're all shooting at the *Reagan* decoy?"

"I see bearing rate on each one, Jake," Remy said. "Six torpedoes, two from each submarine."

"Then we're safe," Jake said. "And helicopters will likely take care of all but the *Romeo*. That's our job."

He thought of his brother's warning about killing and its associated dangers. He noticed the senior Taiwanese officer stir and lean back from his console. In preparation for the expected report, Jake stood straight and faced him.

"Weapon is ready," Jin said.

"Shoot tube one."

*

"That's the activity I wanted to see!" Chan said. "Salvos targeted at the *Reagan*."

"We hear the *Reagan*, too," Gao said. "Shall we shoot?"

Chan considered that the *Kilo* choreographed to parallel him in the last latch of the trap may be skulking behind him preparing backstabbing friendly fire. Balanced between disbelief of betrayal and commitment to cause, he bought time.

"No," he said. "It's still too far. Let it maneuver towards us for a certain shot. Let it take crippling blows from our colleagues. Let it count when we shoot."

"I understand, sir."

Chan leaned over the table and curled his finger. Gao bent forward to listen to his whispers.

"*Kilo* three-six-six hasn't launched yet," Chan said.

"They could be waiting, as we are."

"Or they could be afraid to reveal their position."

"Why? They have no idea we intercepted their orders."

"If they're maneuvering to attack us, they very well couldn't launch weapons at the *Reagan* without arousing our suspicion by being where they should not be."

Gao appeared stoic, his features firm but unforced. Chan wondered if he stared at death's acceptance.

"We're outmatched by the *Kilo*, sir. In every tactical aspect. Sound emissions, hydrophone sensitivity, hydrophone coverage, signal processing, speed, endurance. We're a relic at odds with a contemporary masterpiece."

"Agreed," Chan said. "But despite not knowing whether or not to believe our cracked message, we have a tactical informational advantage. If they intend to kill us, we have a narrow window of surprise over them and must take action."

"And if they don't intend to kill us? If it's a ruse against our adversaries?"

"Then we must also take action. We must attack the *Reagan*."

Chan tapped a pencil on the chart beside his ship.

"If you were *Kilo* three-six-six and you wanted to kill us, where would you position yourself?"

"I'd be anywhere but where we think it is–I wouldn't be in their assigned loitering area. I also wouldn't be between us and the *Reagan* because that's where we're listening, and the *Kilo* wouldn't be able to distinguish our shot at the *Reagan* from a retaliatory shot at them if we were to launch one."

"Correct. So, you'd be in the semi-circle behind our line of sight to the *Reagan*?"

"Yes, sir."

Chan recognized that Gao seemed electrified–everything his underling had learned about submerged warfare blossomed at the needed moment.

"Agreed. And now, assuming they're in that semi-circle, would you launch every available weapon in an equally-spaced spread into that semi-circle? Slow-speed searches to distract them and possibly sink them while we creep away at four knots to the east?"

"Yes, sir. Brilliant! Exactly!"

"You'd also shoot two weapons at the *Reagan*, per plan, in case the message to *Kilo* three-six-six was a ruse. If questioned later in that event, we could say that we heard a transient sound to the west, suspected an enemy submarine, launched our salvo, and evaded."

"Yes, sir!"

Whirring electronic sounds caressed Chan's ear as he realized his conversation of whispers had culminated with Gao's outburst. He patted his executive officer on the back, walked to his chair, and sat.

"You know what to do, Gao," he said. "Make it happen."

*

"Any sign of reaction from the *Romeo*?" Jake asked.

"No, Jake," Remy said. "Our torpedo is going right at them. It's still six minutes out, but it's a kill shot unless they run soon. Even then, you could steer it and accelerate it after them."

Henri stood from his panel and joined Jake by the charting table. He leaned and whispered, surprising Jake by speaking in French.

"Why not end this? You're testing fate. Accelerate the weapon and launch two more, one each on a lag and lead angle, to bracket the target. Maneuver in closer to tighten the shots. You're too far away."

"No."

"For God's sake, why not? If you're not going to do that, at least back off and let a helicopter finish this."

Jake grabbed Henri's starched shirt and, in his anger, switched to English.

"Do you see me flinching? When you know instinctively when to shoot and when not to, you can command your own submarine. Until then, do what I say or relieve yourself. Am I clear?"

The Frenchman nodded, and Jake released him.

"Get back to your station."

"Torpedo in the water," Remy said. "Air-dropped. And now another on a different bearing."

Jake glanced at the lines on the chart corresponding to the weapons' sounds. He recognized them as attacks on the two *Song*-class submarines.

"All submarines are accelerating," Remy said, "except the *Romeo*. The remaining *Yuan* doesn't have a torpedo chasing it, but it's only a matter of time, I imagine."

"Very well," Jake said.

"And there's the torpedo dropped over the *Yuan*," Remy said. "Except for the *Romeo*, every Chinese submarine is under attack and running."

"Is our torpedo active yet?" Jake asked.

"Not yet," Remy said. "Three and a half minutes until the seeker awakes."

"Very well," Jake said. "This will be over soon."

"Torpedo in the water!" Remy said. "Multiple weapons and launch transients from torpedo hydraulic systems. All from the *Romeo*."

"Did they launch at the *Reagan*, finally?" Jake asked.

"Yes, I think so. I don't know. I mean..."

Remy's face contorted in the agony of ignorance mixed with the wonderment of awe.

"What is it Antoine?" Jake asked.

"This is the largest torpedo salvo I've ever witnessed. Ever."

"That ship has eight tubes," Jake said.

"And I think they just unloaded them all. I can't track them all in my head, and Subtics integrators will need time to generate solutions for you."

"But do they all have bearing rate?" Jake asked.

"Most, but one is at near zero bearing rate. And one is on our right bearing left."

"Shit."

"Jake, they've sent torpedoes in multiple directions and multiple targets. I don't understand."

"But one, maybe two is a threat to us?"

"Yes," Remy said.

"Forget about the rest," Jake said. "Focus on the two that we care about."

Remy nodded and tapped the sailor seated beside him. Jake watched them split responsibilities to make sense of the two weapons of concern.

As a dark cloud crept up Remy's face, Jake's concern became fear.

"The zero rate weapon is drawing aft now," Remy said. "But there's still one on the right, drawing left."

"Do you have a solution to it yet?"

"Yes," Remy said. "A perfect shot to intercept us."

CHAPTER 32

Jake bowed his head, unleashed evasion scenarios into his mental optimization machine, and prayed for wisdom to make the right move.

"Left ten-degrees rudder," he said. "Steer course two-zero-five."

From the corner of his eye he watched a Taiwanese sailor wiggle a joystick. The submarine's angling deck forced him to shift his weight, and his stomach felt nauseous as Henri turned in his chair.

"This is hardly an evasion maneuver," Henri said. "You must be decisive. Use a flank bell with countermeasures. We can get away from this weapon if you act quickly."

Jake lifted his chin.

"We will evade," he said.

"Then do something!"

"I am, you son of bitch. I'm relieving you."

"You can't. You need me."

Jake swung his nose at Lieutenant Commander Jin.

"I assume you have a man qualified to handle the ship's control station?"

"I do," Jin said. "I have several. But my best man is not as good as Henri."

Jake lowered his gaze and inhaled to calm himself against his rising heartbeat. He lifted his chin again and sought his colleague's affirmation.

"Henri, my old friend. If you'll take care of your job and trust me, I'll get you and everyone else out of this mess, like I always have."

"At least explain your intent," Henri said. "If I am to trust my life to it."

"If you trust Antoine, you'll believe in his estimates of course and speed for the incoming torpedoes."

"He's the best," Henri said. "But I still fail to see why you would take measures short of a complete sprinting evasion."

Jake watched a crosshair on the chart trace a slow, wide arc away from the *Romeo* and its torpedoes.

"I kept our distance from the *Romeo* out of caution," Jake said, "and that gives us time to evade its torpedoes without accelerating or using decoys. They have no idea we're out here, and I'm going to keep it that way so that they can't steer a weapon towards us."

"I see," Henri said. "And if I trust Antoine's solutions to their torpedoes, we are in no danger."

Henri relaxed and faced his panel, but across the control room on its port side, Remy twisted backwards in his chair and waved a finger towards Jake.

"What's wrong, Antoine?"

"The *Romeo* is turning away. I hear down-Doppler on their screws."

"Maintaining speed at four knots?"

"Yes," Remy said. "I think so. I will confirm after they finish turning."

"They're heading deeper into the ocean."

The sonar expert's brow furrowed.

"I agree, but I just realized something," Remy said. "I don't hear any sounds of weapons reloads. They seem to be content with empty torpedo tubes."

An awareness of an incongruity crept up Jake's spine. His brother's warning about needless violence bothered him.

"How long until our torpedo seeker goes active?"

"Twelve seconds," Remy said.

"Shift it to passive mode," Jake said. "I don't want it making any noise."

"Shifting to passive mode," Remy said. "Our torpedo is in passive mode."

"Henri, Jin," Jake said, "join me at the chart."

Jake watched the men walk to him beside the table in the room's center. Beside Jin, Henri's tone had shifted from defiant to erudite.

"Passive mode?" he asked. "To minimize the *Romeo's* chance

of hearing it and evading?"

"No," Jake said. "Although that's true tactically, that's not why I did it. I just wanted to buy time to make a decision without them knowing we shot at them."

"What decision?" Henri asked.

"To let them live."

"You called us here to ask our opinions?" Jin asked.

"Yes. We've just heard four submarines get pummeled, and part of me is just tired of needless killing."

"I see," Jin said. "But I am aware of your history. You have caused the death of many adversaries. You are not one for showing mercy without justification."

"Mercy is its own justification," Jake said. "But I see your point. You mean that I need a good reason."

Jin nodded.

"Review the facts," Jake said. "Taiwan and America want that submarine sunk. China wants it sunk, too. So, since everybody wants that thing sunk, the right answer is to sink it, right?"

"That's the obvious answer," Jin said. "But I see that you question it. If you consider that adversaries desire the same outcome, then one of them may be drawing the wrong conclusion."

"Right," Jake said. "And I just figured it out. We have drawn the wrong conclusion. China is the side that wants that submarine dead. Not us."

"But why?" Henri asked.

"Survivors," Jake said. "That's the biggest risk. A cracked North Korean submarine hull at the bottom of deep water coupled with North Korean torpedoes blowing up underneath the *Reagan* makes you wonder if the Koreans actually pulled this off by themselves."

"I see," Henri said. "But if men on the *Romeo* survive and tell stories of deception, then you've eroded most of your plausible denial about China's participation."

"Right. And I mean to track that thing to its end. We're quieter, faster, better, and with a ton more endurance with our MESMA system. And they can't drive home because we've got that hydrophone defense line. They're stuck in open water for a long time, at our mercy. We just need to get a message off to friendly forces to let them know our plan."

"I will draft that message immediately," Jin said.

Jake verified that the closest hostile torpedo passed far north of his ship before looking up to Remy.

"Antoine," he said.

"Yes, Jake?"

"Shut down our weapon."

*

"What's going on out there, Gao?" Chan asked. "Are any friendly torpedoes finding their mark?"

Gao stood from his stooped perch behind a sonar technician. He appeared fierce, his sharp, angular features casting shadows on his face.

"Weapons are either circling the *Reagan* or vectoring to oblivion. This is impossible. It's as if the carrier is somehow invisible to torpedo seekers."

"Our salvo of weapons is faring no better against an unknown enemy that may not exist–the wide sector of water we attacked?"

"Correct, sir. Not so much as an active sonar return from a single weapon. But if there were a submarine out there, I believe you've distracted it enough to let us drive away, hopefully unnoticed."

"And no sign of *Kilo* three-six-six?"

"No, sir. It's as if they no longer exist."

"Given the results of this so-called attack on the *Reagan*," Chan said, "they're just as well off elsewhere, whether dead or alive."

As Gao moved to his side, Chan smelled pungent body odor.

"The Americans must have known about our attack," Gao said. "Their anti-submarine defenses aren't this strong, even in waters they know to be hostile."

"But somehow, we have survived," Chan said. "We, the least capable vessel in this exchange and the vessel with the most subterfuge surrounding its agenda."

"Our fate is beyond reckoning," Gao said. "We should already be dead."

"But we are alive and will remain that way. And we seem to be succeeding in evading the only way we can–slowly, optimizing our silence, and praying that none of the carrier strike force assets stumble across us."

"We are on the correct course for giving ourselves that chance," Gao said.

"Let's continue this evasion before we discuss subsequent actions. But once I'm convinced we're free of this mess, I'll want to create a plan for getting our feet back on dry land."

Over the next hour, the fusion of heightened emotions drained from Chan's frame. His fingers tingled, and he wondered if fatigue and numbness would consume him. He accepted that the failed trapping of the *Reagan* had been a reverse ambush, and he stuffed the frustration deep inside himself for future processing.

He watched Gao stand from beside a seated sailor. His executive officer yawned and stretched. Their eyes met, and Chan waved him to the table.

"We're done with this cursed engagement," Chan said. "It's time to plot our escape."

"There's no rescue ship," Gao said. "You've looked for signs of it in the message traffic. You're not hoping to reach snorkel depth and learn that the East Sea Fleet has decided to send us a rescue ship?"

"Hoping–yes, Gao. Expecting–no. That would be folly. However, I mean to complete my mission."

"Sir? The *Reagan* survived, our comrades were defeated, and it's likely that our homeland attempted to sacrifice us in betrayal. What mission would you define?"

"Given that we are alive, I am uncertain of the betrayal. I will give the fleet the benefit of the doubt."

"It hardly seems to matter now."

"It matters only that I refuse to head home."

Gao scrunched his face in thought.

"I admit I hadn't considered it," he said. "We could avoid the Taiwanese hydrophone line and get home by driving north around Japan, but you bring up a good point in seeing possible danger in returning home at all."

"We could attempt docking at a remote port far from the influence of whoever may have betrayed us," Chan said, "but the power of the party is vast and quick. I will not risk it."

"Then where will we go?"

"Taiwan," Chan said. "We will complete the charade that this is a North Korean submarine by scattering the bodies within it and turning it into an inferno before commandeering a passing vessel."

"Have you considered just driving this submarine into Taiwan?" Gao asked. "It's far simpler."

"But it would be treason," Chan said. "We must straddle the line between assumed betrayal and loyalty to our cause."

"Then we must find a vessel willing to rescue us as we burn and abandon this one."

Chan straightened his back.

"A willing vessel," he said, "or a vessel we can take by force. We have torpedoes to slow it and small arms to raid it. Then we can redirect the vessel to Taiwan and earn time to think and react to the publicity surrounding this failed attack on the *Reagan*. We could possibly reach Taiwan and blend in, find our way to a friendly outpost."

"We must make the attempt."

"Are you ready to lead a boarding team onto a ship that may be unwilling to carry our crew to safety?"

A sardonic smile spread across Gao's face.

"I am, sir. By force, if necessary."

"Excellent," Chan said.

He bent over the plotting table to review the myriad merchant vessels strewn over the chart.

"We don't know which vessels belong to which nation," he said. "I'm unsure if any would willingly help us, or if verbal radio threats would compel one to stop for us."

"If one defies us and we must sink it with a torpedo," Gao said, "its distress calls would be heard by the next ship we threaten to board."

Chan shifted his gaze to the *Reagan*, and he accepted that the ghostly carrier had steamed into his past.

"I agree," he said. "We can afford to make noise now. Reload tubes one and two."

Gao acknowledged the order and walked forward toward the torpedo room, leaving Chan in a silent room filled with men consumed in private thought.

He exhaled and let his head droop between his arms. Ascertaining the challenges of commandeering a nearby vessel, he visualized the dossiers of the men he had recruited to his crew.

In varied degrees of aptitude, they knew the languages to communicate with most passing ships. They covered the foreign tongues he expected to encounter–English, Japanese, and Korean–and he would identify those on his team with the strongest skills to translate.

Turning his thoughts to small arms combat, he recalled that one sailor had survived three months of commando training prior to suffering a career-altering foot injury, and another sailor had military police preparation. They would lead two, four-person small arm teams.

He decided that once he had weapons in his tubes, he would ascend to snorkel depth, give the fleet a final chance to assign him a rescue option, and then set his escape plan into action.

CHAPTER 33

"Who is the other?"

Dun Lu surveyed the scullery to assure himself nobody had heard his whispered question.

The failed commando considered his submarine compatriots a lesser species versus the warriors with whom he had trained in the special forces pipeline. An excellent specimen of strength, agility, and resilience, Lu had thrived as a leader among China's best, until an accident had ended his career.

During a small boat exercise, the surf had capsized his Zodiac. He remembered his foot becoming wedged between rocks and the water pounding him against stone. He had swallowed the ocean, inhaled fluid, and died.

Revived, he remembered coughing water aboard a power-boat. When he had realized that he had drowned, the searing pain in his pulverized foot had verified that he lived again. The quick action of his instructors had allowed him to cheat death–but not pain.

When Lieutenant Commander Dao Chan had approached him at his hospital bedside with an offer to join a submarine crew with a covert mission, he grabbed hold of the opportunity to do something–anything to distract himself from the nothingness of his empty future.

While learning basic submarine training and minimal culinary skills to serve as the ship's cook, Lu realized that his promised adventure would pale in comparison to the life he deserved as an elite warrior. He had nothing but agony with each step that he placed weight on his reconstructed bones.

Two months before setting after the ill-fated North Korean *Romeo*, two senior officers in uniform had approached him at his quarters. His wife had answered the door, and he recalled feeling the premonition that starting a family had been a vulnerability and that having widowed his pregnant wife in the surf would have been his kinder fate.

The officers had been blunt in recruiting him for a covert

mission within a covert mission. Lieutenant Commander Chan would remain ignorant of it, but another member of the crew would work in parallel with Lu to assure the mission's completion. The two-operative approach would serve as a redoubling of commitment in case Lu decided that his family's welfare fell short of proper motivation.

Promised financial security for his wife, his parents, and even his siblings, Lu accepted death as his calling.

With the escape from the torpedo that *Kilo* three-six-six had never launched, Lu buzzed with energy. The *Romeo's* survival transformed him from an insurance policy into an operative. He tucked the largest blades from the cutlery set into his overalls' pockets and marched to the engineering spaces where he expected to meet the other operative.

As he turned the corner to the electric control panel, the pressure on his foot ached. For the first time, he welcomed the pain. Anticipating death, he welcomed all sensations.

Two sailors glanced up at him from their panels, and he uttered his memorized phrase.

"Communism succeeds as a form of government when paired with capitalistic economic practices."

One man frowned while the other scowled at Lu.

"Are you well, Lu?" he asked. "You must be in a worse state of shock than the rest of us."

"Never mind," Lu said. "I was just seeking a conversation to get my mind off our fate."

He slipped deeper into the spaces and found Park tapping at keyboards among a sea of laptops. Chan's hand-picked cryptologist had failed in uncovering anything useful that Lu knew about, and he, like most of the crew, considered the hacker extra baggage. As he uttered his phrase, he prayed that Park would ignore him.

The spooky hacker kept his face buried in his screen.

"Go away, Lu."

Lu obliged and sought the final man in the engineering spaces as he hunched over bearing temperature gauges on the ship's electric drive motor.

"Communism succeeds as a form of government when paired with capitalistic economic practices."

As the man scanned the room to assure their solitude, Lu recognized his partner.

"We are the first nation to achieve this," he said. "And we must protect the nation at all costs."

Lu formed a desperate and instant bond with his accomplice.

"We should already be dead, but we are not," he said. "We have work to do. Are you committed?"

The man's eyes became steel.

"Of course, I am. They threatened me. They threatened my family. They promised wealth to my family. In fact, they've already paid. I only need assure that this submarine finds its way to the bottom of the sea to see to the future of my loved ones."

"Why do you accept death so readily?"

"I'm already dead."

The man pointed to his lungs.

"Cancer?"

"Yes. I could possibly live with radiation therapy and endless surgeries, but why subject myself to such torture for a miniscule chance of survival?"

"Then let's get to business," Lu said. "You start the air compressor. Let me know when we've reached low enough pressure in the space to assure that the door remains shut."

The man darted around a corner and Lu followed him to a silvery rectangular obelisk. He checked the position of a few small valves, opened an intake, and depressed a button. A plate on the end of the pump started rotating, driving cyclic cylinders.

"That's it," the man said. "The cylinders will suck air from the compartment and compress it into our high-pressure air tanks."

"The ventilation lines to the forward spaces are closed?" Lu asked.

"Correct. They are controlled from the engineering spaces and will remain closed."

"How long until the compartment is inaccessible?"

"About five minutes."

Lu felt a sick impatience, knowing his ensuing task.

"Open the drain valves," he said. "Bring water into this doomed coffin of a submarine while I neutralize those who might oppose us."

Sliding his hand into his pockets, he grabbed the hilt of his knives. He considered Park, nestled in his forest of computers, and he decided that nothing would distract the hacker. He would begin by killing the others.

He walked forward to the electric control panel, turned the corner, and spied his two seated victims. His commando training became adrenaline-instinct.

Refusing to overthink his tandem kill, he stepped to the closest man and drove an underhanded thrust through the overall fabric covering his belly. The wound might prove nonfatal, he reflected, but the lower torso presented a large target, hard to defend and easy to hit, and it incapacitated his victim.

As the man fell to the ground, Lu twisted his torso, raised two blades, and lunged. The man raised his arms in defense while standing, and Lu's daggers carved flesh wounds.

He flailed his blades across the man's forearms, slicing red lines until he saw an opening below an elbow and backhanded a tip through the coverall stitching and between ribs. The man doubled to his side, and Lu finished him with a slicing motion through his jugular vein.

He turned and noticed the labored breathing of his first victim, doubled over on the deck. He eased the man's passing by maneuvering a blade between ribs and through the back of his heart.

His weapons concealed in his pockets, he smelled splattered blood in his coveralls as he marched aft toward Park. Relieved that the hacker ignored his approach, he moved to within arm's reach of his neck.

"Park," he said.

"What?" Park asked.

"Look at me."

The young computer geek lifted his chin toward Lu, who sliced a rapid red line through his Adam's apple.

Park lowered his gaze to his computer screen and extended his fingers towards the keyboard in what Lu thought resembled some bizarre hope of finding an undo function. The young man then grasped his throat and curled forward, his laptop following his carcass to the deck.

Alone with his accomplice in the engineering spaces, Lu slid the knives back into his pockets and walked forward toward the door.

Its round shape appeared large, supporting his desire for the pressure difference on its opposite side to seal it shut via force over its surface area.

He unlatched the handle and pushed. It didn't budge. Lowering his shoulder into its steel mass, he drove his sneakers into the deck and strained with his legs and back. The door cracked open, and he felt the whistling rush of air from the forward spaces jetting over him. Yielding to the force, he let the door shut itself and reset the latch.

His companion crept up beside him.

"You have blood all over you."

"It makes no difference, does it?" Lu asked.

"Are they dead?"

"Yes," Lu said. "We are alone. But I can still open the door, slightly. A team of men on the other side might succeed."

"The differential pressure is hardly fourteen kilopascals. It will reach twenty-five within minutes. At that point, there will be no opening the door. The latch will break off before it would open."

"Regardless," Lu said, "I will stay here and hold the latch shut, in case a random crewman happens by."

"That is the only thing that could stop us now. I've opened drain valves for the diesel seawater and propulsion motor cooling systems. It is a slow infiltration of water, but it is enough to sink this ship."

"The estimates say that we need an hour before the ship could not recover from the water ingress, correct?"

"Correct. At that point, not even blowing ballast tanks would matter. Even if the ship does reach the surface, the continued inflow will eventually sink it."

"You've shut all valves that would allow pumps to suck water from the engineering spaces?"

"Yes, of course."

"Then all that is left is to secure the shaft so that the ship has no propulsion to drive to the surface."

"It's best to wait until they notice the water weight."

"How will we know they've noticed?" Lu asked.

"I'm sure they will call to ask."

"Then we appear to have a successful plan in motion," Lu said. "Will you show me the influx from the drain valves? Excuse my curiosity."

"Follow me."

As his accomplice turned, Lu stepped forward to finish the final step in his mission. He grasped the hilts of both pocketed blades, flexed his arms, and drove steely death into the back of the other saboteur's lungs.

Walking over the corpse, Lu glanced between floor gratings and saw shiny surface oil dancing atop the dark water rising in the bilge. The smell of seawater became noticeable, but he wondered if he fooled himself.

He fixed his eyes on a section of drain line from a refrigerant cooling system that opened above the waterline. As the sheen surface tickled the vertical copper drain pipe, he knew the water level was rising.

CHAPTER 34

Chan watched from the corner of his eye as Gao gathered input from animated sailors. He disliked the look of concern in his executive officer as he approached.

"What's wrong?" Chan asked.

"The ship control station reports that he's needed excessive pump usage to move water from the after trim tanks. Apparently, we've been getting heavier aft, taking on water, gradually."

"What does the engineering watch say about it?"

"The engineering spaces aren't responding," Gao said. "I've sent a man to investigate. I fear a possible casualty, possibly a refrigerant leak or a fire, that has incapacitated the staff back aft."

"Send messengers throughout the forward compartments and have everyone be ready to don forced air masks."

"I will pass the word, sir."

After Gao disappeared, Chan decided to come shallow to get closer to the clean air above.

"Helm," he said, "increase speed to five knots."

Watching the speed gauge, Chan awaited the slight increase in ship's speed. Instead, he noted the down-counting decimal inching toward three knots.

"Damn," he said. "We're losing propulsion. Get us up by pumping water overboard from our trim tanks, and use an aggressive up angle to use what momentum we have."

The *Romeo* angled upward while it slowed against Chan's will. The jettisoning of water weight from the tanks enabled its climb, where it stalled at forty meters depth.

When Gao returned, his words numbed Chan.

"We can't get into the engineering spaces," he said. "There's a differential pressure across the watertight door, and it's too great for us to open it. We would rip off the door handle before we could. However, I saw no sign of fire through the portal glass."

A sickness billowed in Chan's stomach as he walked to the

ship's control station and looked over a sailor's shoulder.

"There's no fire," he said. "A fire would heat the air and make the pressure higher in the engineering spaces. But it's lower, and I verified this with evidence. The after high-pressure air banks are at abnormally elevated levels. Someone has been compressing air into the banks."

"Why?" Gao asked. "That's wasteful."

"To create a vacuum in the engineering spaces," Chan said. "Patiently, while we weren't paying attention. To create a differential pressure across the door of just a few pounds per square inch. Just enough to prevent us from gaining access to the spaces."

"This is nonsense, sir."

"Is it? We've lost communications, propulsion, and access to the engineering spaces, and we appear to be slowly taking on water."

"Slowly, sir. That's my point. If someone is working against us, why not inundate the engineering spaces by opening the hatch or overriding interlocks to torpedo tube doors?"

"Too much backpressure on the hatch," Chan said. "Too much sophisticated knowledge of the interlocks required to open the breach and muzzle doors simultaneously on the after torpedo tubes. No, Gao, this is someone doing their best to kill us with the drain valves at their disposal. Their methods are slow but proving effective and a challenge for us to counter."

"This is madness, sir," Gao said. "After all we've encountered, now we face a saboteur."

Chan reviewed the ship's control panel.

"Our after trim tanks are almost dry," he said. "We will soon have nothing left to counter the water ingress."

"Then we'll have to blow the after ballast tanks."

"That brings its own risks," Chan said. "It could pin us to the surface where we would be exposed."

"I agree, sir, but we're running out of time and choices," Gao said.

"Can we drill through the viewing lens of the watertight

door?" Chan asked. "To equalize pressure, gain access, and re-take the engineering spaces."

"It's possible, sir, but it might be just as fast to cut through the steel of the door itself."

"Assemble a team with drilling and cutting equipment to puncture through that door any way possible–attack glass and steel. Also, send men to the ventilation line isolation valves to attempt cutting through them, or perhaps unseat them. All we need is a pinhole leak to balance the air pressure. Also, send a team with small arms to storm the engineering spaces once you break through the door."

"I will, sir."

Gao departed to loosen the saboteur's grip on the submarine, and Chan watched the slow battle of water management unfold on a panel. Vertical bars rose and fell as the ship's trim pump funneled water from the empty rear trim tanks to those near the ship's bow.

Minutes ticked away as Chan teased his brain for new ideas to break through the engineering door. Nothing.

Expecting a sailor beside his executive officer to be listening, he lifted a sound-powered phone from its cradle.

"This is Chan," he said. "Give me Gao."

Chan heard the high-speed whine of a drill in the background as he waited.

"This is Gao, sir."

"Any progress?"

"Progress, yes. Drilling through the glass appears the fastest option, but this is going to take at least thirty minutes–probably more. And that's just to create a small hole. It may take another thirty minutes of pressure equalization before we can open the door."

"Have we thought of everything?" Chan asked.

"There are no more vulnerable ways into the engineering spaces than the door and the ventilation lines," Gao said. "The electrical and piping lines are as resilient as the ventilation lines and harder to access with cutting equipment."

"That's it, then," Chan said. "Continue your efforts to retake the engineering spaces, Gao. We may yet have use for this complete submarine. But now it's time to surface and seek a vessel of opportunity to deliver us from this steel sarcophagus."

*

In the reddish lighting of the control room, Jake watched Remy spring half way out of his chair.

"What's going on, Antoine?"

"They're blowing to the surface!"

"You heard their high-pressure air compressor running, you heard their trim pump practically spinning off its bearings moving water around their boat, and after all those boring tasks they're all of a sudden hitting an emergency blow?"

"Yes!"

"No warning. No flooding. No explosions. Nothing banging. No ship-wide alarm klaxons blaring. Just business as usual and then blow for their lives."

Remy squinted and cocked his head.

"Well, I heard some maintenance sounds, like welding or cutting, but I thought nothing of it."

"Fair enough," Jake said. "We don't know why they're surfacing, but they needed to get there in a hurry, and they'll probably be there for a while."

"We should probably have a look," Remy said.

"Darn right," Jake said. "Henri, get us to periscope depth fast. Feel free to broach if you need. I never thought I'd say this, but in this case, speed is more important than stealth. I need to see what they're doing."

"I shall see to it," Henri said.

"Also, raise our radio mast," Jake said. "I want to listen, too."

As the *Hai Ming* angled upward, Jake raised the periscope, stuck his eyes to the optics, and saw darkness in the sea's shallow layers.

"We're at periscope depth," Henri said.

Jake digested the Frenchman's report and realized his lens had broached, and he stared at a starless horizon. He swiveled the optics upward, let his eyes adjust, and proved to himself that the outside world existed by blinking until his brain registered the appearance of constellations.

He walked the periscope counterclockwise.

"Henri," he said. "Let me know when I'm on the bearing to the *Romeo*."

"Five more degrees," Henri said. "There!"

"Nothing," Jake said. "They're too small, even this close. I can't see a thing."

Jake pulled his face back from the optics.

"Jin," he said, "capture an automated three-hundred and sixty-degree sweep from the periscope, and then lower it. There's no reason to keep looking at nothing."

Expecting Jin's habitual professional compliance, Jake felt a strange arousal when the Taiwanese officer hushed him with a stern finger. Jake watched with fascination.

Jin pulled back one of the muffs from his ear and flipped a switch at his console. A voice, deepened with its higher frequencies clipped by radio transmission, filled the control room. Jake recognized the inflections and rhythm as Mandarin, but the foreign meaning eluded him.

However, his intuition grasped the emotions in the man behind the words. He sensed fear and, to lesser extents, hope and relief.

Jake looked to Henri.

"Make sure we're recording this. Also, get some Taiwanese guys up here who aren't manning stations so that they can listen and take notes."

"Immediately," Henri said.

Then Jake heard a second voice. It also spoke Mandarin, but it carried more excitement and enthusiasm than the first. He turned to Jin.

"Who is it?" he asked. "What are they saying?"

Jin twisted in his seat.

"I believe the captain of the *Romeo* has had good fortune," Jin said. "He's seeking a vessel to rescue his crew from his submarine, and he's found a mainland fishing vessel that is happy to assist."

Jake recalled that Chinese merchant and fishing vessels maintained free reign within international waters despite the boundaries their navies had set between themselves.

"Sounds like the *Romeo's* captain is a lucky man," Jake said. "So is his crew."

"They're going to abandon the submarine and seek transfer via life rafts to the fishing vessel," Jin said. "They need only wait two hours for the fishing vessel to arrive at its best speed."

Jake glanced at the chart and sought the nearest friendly combatant. A stealth patrol craft one hundred miles away caught his attention.

"If you can convince the captain of this stealth craft to leave the hydrophone line partially unattended for the night, he could be here in less than three hours to offer the *Romeo's* captain a second option."

"The option to escort the fishing vessel and the submarine crew to Suao?" Jin asked.

"To escort them wherever the heck the admirals in Keelung want to accept their new, special guests," Jake said. "This scenario is why the mainland wanted them dead. This is why I let them live."

Jin tapped buttons on his screen and called up the overhead chart.

"Ah," he said. "That patrol craft belongs to Yang Lei. He's a good man. A year ahead of me at the academy. I'm sure he'll find a way."

Jake sensed that for the first time in his life, sidestepping the dealing of death had created his success. He walked to the foldout captain's chair and planted himself on its seat.

"This is our ultimate victory," he said. "Vector in that patrol craft, Jin, and make it happen."

*

Chan stood beside Gao as a sailor pushed a drill through the portal glass of the watertight door. The sailor wiggled and wrestled the bit backwards, and air whistled through the hole.

"That's it, Gao," he said. "That's all we need. Leave me with these two armed men and take the rest of the crew topside. Assemble them into life rafts, assure each man is dressed for the weather, and arm the officers and senior enlisted with side arms."

As Gao and the drill worker departed, Chan unlatched the door and pulled. It resisted him.

He stepped back and looked to the larger of the two armed sailors who remained.

"You," he said. "You look strong. See what you can do. If you can even crack it open, we can hold that crack with the crowbar."

The larger, strong-looking sailor stood and grabbed the latch. He braced his shoes against the deck and waited for Chan and the other sailor to poise the crowbar's tip at the door's lip.

"Go!" Chan said.

The sailor grunted and strained, and the door popped from its seal. Chan jabbed the bar toward the opening, but the door slammed shut.

"You had it!" he said. "Try again. It will only get easier as the pressure continues to equalize."

The man yanked again, and when air whistled between the door and its seating, Chan rammed the bar downward. Air pressure forced the door shut again, but the second sailor stabilized the bar and held open the gap.

Chan placed his palm on the crowbar and leaned his chest into it to counter the torque. He ran his free hand over the arced sliver of light into the engineering spaces, feeling the rush of air.

His chest heaved, and he noticed that the sailor at the latch also labored to breathe.

"There's a point at which the door opens enough," he said, "where so much air begins to pass by that the pressure differential no longer matters. I believe we can open the door enough now to reach that point. Pull with all your might, and I will risk my fingertips in the crack this time to help you."

Chan ran his fingers on either side of the crowbar, using friction against metal to assist the man at the latch. The sailor tugged, Chan walked his fingertips over the edge of machined metal, and the door swung.

"Pull!" he said.

With a grunt, he fell backward, and the door pivoted open on its hinges. Air bowled over him, and he rolled to his side. He reached to the deck where he had rested his pistol, grabbed the weapon, and looked up. The entrance to the engineering spaces remained empty as the wind subsided.

He stood, pointed the barrel ahead, and stooped through the doorway.

"Follow me," he said.

The engineering spaces revealed carnage. A corpse bled from its back and another from its neck and stomach. One bled from its wrists, and he stopped to inspect it.

It opened lifeless eyes.

"Lu?" Chan asked.

"I'm sorry," Lu said. "I was pressured. They had my family."

"Curse you, Lu," Chan said. "You're the last one I expected to turn against me."

The two sailors stood beside Chan, but he redirected them to seek other saboteurs, survivors, and the sources of inrushing water. He glanced through the deck girders and saw that the water had risen a meter up the side of the ship.

"Forgive me," Lu said.

"I cannot forgive you," Chan said. "You've done me no wrong. Our ascent to the surface was perfectly timed. A ship will carry us away. It is the dead you've killed from whom you must beg forgiveness. You will join them soon."

Chan knelt and examined the sliced wrists.

"Can we agree that it's best that I let you die by these self-inflicted wounds?"

Lu nodded.

"I didn't want to drown again," he said.

"I could end it with a bullet to your head."

"No," Lu said. "I will pass soon enough."

Chan's sailors returned, each dripping seawater from their coveralls. They reported that nobody else breathed within the engineering spaces. They had shut the valves allowing water into the ship, and they had opened the ones allowing pumps to suck water from the bilges.

"Then I've failed," Lu said. "My family."

"If your intent was to see this ship destroyed, you have no worries. I will soon burn it and abandon it, as is my mission. Does this please you?"

Lu nodded, life waning from his eyes. Chan knew that death was claiming the traitor.

"Pull the Korean body bags from their storage areas and place them on the decks," he said. "Then set an oil fire in the lagging and exit through the nearest hatch. I will close the watertight door behind me."

Chan walked forward and met Gao in an empty control room.

"The crew is topside," Gao said. "We have bridge-to-bridge radio contact with the fishing vessel, and they are visible on the horizon!"

"Excellent! Now help me finish the mission."

Chan flipped switches on the ship's control station and set the drain pump to sucking water from the after bilges so that his inferno would stay afloat.

"Drag the body bags about the ship," he said. "Start in berthing. I will start in the torpedo room."

Chan walked forward and tugged a bag from a pile of three corpses. It hit the deck with a thud, and he scooted it across deck plates to make room for the other two.

He tugged at the next two bags and left them in a haphazard pattern, trusting that fire would melt the bags, the bodies, and the clothes. With the heat of the confined burn, he suspected that even the bones might become powder.

Ten corpses later, he met Gao in the control room.

"I laid out thirteen corpses," he said.

"Fifteen for me," Gao said.

"That's enough."

The ship's buoyancy assured, Chan stepped to a control station and secured the pumps.

"Head topside, Gao. I will set the blaze in the forward spaces and then follow you."

Alone on his hijacked *Romeo* submarine, Chan entered the scullery and dipped a rag into cooking oil. Recalling the story of the USS *Miami* and its disastrous arson attack, he marveled at the ease of his task. He returned to his stateroom, grabbed a cigarette lighter, and passed the flame under the rag until it caught.

He dropped the rag to his bunk, waited, and watched his bed burning. Confident the flames gained life in the insulating lagging that encircled the ship, he coughed out smoke and retreated.

As he climbed out of his captured prize, he inhaled cool, fresh sea air and reflected that he had fallen short of his mission by one ghost-like aircraft carrier. But that carrier had proven invulnerable, and he alone had escaped it.

Uncertain if an approaching vessel, claiming to be friendly, would carry him to safety, he considered his mission a success–no matter what cruel twist fate could strike him with next.

CHAPTER 35

Yang Lei held a polished rail as his thighs absorbed the patrol craft's flank speed bouncing. A glance at his console showed an infrared camera's perspective of dual billowing plumes over the horizon.

As his craft neared the smoke's source, he discerned two separate columns. Expecting to see a submarine conning tower between the dark clouds, he grunted as the largeness of the fishing vessel struck him with its eclipsing of his hunted *Romeo*.

He flipped his boom microphone to his lips to get his executive officer's thoughts.

"I'm not sure our cannons are powerful enough to stop a vessel that big if it decides to defy us."

"Agreed, sir. I think we should ask Keelung to send a frigate, just to be certain."

"Make the request," Lei said. "Also, see if they have air support available. But in the meantime, there is something we can do."

"What's that, sir?"

"Clear that submarine of mainland personnel and board it with a small boat detachment. We need to shut its hatches and suffocate the fire."

"Shall I lead the boarding team?"

"By protocol, you should," Lei said. "But leave this task to me."

Thirty minutes later, Lei stood atop an abandoned *Romeo*-class submarine, its hatches closed. The fishing vessel next to it floated dead in the water as its crew lifted the last of the *Romeo's* crew aboard.

His crew outnumbered versus the fishing vessel and its new inhabitants, Lei opted for patience. He instructed the vessel to remain motionless, and with nowhere to run, its captain obeyed his radio request to await boarding from an inbound frigate and a helicopter boarding team.

*

Pierre Renard's tail bristled as his vulpine eyes spied his prize. His prey ensnared, the French fox salivated as he savored success as the chauffeured Cadillac XTS descended toward Keelung's concrete pier. Gazing over Admiral Ye's shoulder, he saw the stealthy lines of a *Kang Ding*-class frigate, nylon lines securing it to its berthing below an overhead crane blocking his view of the bow.

On the fantail, armed men with digitized patterns covering their camouflaged uniforms pointed rifles downward as they walked slow ovals around genuflected men.

"That's the *Si Ning*," Ye said. "The detainees are the crew of the captured *Romeo* submarine. It took the crew aboard with small boats during the night, and what you see below is the crew without its officers. We've flown them to the command center and are already questioning them."

"Separating the crew from its leadership was wise," Renard said. "I'm sure the stories that will be told will corroborate the facts we already know and add to the gaps about which we've only speculated."

Ye curled his arm across his body and pointed out the side window at the channel.

"There," he said. "The *Hai Ming*."

Renard strained his eyes but saw the surfaced submarine's conning tower backlit by the early morning sun. He looked forward to a reunion.

Ye's mobile phone chimed, and the admiral placed it to his ear. He listened, uttered few words, and smiled.

"One officer from the *Romeo* has already requested asylum," Ye said. "Others are ready to break. Apparently, they are more afraid to return home than to remain in our custody."

"Excellent news," Renard said. "It's as if they know they've been betrayed."

"We will learn what they know," Ye said. "It's only a matter of time and questioning."

"What of the *Romeo* itself? Have your men been able to keep it afloat?"

"It stayed afloat as it burned," Ye said. "The first commander to arrive on the scene was wise enough to board it and close the hatches, and that suffocated the fire. But initial reports indicate that the ship is charred badly."

"But perhaps useful for your future needs after repairs," Renard said. "And perhaps containing forensic evidence of its fate."

"I've sent a second *Kang Ding* frigate to guard it while tugs head out to tow it back to port. We'll conduct a detailed investigation once it's beside the pier."

Renard reflected in silence upon the outcomes his scheming had created. He sensed a dizzying array of new possibilities opening to him, but as the car approached the dock, he thought of friendship.

He stepped from the car and straightened his blazer. Accented by the stench of brackish water, the dawn air smelled crisp. Standing beside Ye at the empty pier, he lifted one foot atop a cleat and folded his arms across his thigh. Craning his neck, he saw the rounded bow of the incoming *Hai Ming* jut from a jetty, followed by a tug mated to its starboard side.

"The heroes return," he said.

"We've had many of them in this campaign," Ye said. "I hope that we've placed the major hostilities behind us."

Ye's mobile chimed again, and Renard studied his companion's softening features as he digested its message and lowered the phone to his pocket.

"More news from the interrogations?" Renard asked.

"The executive officer apparently is the son of a high-ranking party member," Ye said.

"This calls into question why the mainland would sacrifice the vessel," Renard said.

"There was a mutiny in the engineering spaces," Ye said. "Someone tried to sink the ship. There's also a rumored suspicion that the commanding officer intercepted and decrypted the orders to the *Kilo* to sink it."

"That would be interesting," Renard said. "Has the commanding officer confirmed this?"

"He's maintaining his silence. So is the executive officer. There's no need yet to use more coercive techniques, but I expect that we'll have enough of the story from the rest of the crew to place before them that they'll realize they have no secrets to protect."

As Renard lowered his foot from the metal cleat, a crane swung a steel girder walkway across the sky. He craned his neck and watched the hook lower it towards the *Hai Ming* as a tug pushed it against the concrete. Rapid line handling and rigging mated the submarine against the pier and gave access to it.

Wearing a white working uniform, Lieutenant Commander Jin appeared on the walkway. The men following him wore starched white shirts and moved with springs in their steps. When they reached Renard and Ye, Jin saluted.

Ye returned the salute, ending the formality.

Renard surprised himself by stepping to Jake and embracing him across his broad, hard shoulders.

"I thought you didn't like hugging," Jake said.

"I've become soft in my old age," Renard said. "Either that or I'm overcome with joy in the way you've resolved this conflict. Wisdom, patience, and skill."

Renard released his protégé and greeted his countrymen with a traditional kiss beside their cheeks.

"Congratulations, to all of you," he said. "I'm buying dinner tonight."

"I thought you'd be leaving," Jake said. "Getting home to Marie and the kids."

"Soon, my friend. But first, tonight, I demand that you all tell me what happened. I wish to know everything."

*

Admiral Brody relaxed, enjoying coffee in an austere break area. As he lifted his shoe from the linoleum and crossed it over his leg, he questioned how to craft his legacy.

His phone rang, and he arched his back to wiggle his wrist

deep into his pocket. His curiosity rose as he recognized the caller as the young senator who sought to elevate Brody to the Republican presidential ticket while carving himself a spot as the vice presidential candidate.

"What can I do for you, Tom?" he asked.

"Capitalize on this victory, admiral."

"You don't waste any time, do you?"

"There's no time to waste. The media knows something big happened, and it's hungry for a story. Either the Rickets camp can spin it, or we can."

Brody's mind raced with the alien viewpoints of politics. He grasped that the truth he respected as a military warrior would end upon his retirement from uniformed life.

Part of him wanted to tell the senator to shut up and find a better presidential candidate, but he knew that accomplishment in the public sector required the management of perspectives. Whoever won the ticket would do so through the manipulation of facts to craft an image, and it may as well be him.

The bovine beast within him envisioned Rickets within range of his horns. Before attacking, he needed to know if his adversary had become a fallen rodeo cowboy, or if he had transformed himself into a skilled matador.

"How's Rickets' camp going to proceed?" he asked.

"He's going to claim that this campaign was a matter of diplomacy, minimizing the risk to American lives and sparing the world economy through his support of Taiwan. He wants Americans to believe that he can protect them by empowering our allies to defend themselves."

Brody shifted the phone to his other ear.

"Well, shit, Tom," he said. "That's what he did."

"But he couldn't have done it without the U.S. Navy, or at least its presence and threat of intervention."

"Actually, I hate to say it," Brody said, "but he got most of it done without me. I hardly mattered."

"That's your opinion admiral, but it's just one in a chorus. The truth is that you've got a carrier strike group within flight operations range of Taiwan."

"Yeah, and I just sent another one. You'll probably read about it in the papers tomorrow. So what?"

"Rumors are spreading that there's not a Chinese submarine remaining in the ocean that can stop you. China needs to hear you bragging about it to give the Secretary of State leverage for negotiating a ceasefire, and America needs to hear you bragging about it to believe in its leadership."

Brody bit back the shame that he had needed Rickets and Renard to spare him from a trap and create his opportunities for him. He questioned if Rickets were the better man.

"For God's sake, Tom," Brody said, "If you knew how bad I really screwed this up, you'd be talking to someone else right now. I got lucky, and I owe most of my good fortune to Secretary Rickets."

"Whose side are you on?"

"I serve America."

"Not for much longer if you don't start fighting for your public image. You have to decide right now if you want to become the next president or if you want to fade away as a footnote in the greatest naval campaign in modern times."

"I can't sacrifice my integrity," Brody said.

"You don't have to. Just take credit for having done your job. Leadership isn't about having the brightest idea. It's about marshaling the forces at your disposal to create the vision that has to be created. It doesn't matter if you ran into snags. It doesn't matter if you got lucky. And it doesn't matter if Rickets helped you. You are the Chief of Naval Operations, and you succeeded."

In his mind, Brody replayed the video tapes of Chinese detainees from the *Romeo* submarine that he had seen hours earlier in Rickets' office.

"You know there's more leverage to this than just a carrier strike group, right?" he asked. "We have enough political firepower to reduce China's military presence in Taiwan to a foxhole."

"I think I know what you're talking about, but better to leave it unspoken. But if you're talking about what I think you are, and if it gets declassified soon enough, the first person between you and Rickets to claim credit for it will earn the edge."

Brody pinched the bridge of his nose and tried to stop time. His inner voice tormented him with fears, doubts and second thoughts, but decided to take the first baby step in his presidential campaign.

"Okay," he said. "I'm in. What do you need me to do?"

"Attend a press conference. I'll call it, and I'll have a speech written for you. There will be members of the cabinet present who've already chosen you over Rickets, and they'll do most of the talking. You just need to be ready."

"Is anyone ever ready for a transition like this?"

"No, admiral, they are not. Which is exactly why I think you're the man for the job."

CHAPTER 36

Through the passenger window, Jake watched the faces of pedestrians on the Taipei sidewalk. The Cadillac's reflection in a bank's window reminded him of the economic value he had protected. The determination in the face of a suited man marching into that bank reminded of the resilience he had inspired.

"They look scared," he said.

"At least they're out in strength again," Renard said. "Two weeks ago, there were perhaps thirty, forty percent fewer people who felt safe enough to be outdoors."

The XTS accelerated through a stoplight, carrying Jake toward Chiang Kai-shek International Airport. He had declined military transportation home to experience the benefits of his efforts in Taiwan, and he requested taking a scenic route through the downtown area for the impression to take full effect.

He also desired extra time with Renard, who agreed to employ public transportation for his return to France.

"I need to tell you something," he said.

"Anything, my friend," Renard said.

"When I was back in the states, I never went home."

"Then Linda must be impatient to see you. And you her, I imagine."

"Right, but that's not what I meant," Jake said. "I needed to tell you that I visited al-Salem."

"Dear God, man! Why?"

"I really don't know. Looking back, I didn't have a good reason. I just needed to talk to him."

Renard squirmed, wrinkling his blazer's sleeve as he shook his palms at Jake.

"You come to me when you're not sure who to talk to. I love you like a son and will always look out for you. If you don't go to me, you go to your wife, or you go to your brother. You don't go to pond scum that came within inches of flinging the United

States into eternal chaos."

"I don't think I'm that much different than him," Jake said. "In fact, I'm afraid I'm more like him than I know."

"You need a psychologist, and I'm not being facetious. I find your perspective disturbing."

"Shit, Pierre. I was so angry when you found me that I would've done what al-Salem set out to do, only ten times worse. You can't know what's wrong in my head until you've been in it. And you can't get there. I wouldn't do that to you. There's still shit disturbed in there. Deep."

"My point exactly, about the psychological help. Friends and family can only do so much for you without you exhausting them."

Jake wondered if Renard had a valid point.

"You sound like you know firsthand."

"I do," Renard said. "After the drunk driver killed my first family, it was all I could do to avoid taking my own life. It takes a strong man to admit his weakness. I turned to professional help and am glad I did."

"I'll think about it."

"Please do."

"But he was right."

"Al-Salem?" Renard asked.

"Yes."

"About what?"

"That I was being selfish. That helped me see that I needed to call you, you know. He helped me see that."

Renard sighed.

"Even a broken mechanical wristwatch is right twice a day," he said. "Don't read too much into it. Stick with your commitment to consider professional counsel."

"Linda thinks I need a relationship with God."

Jake eyed the Frenchman with his peripheral vision, scanning for a reaction. Renard remained unresponsive for a moment that dragged to the point of discomfort. When his friend broke the silence, he seemed more distant than Jake had remembered seeing him.

"That," Renard said, "is also a place I once turned."

Before Jake could decide if he wished to pursue the question, Renard redirected the conversation.

"You'll have to forgive me," he said.

"For what?" Jake asked.

"For having withheld the information I'm about to give you. I was instructed to do so."

Anxiety rose in Jake's chest.

"What is it?"

"A message from an old friend."

"I don't have any old friends," Jake said. "If you don't remember, I left an identity and a life behind a few months after I met you."

"Not all of it," Renard said. "Admiral John Brody remembers you, and he knows you're still alive and have just helped him in his recent naval victory."

"No kidding! Sweet! Can I see him when I get back?"

"I'm afraid not, at least not immediately. He's soon to be launching a presidential campaign, and he can't be seen associating with treasonous ghosts."

"What did he say? You said he had a message."

"He says thank you for turning your life around and helping him and your country. And it is your country, despite what you did with the *Colorado*. He's trying to forgive you for the sailors lives he holds you responsible for taking, but whatever came over you, he's sure there was a reason. When he can meet you with the assurance of secrecy, he would like to do so."

"When's that going to be?" Jake asked.

"I'm afraid that will be difficult to ascertain," Renard said. "The man who holds the most power over your head in the states is also about to become Admiral Brody's political enemy. You may have to wait until the Republican primary has ended before Brody could ask the favor of Rickets allowing the connection to you without exploiting it."

"Rickets? He's got the tact of a rhinoceros, but he wouldn't screw John like that. It would be hitting below the belt."

Renard looked out the window, the nearest terminal catching his gaze.

"Good men behave poorly when fighting over something they covet," he said. "Best to avoid the temptation of letting them place you between them."

*

From the first class cabin, Jake watched the lights of Taiwan recede into a glow over the horizon. He wondered about the spirits of the men around and below him who patrolled the air and sea, allowing himself a moment of pride in his service to them.

He reclined into a deep sleep, woke up in mid-flight for three hours during which he distracted himself with a movie before falling back asleep. Turbulence on the descent into Los Angeles International Airport shook him from a dream that escaped his memory upon awakening.

When he deplaned, he jogged toward the immigration booths, his thumbs stabilizing his backpack's shoulder straps. He found short lines remaining from the prior international arriving flight, and when he reached the counter to present a fake passport and false story about a business trip, he felt vulnerable. But a smile and a stamp later, the agent dismissed him.

Skipping baggage claim to seek his next flight, he found easy passage through customs. But when he exited the doors to freedom from government controls, a visitor surprised him.

Dressed in open-toed Birkenstock shoes and a striped hemp pullover, his older brother Nick stood in the throng of passengers who paused in transit to collect their bags and chart their routes to their next gates.

Incredulous, Jake wrapped his arms around his lithe sibling's shoulders and then released him.

"What's going on?" he asked. "You couldn't wait six more hours to see me?"

"There's more to it than that."

"I figured."

"Pierre told me to meet you here, outside customs."

"Ah, Pierre. That explains a lot. What's this about?"

"He said he wanted me to make sure you went straight home after arriving in the states. I guess he didn't like your hopping around airports the last time you were here."

Jake thought of the incarcerated terrorist with whom he had sought counsel.

"I'm sure he didn't," he said. "I told him about who I visited on my travels, and I guess he didn't want me going to the same places. He wants me to get home to Linda."

"So do I," Nick said. "But I want to talk to you first before we get home."

"Sure, but wait until we're at the gate," Jake said. "We need to hurry to catch the next flight."

After boarding the plane to Detroit minutes before cross-check, Jake reclined in the first class chair beside his brother.

"What's on your mind?" he asked.

"I sense that you've grown recently," Nick said.

"No shit. It doesn't take a genius to make that general statement."

"You listened to me, didn't you?"

"About what?"

"About finding a new channel for your anger other than killing. You still have the anger, but you're developing wisdom and peace to better contain it."

Jake tested his brother's conviction.

"What if I told you I killed more people in the last three days than in my entire life up to that point? Huh? What would you say to that smart ass?"

"I'd say you were lying. Some things I just know, and you crossed over an important line since I last saw you."

"Yeah, okay," Jake said. "You got me. So, what's next on your agenda for dissecting me?"

"You need to find a new perspective on life and spend time working on your lingering anger."

"Fine, Nick. I have to hand it to you. You're making sense. You're getting through to me. I think I can work on this, especially if I can keep Pierre and Rickets out of the picture for a while."

Nick twisted in his seat, clasped his palms around Jake's hand, and closed his eyes.

"Now? Aren't you afraid of collapsing to the ground again?"

"No. Quiet please."

Jake looked out the window and noted that the aircraft rolled away from the gate. Nick released his hands.

"Well, what did you find? Or feel, rather?"

"You're not ready yet," Nick said. "You've made a lot of progress, but you're not quite there. And you need to hurry. I think Linda is pregnant."

Jake's body bristled, and he slipped into a warm bath of enthusiasm and anxiety.

"Linda's pregnant? Did she tell you? Are you sure?"

"No. I doubt she knows yet. In fact, I'm sure she's only beginning to suspect. I just noticed the life auras in her womb recently."

"Don't screw with me and get me excited about this because of your intuition and your sixth sense."

"You don't have to trust me," Nick said. "Nature will take its course and prove me right soon enough. But assume that I am right, and then consider the changes you need to make, or at least continue making, in your character to be a father."

"I'm already a stepfather."

"This is different, and you know it."

Jake knew it, despite his protestations. He pondered his brother's advice in silence as the ascending plane pressed him against his seat.

Once at level altitude, he spoke over the humming engines.

"Okay. So, if I agree with everything you say, then I need to start taking my anger seriously. I think I can do that. I know I can. And if you're wrong, then I've still done something I should be doing anyway."

"Yes," Nick said. "That's a very constructive attitude about it."

"Wait. Hold on," Jake said. "You said auras in her womb, right?"

"More than one," Nick said. "But they were overlapping and too amorphous to tell how many. Twins, triplets, I don't know. There's no guarantee that she'll carry all of them to term, if any, and you have to be ready to deal with all the outcomes."

Jake released a long, tense sigh.

"What if I'm not? What if this isn't me?"

"It's no longer your call. It's out of your hands. Based on what little I really know about your escapades with Pierre, I know that you can shape the fate of nations. Now you need to learn to shape the fate of people close to you that you love."

"This sounds hard. I mean, there's no training for this. There's no way I can really prepare, is there? How do I get ready for this?"

Nick's smile assured Jake.

"For the first time in your life, you let your older brother teach you something."

"Okay, sure. What do I need to know?"

"You forget about trying to be a god who changes the entire world with each magnificent mission you take on," Nick said. "And you try your hardest to make the world a better place by caring about it one person at a time."

"Sounds hard."

"Remember how I said you have the same gift I have, maybe stronger, to read people? A sense of augury, how to behave, and figure out what to do next?"

"Yeah. Sure."

"I recommend you start using it when you get home."

*

Nick met Linda's kids in the garage to take them to dinner, freeing Jake for his reunion.

Jake sauntered through the entryway into his warm home.

In the entryway, feminine lines drew voluptuous curves under a pink robe, and dark hair touched his wife's shoulder. She ran to him, and he saw a smile spreading across her face before she hugged him.

She bounced and wiggled in his arms, and he squeezed to lessen the repeated impact of her head on his jaw.

"Careful!" he said.

She stepped back.

"Sorry. I just missed you."

"I know. I missed you, too."

Jake stared at her belly. He thought he sensed new life but could only speculate if his brother had planted a false image in his mind.

"What? Do I look fat?" she asked.

"No," he said. "Just wondering. I mean, how are you doing? How do you feel?"

"How do I feel? You've never asked me that."

"Well," Jake said, "I think I'm learning how to care."

THE END

About the Author

After graduating from the Naval Academy in 1991, John Monteith served on a nuclear ballistic missile submarine and as a top-rated instructor of combat tactics at the U.S. Naval Submarine School. He now works as an engineer when not writing.

Join the Rogue Submarine fleet to get news, free audiobook promo codes, discounts, and your FREE Rogue Avenger bonus chapter!

Rogue Submarine Series:

ROGUE AVENGER (2005)
ROGUE BETRAYER (2007)
ROGUE CRUSADER (2010)
ROGUE DEFENDER (2013)
ROGUE ENFORCER (2014)
ROGUE FORTRESS (2015)
ROGUE GOLIATH (2015)
ROGUE HUNTER (2016)
ROGUE INVADER (2017)
ROGUE JUSTICE (2017)
ROGUE KINGDOM (2018)

Wraith Hunter Chronicles:

PROPHECY OF ASHES (2018)
PROPHECY OF BLOOD (2018)
PROPHECY OF CHAOS (2018)
PROPHECY OF DUST (2018)

John Monteith recommends his talented colleagues:

Graham Brown, author of The Gods of War.

Jeff Edwards, author of Steel Wind.

Thomas Mays, author of A Sword into Darkness.

Kevin Miller, author of Declared Hostile.

Ted Nulty, author of The Locker.

John R. Monteith

ROGUE DEFENDER

Copyright © 2013 by John R. Monteith

Stealth Books

www.stealthbooks.com

The tactics described in this book do not represent actual U.S. Navy or NATO tactics past or present. Also, many of the code words and some of the equipment have been altered to prevent unauthorized disclosure of classified material.

ISBN-13: 978-1-939398-04-8

Published in the United States of America

Made in United States
North Haven, CT
02 June 2022

19780595R00150